BITTER END

JENNIFER BROWN

Little, Brown and Company
New York   Boston

Little, Brown and Company

Hachette Book Group
237 Park Avenue, New York, NY 10017
Visit our website at www.lb-teens.com

Little, Brown and Company is a division of Hachette Book Group, Inc.
The Little, Brown name and logo are trademarks of Hachette Book Group, Inc.

The publisher is not responsible for websites (or their content) that are not owned by the publisher.

First Paperback Edition: May 2012
First published in hardcover in May 2011 by Little, Brown and Company

Library of Congress Cataloging-in-Publication Data

Brown, Jennifer, 1972–
Bitter end / by Jennifer Brown.—1st ed.
p. cm.
Summary: When seventeen-year-old Alex starts dating Cole, a new boy at her high school, her two closest friends increasingly mistrust him as the relationship grows more serious.
ISBN 978-0-316-08695-0 (hc) / 978-0-316-08696-7 (pb)
[1. Dating violence—Fiction. 2. Best friends—Fiction.
3. Friendship—Fiction. 4. Grief—Fiction. 5. Mothers—Fiction.] I. Title.
PZ7.B814224Bi 2011
[Fic]—dc22   2010034258

10 9 8 7 6 5 4 3 2 1

RRD-C

Printed in the United States of America

For Scott
and for Pranston

CHAPTER ONE

If I had to describe my best friend, Bethany, in one word, it would be *persistent*. Or maybe *unrelenting*. Or, if I were writing her into a poem, I might use *importunate*, because words like *importunate* impressed Mrs. Moody, and when I used them she told me I was a born poet, which was kind of cool.

Doesn't matter; all of those words mean the same thing—*determined*—and Bethany was nothing if not determined.

It was one of the things I liked best about her. She always had a clear sense of where her life was going, or, more accurately, where she was steering it. For all the ways we were totally alike, that was one of the ways we were different, and it was part of why I liked hanging out with her. I think I kind of hoped her importunateness might rub off on me and someday I'd find myself behind the steering wheel of my own life, certain where I was going to end up.

Sometimes Bethany's persistence could be a little hard to ignore. It didn't matter that we were just recovering from lunch rush and that I was busy wiping a mountain of trays taller than myself, or that my manager, Georgia, was standing right next to me. Bethany marched into The Bread Bowl in her untied high-tops, her giganto-purse bouncing against her hip, and sat down at the dirtiest table in the dining room.

"*Psst!*" she hissed, pulling a handful of papers out of her purse and waving them at me. I ignored her, keeping my eyes glued on the tray I was holding. So she did it again. "*Psst!*" And then she cleared her throat elaborately.

"I think someone sprang a leak over there," Georgia said, pulling a wad of twenties out of the cash register drawer and then shutting it with her hip. "Or a lung, from the sound of it." Bethany's persistence was no stranger to Georgia, either. Georgia liked Bethany and often joked that Bethany would for sure be the first female president.

I stacked the tray I'd been wiping and dropped the wet rag on the counter. "I think I've got a table to clean," I said.

"Looks like it," Georgia mumbled. She headed toward the office, turning all of the twenties so they were facing the same direction. "And with her spitting all over it like that, it's getting dirtier every minute." Then she added over her shoulder, "And get that customer a drink. Might help her with that throat problem."

"You're all about the humanitarianism, Gee," I responded, grabbing an empty cup on my way.

Cleaning the dining room was probably my least favorite duty at The Bread Bowl. People could leave some really disgusting trash behind. Sometimes, though, if Bethany happened to be hanging out at The Bread Bowl, having cleanup detail wasn't so bad. That way she and I could talk while I picked up shredded pieces of napkin and half-eaten sandwiches, trying to look a lot busier than I actually was.

"Look at this," Bethany said as soon as I plunked a Diet Dr Pepper in front of her and got to work on her table. She bumped my leg lightly with her knee. "Hot tub!"

I straightened and grabbed the stapled stack of papers out of her hand and scanned the top one, which included a grainy photo of a twelve-person Jacuzzi.

"Oh, man," I said, reading down the list of amenities: hot tub, indoor pool, fitness room with cardio machines. It sounded like bliss. Expensive bliss. "This is amazing. No way we can afford it. You think we can actually afford it?"

I flipped the page over and started to read about nearby attractions. Across the room, Georgia cleared her throat. I glanced up. She was stacking take-out menus next to the register. She shifted her eyes meaningfully to Dave, the owner of The Bread Bowl, or Granite-Ass, as he was not-so-lovingly called by some of the line cooks. For some reason Dave had been hanging around lately, which put a real damper on everyone's mood, not to mention my ability to drool over hot tubs and hotel fitness rooms with Bethany.

I thrust the papers back at her and resumed picking up crumpled sandwich wrappers and stuffing them into a cup.

"Oh, and look!" Bethany was saying, totally ignoring both my question and Georgia's not-so-subtle warning. "It has a huge fireplace in the lobby. I bet you could get hot cocoa and sit there celebrity-watching all day long. Just think, we could end up making out in the snow with a star." She gasped, slapping my shoulder with the papers. A handful of napkins fluttered out of the cup and back onto the table. "We could end up in a tabloid!" She held her hands up in the air as if she was envisioning a title. "Who Are the Mystery Beauties on the Slopes Breaking Boy Band Hearts?"

I giggled. "More like, 'Who Are the Mystery Klutzes Who Broke Boy Band Legs by Falling into Them on a Ski Slope?'"

"Well, I wouldn't mind breaking a leg if it meant a hottie broke my fall."

"Uh-uh, I get dibs on the broken hottie," I said.

"No way, I thought of it first."

Georgia cleared her throat again. Now she was starting to sound like Bethany. Dave had moved into the dining room and was standing with his hands on his hips, assessing it slowly with his eyes. The last thing I needed was to get on Dave's bad list. I most liked Dave when he pretended I didn't exist, which was 99 percent of the time. He reminded me of my dad that way. I was used to being ignored by the men in my life. "Listen, can we talk about broken boy bands and tabloids later? I've gotta clean this up."

Bethany sighed. "Work, work, work."

"Yep. And if I get fired, you'll be ordering cocoa for one, one, one."

Bethany eyed Dave and gave a frustrated grunt. "Sure. Okay. Call me, though. I want to see what you think about restaurants. Zack and I've been researching."

Zack. Our other best friend. If I could describe him in one word, it would be... well, you just can't sum up Zack in one word. He was like an overprotective big brother, pervy uncle, and annoying little cousin all in one. He was a traveling comedy show. A musical genius. An amazing friend. If I was being completely honest, Zack was probably the only reason Bethany and I weren't relegated to "too nerdy to notice" status at school. The enviro-nut and the poet—invisible and invisible. But it was impossible not to notice Zack. Everybody adored him. However, we adored him best, and we adored him first, so we were okay by association.

If I were to write Zack into a poem, I'd definitely use the word *sanguine*.

Bethany stood up and tossed her empty cup in the trash before coming back for her things. I knew she was going to go home, flop on the couch with her laptop, and scan every restaurant listing in the state of Colorado until I called. It's all she'd done since we came up with the idea for this trip.

"Oh!" She snapped her fingers. "I almost forgot. Guess what idea Zack had?"

"I can only imagine," I said, patting the last of the trash

into the cup and straightening the salt and pepper shakers. Bethany picked a piece of lint off the bottom of her shirt.

"Tattoos," she said.

"Tattoos?" I repeated.

She nodded, biting her lower lip as she smiled. "Yeah, he thinks we should get matching tatts while we're there. Like a mountain or...or I don't know...something sexy."

"You do know what Zack's interpretation of 'sexy' is, don't you?" I imagined us all leaving Colorado with half-dressed, big-boobed women in stilettos permanently emblazoned on our bodies.

I picked up the cup and headed for the farthest trash bin—the one by the front door—nonchalantly tugging Bethany's shirtsleeve so she'd follow me.

"Well, yeah, but..." She paused as I leaned over to throw away the trash. "I don't know. It could be fun."

"And painful," I reminded her. "And permanent."

"And fun," she repeated.

Dave's voice cut through the restaurant. He was griping at someone in the kitchen, which reminded me that I needed to get back to work before he turned on me, too.

"I'll call you," I said. "We can talk later."

Bethany dug out her car keys. "You better," she said, pushing through the glass doors.

Pressing my fingers lightly against the necklace under my shirt, I scurried back behind the counter and resumed wiping trays, daydreaming a little about Colorado.

Bethany and Zack and I had been planning this trip

since we were eight years old, back when Zack's mom still called us the Terrible Three. It started out as my idea—go to the place my mom was headed when she died and see if I could figure out what was there that was so important to her that she would leave her family the way she did.

But it wasn't long before Bethany and Zack wanted in on the plan. Partly because they were my best friends and they knew how important it was to me. But mainly they wanted in because the trip sounded fun. And glamorous, like something people do in a movie. Best-friend cross-country mystery-solving road trip. Does it get more feature-film than that?

We decided that the trip was going to be our graduation gift to ourselves, and ever since the last day of junior year, Bethany had been practically obsessed with planning it. She talked about it constantly and even instituted a standing Vacay Day, where we'd get together to go over details every Saturday (Bethany's idea). Rotating between our houses (my idea). Complete with pizza and video games and lots of crude jokes featuring female body parts (Zack's idea). We'd been meeting all summer, and so far all we'd managed to accomplish was inhaling about fifteen large pepperoni pizzas and beating level nine of some zombie video game Zack had gotten for his birthday.

Truth be told, I didn't care about hot tubs and ski gear and restaurants. All I cared about was Mom and what happened to her. Which Dad didn't seem to care about at all. When I told him after our first Vacay Day meeting that I was going to Colorado after graduation, he made a non-committal noise but didn't even look up from the newspaper he was reading at the breakfast table.

"I'm going because of Mom," I said, standing in the kitchen doorway, staring at his back, as usual.

"What's your mother got to do with it?" he asked.

"I don't know," I said. "That's part of why I want to go." I took two steps into the room and then stopped and crossed my arms over my chest. The room always felt lonely when Dad was in it. Lonely and chilly. "I want to know why she was leaving. What was so great about Colorado?"

He stood abruptly, closing the paper with one hand and picking up his coffee mug with the other. "You want to go, that's fine with me. But we don't have the money for it. With your sister's college tuition and no second income..." he said, setting his cup in the sink. But he never finished, and before I could ask another question, he was out the door.

Ever since my mom died, it seemed as if my dad always talked in open-ended sentences like that—especially when she was the subject. "You know what your mom would've said..." or "Your mom would've thought your behavior right now..." or "If only your mom were here..." He always looked so sad and meek when he said it.

It was the Big Mystery of my life. My mom. My dad. What happened between them and why we didn't talk about it. Sometimes it seemed as if I was the only one in the house who even cared.

The only time I'd ever heard Dad say anything real

about our mom was when I was eight. He drank a six-pack at a block party, and then he came home and sat at the kitchen table, with a shoe box of old photos in front of him. That night he said our mom was "crazier than goosehouse shit," whatever that meant.

My baby sister, Celia, and I had giggled nervously when he said that, not sure if it was some sort of joke, imagining our mom as a white and goopy puddle, stuck to someone's windshield or a fence post, eyes rolling around insanely. Neither of us remembered our mom. We were really little when she left.

But Shannin, our older sister, was there when Mom left, and she didn't laugh.

Dad had gotten up, taken the shoe box, and tossed it into the garbage, muttering something about being an old fool. After he left the mudroom, though, I crept in and pulled the shoe box out, took it up to my bedroom, and hid it under the bed. I didn't know why, but saving that box just felt like something I had to do.

Later that same night, when we were alone, Shannin took us into her bedroom and told us the Real Story. How she'd awakened one night to the phone ringing. How she'd crept out of her room and into the hallway to look around the corner, crouched against the wall with the skirt of her nightgown pulled over her legs. And then how the phone rang again and how Dad's voice sounded really upset when he answered it.

"She's gone off the deep end this time, Jules," Dad had said. "I don't know. I don't know where she's gone."

Shannin told us about how, just as Dad hung up the phone, the front door banged open and Mom barged through it, saying something about going to Colorado—to the mountains. Dad had pulled on her elbows, saying she was drunk, and begged her to stay, to "see someone," and Mom argued that she was already "seeing someone," just not how he meant it.

And then later, after Mom had left and Dad had disappeared into the kitchen and the smell of coffee started to fill the air, Shannin had gone back to bed. And in the morning Shannin found out that while she slept, the police had come to the door and told Dad that Mom had wrapped her car around a light pole and died. Just like that.

"Knocked her brains out onto the road," Shannin whispered as Celia and I sat cross-legged on her bed, clutching each other's hands and shivering. "That's what Dad told Aunt Jules at the funeral. Mom's brains were knocked out onto Forty-first Street, and they had to shut it down until they could get a hose and wash it off. And Aunt Jules patted Dad's shoulder and said she knew he loved Mom a lot and that he should never have had to hear something like that, and Dad cried and said, 'I know, and now I can't forget it.'"

After Shannin told us the story, I went back to my room and locked the door. I pulled out the box of photos of Mom and Dad and dumped them onto my bed, flipping through them carefully and secretively, as if I were doing something wrong just by looking at them.

I stared at those pictures for hours. I'd look at Mom, so happy and thin and glowing, and would imagine her being drunk and crazy like Shannin said. It didn't seem to fit.

There were dozens of them. A photo of high school graduation. Two of a birthday party. One of their wedding day.

I had my favorites. Ones I'd look at over and over again.

A photo of them at a party. Dad sitting in a folding chair, Mom in his lap. Her hair was very short, and she was wearing a vest over a button-down shirt. His hands were looped across her belly and clasped together. She had her hands resting on his and a big smile on her face.

Another one, of the two of them sitting in a mossy space between two trees. Each of them was barefoot and cross-legged, facing each other with their knees touching. Their faces were shadows. They looked like they were telling secrets.

And another one, Dad and Mom standing in Grandma Belle's kitchen, wrapped in a kiss. Dad had Mom in a deep dip toward the floor. Her arms were hanging limply at her sides. The back of the photo read: *First day back. Reunited!*

One after another, the photos telling a story. Only it was a story with no ending because Mom left and Dad never told us why, and the ending we knew just didn't make sense when I looked at the photos.

The Mom in the photos looked so gentle. The Mom who left us must have been a whole different person.

When I was little, I'd ask Dad about it. Why was she going to Colorado? We didn't know anyone out there. We'd never even been there. But Dad would just mumble that Mom "wasn't in her right mind and didn't know where she was going." Once he said something about Mom being "too trusting for her own damn good." But something in his eyes when he said it told me he wasn't telling the whole story. There was something more to Colorado for Mom. There was something important there. I wanted to shout at him, *You heard about her brains on the road, Dad, and you said you couldn't forget it, but you have! You have forgotten it!*

Eventually Shannin told me to stop asking about it because it upset Dad too much to think about Mom. So I did. But I couldn't forget the story. It haunted me. Literally.

That year, I had nightmares. Always, they were the same. Dad screaming into a pillow, Mom standing at the top of a mountain cackling, her face soft and sweet, her hair billowing out behind her. In the dream, she dangled me over the jagged mountain edge.

"This mountain is mine," she said, puffs of smoke billowing out of her mouth. "I don't want you here. I don't want you at all, Alexandra."

She laughed as I kicked and thrashed and begged to be let go.

"Oh, Alexandra," she jeered. "Stop making such a fuss. Just think, they'll have to shut down traffic while they find a hose to wash your brains off the street. Isn't that exciting?"

And always, just as she opened her hand and let me fall, I woke up.

It got so bad I refused to go to bed at night. Dad eventually took me to a therapist, who said some stuff I didn't understand about "closure" and "healing" and suggested that Dad give me something of my mother's to help me feel closer to her.

Dad came into my room that night clutching a folded yellow envelope.

He cleared his throat. "Alex, honey, I know you're having a hard time being without your, um..." His eyes filled up and he swallowed. Then he pushed the envelope into my hands. "This was your mother's. I bought it for her on our honeymoon.... It was in her purse the day she, um..."

I held the envelope in both hands, looking up at him as he swallowed and swallowed, unable to finish any sentence, it seemed, that had anything to do with my mother. He nodded at me, and I opened the envelope. Inside was a necklace — a thin leather strap with a small hoop on the end of it, a web of flossy clear thread strung inside the circle. Tiny beads dotted the delicate web; two white feathers, so small they might have come from a hummingbird's tail, dangled from the bottom of it. I gently prodded the beads with my finger.

"That's called a dream catcher," he said. "It's supposed to keep nightmares away."

He pulled the necklace out of the envelope, held it in midair to straighten it, and then carefully slipped it around my neck. It smelled oddly familiar to me—perfumey and alive, almost like a memory—and instinctively my fingers drifted to it.

Right then, at eight years old, I knew. Just as I knew I'd never take the dream catcher necklace off, I knew that someday I'd get to Colorado, where Mom had been going.

The therapist was wrong. The necklace didn't give me closure. Instead, not knowing anything more than this about my mom made me feel like a piece of me was missing, and I almost felt as though, just like Dad, I could break if I didn't fill in that piece. That there would always be a hole in my heart where Mom should have been, and if I didn't fill it in, I could end up empty and dull, like him. That I might forget hearing about her brains on the street, just as he had.

The next day as Zack and Bethany and I played on the woodpile behind Bethany's house, I showed them the necklace and told them the whole story. My mom wasn't just gone, and my dad wasn't just quiet. I told them about the photos and about Mom going crazy and dying on her way to the mountains and about my plan to go where she was going. And just like that, the trip planning officially began.

I needed to know that she was going toward something, not away from us. Not away from me. She loved me. I needed to know that she loved me.

Whenever Aunt Jules or Bethany's mom or someone else tried to tell me that my mom was an angel watching down on me from heaven, I never could envision it.

To me, my mom was in the mountains, waiting for me to arrive.

"Really, if you're not gonna be some stick-up-the-butt English teacher, who gives a crap about direct objects, anyway?" Zack said, leaning back in his chair and crossing his arms. His toothpick—Zack's new signature look was a toothpick—rolled from one edge of his mouth to the other.

I picked up his pencil and held it out to him. "You should, that's who; because if you don't pass this class, you don't graduate." It was only the second week of our senior year, and already Zack's teachers were worried about his ability to stop goofing off long enough to earn the credits he needed to graduate.

Zack shrugged. "And your point is?"

I gave him a look. "I thought the point was pretty self-explanatory." He rolled his eyes at me. The toothpick, which had made its way to the middle of his lips, was bumping up and down as if he was flicking the other end of it with his tongue. I sighed and put down the pencil. "Fine. Whatever. Just don't come crying to me when your mom takes away the crapmobile again. And don't expect me to give you a ride anywhere, either."

Zack raised an eyebrow. "So that's how it is now? Been covering your ass since forever. Saved you more times than I can count. And you just leave me hanging out to dry. Hurts, my friend. Hurts."

I grinned. "Yeah, pretty much. I'm doing you a favor. Someday you'll thank me."

"Now you sound like my mom. What's next? You telling me this'll hurt you more than it'll hurt me?"

"Trust me, helping you can be pretty painful sometimes." I cleared my throat and began writing in Zack's notebook, which was spread out on the desk between us. "Okay, seriously. We've gotta get to work. Here, look at this sentence. What's the direct object?"

Zack uncrossed his arms. He leaned forward over the paper and studied the sentence I'd written. "God, you're a pain in the ass," he muttered around his toothpick. "Good thing you put out. That?"

I smacked his arm. "Close, but no. And you wish I put out, you perv. Okay, remember, to find the direct object, you..."

"Alex?" Mrs. Moody, the tutor lab sponsor, called from the doorway, interrupting us. She waved me over.

"I'll be right back," I said. "Why don't you write five

random sentences, and when I get back we'll find the direct objects together."

"Can I use any words I want?" he said, arching his eyebrows at me deviously.

"Yes, such as 'fail,' 'forever a senior,' 'degenerate,' 'grounded for life'? Go ahead."

He made a face at me and picked up his pencil. I pushed my chair out and headed to the door, where Mrs. Moody was still standing, half-in, half-out, talking to Amanda, one of the other tutors. Mrs. Moody was pointing over her shoulder with her thumb at Zack, and Amanda was nodding. I waited, half-wondering if I'd done something wrong. Maybe she'd heard Zack and me bantering and was firing me, which would totally suck because, without the tutoring lab seventh period, I'd probably get stuck in ceramics or some other art class, in which I would, without a doubt, be a complete failure. Plus, I liked tutoring. Especially tutoring Zack. Zack was a great stress-reliever, pervy jokes included.

Mrs. Moody finished talking with the other tutor and put her hand on my shoulder. "Alex," she said with a wide smile. Mrs. Moody always smiled, even if you were in trouble. Talking to her was like talking to a cloud. She was soft, graceful. She smelled like honeysuckle and vanilla, and her clothes always drifted around her like ribbons on a breeze, giving the illusion that she was moving faster than she actually was. When she spoke, she had this even, measured rhythm to her voice that made me automatically think of bedtime stories. She was easily my favorite teacher. Hell, she was easily *everyone's* favorite teacher. "Come with me. I've got a new student for you."

She turned and headed down the short hallway to her office, her shirt and skirt billowing out behind her, and I followed.

"He's transferred over from Pine Gate," she said over her shoulder. "Just needs to do some catching up so he can hit the ground running in senior English. I thought you'd be the best choice for him, being our expert writer and all." She flashed me a smile as she paused at her office doorway, then stood to the side and ushered me through.

"Oh," I said. I didn't even know we had a new student from Pine Gate. But then I stepped into the office and there he was, standing next to Mrs. Moody's file cabinet, holding a little ceramic duck. He saw us come in and quickly set the duck back down on top of the cabinet, as if he was embarrassed to be caught holding it. "Hey," he said.

"Hey." There was an awkward pause between us while Mrs. Moody grabbed the doorknob and pulled the door shut. "I guess I'm your new tutor."

"Totally unnecessary," he said. "But Coach Dample disagrees, so…" He shrugged and then added, "Cole," and he stuck out his hand to shake mine. When I put my hand in his, it felt warm and strong and comfortable. And kind of weird. Like we were business partners or something.

Mrs. Moody took a seat behind her desk, and we both fell into place in chairs across from her. I sat on my hands, while Cole lounged comfortably in the chair next to mine, one foot tilted sideways and propped up on top of the other, his legs stretched out in front of him.

"Um, what about Zack?" I asked. "He really needs help with his sentence diagramming." *Plus*, I didn't add, *we were having fun in there.*

Mrs. Moody spoke up. "I've moved Zack over to Amanda for tutoring from here on out. She can handle sentence diagramming just fine. Cole, I'm sure you'll find Alex to be just what you need to get caught up and secure that spot you're looking for on the basketball team." She glanced at her watch. "We've got a few minutes before the final bell. Why don't you two go to the lab and get acquainted? You can start working on assignments tomorrow."

"Yes, ma'am," Cole said with a pleasant grin. He had a dimple, just one, on the left side. But the dimple was kind of cute. I didn't even notice I was staring.

"Do you have questions, Alex?" Mrs. Moody said, snapping me out of it. I jumped.

"Uh, no. I'll tell Zack to go with Amanda."

But Zack had already moved to Amanda's room when I got back to the lab, leaving my room completely empty for me and Cole.

I sat in the chair I'd been sitting in before, but Cole moved to the window and looked out, his hands on the sill in front of him. I gazed at the back of his letter jacket, which was so full of patches there was hardly any jacket showing.

"Wow," I said finally. "Pine Gate must really be missing you."

He turned. "Why do you say that?"

I pointed at his jacket. "Looks like you're a sports star."

He glanced down at the front of his jacket, where there were even more patches and a few medals. "Yeah. I did okay. I thought maybe you meant they were missing my sparkling personality and unforgettable good looks."

I blushed, hard, and looked down at my hands. "No, I didn't mean..." I said, mentally kicking myself for sounding like such a dork.

He laughed, crossed the room, turned around the chair Zack had been sitting in, and straddled it backward. "I'm kidding! Don't worry about it. It was just a joke."

I peeked up at him, hoping my face wasn't too red. He was looking right into my eyes, which made me feel more awkward. I missed Zack.

"So," he said, "Mrs. Moody says you're a writer. What do you write?"

I waved his question away. "She exaggerates," I said. "I'm not great or anything. Some poetry. Some short stories. Nothing major."

"If you can do it, I say it's major. Writing's a lot harder than dribbling a basketball or catching a football."

I chuckled. "You haven't seen me try to catch a football. It's not pretty. But I get what you're saying. I won a contest last year with a poem I wrote for lit class."

"Really? That's cool. I'd like to see it sometime," he said.

I glanced at him. He was still looking directly into my

eyes. How did he do that? I could feel his gaze all the way down to my toes. "Really?"

He nodded. "Yeah. Mrs. Moody says you're really good. I think you're her sports star."

"Well, you know," I said. "Must be my sparkling personality and unforgettable good looks."

His eyes widened, and he pointed at me. "Good one!" We both smiled.

We were silent for a few seconds, and I busied my fingers, picking ripped pieces of paper out of my spiral notebook. He leaned back and started casually drumming against the desk with his thumbs. "It must suck," I said after a while. "You know, to move to a new school your senior year. Especially to leave your team. I'd hate it."

He shrugged. "It's not really a big deal. My dad got a new job, and we got a bigger house. It's a chance to start over." His eyes drifted back to the window and held for a second, like he was seeing his old school out there. Then he leaned forward across the desk again. "Plus," he said, "I get to share my sparkling personality and unforgettable good looks with more of the world. A humanitarian effort."

This time I pointed at him, and we both laughed without me saying a word. The bell rang. We stood up, and I began gathering my books, still spread out from reviewing direct objects with Zack. Cole didn't have any books, so he reached down and picked up my backpack off the floor. He held it open for me while I stuffed my homework into it.

"Thanks," I said. "I can honestly say that's something

Zack never did." Zack was much more likely to spend most of our tutoring session trying to bounce cheese balls off my forehead.

"No problem," he said. "Same time tomorrow?"

I zipped the backpack and shouldered it, nodding, but he was already at the door. He slapped the doorjamb with his palm, looking out into the sea of students filling the hallway. He waved at someone. Was it possible that he already had friends?

I opened my mouth to tell him good-bye, but he had already plunged out into the hallway and disappeared. Instead, I straightened the chair he'd been sitting in, then shuffled to the door, hoping I could catch up with Bethany outside the band room.

But just as I was reaching to turn out the light, he popped back in the doorway, almost bumping into me. He was slightly out of breath, as if he'd run back to the classroom.

"Hey," he said. "And don't forget to bring that poem, okay?"

"Okay," I said, but he was already gone again before I could get the word all the way out.

After I turned off the light, I stood in the shadowy classroom and grinned until the hallway was empty and the sounds of cars leaving the parking lot filled my ringing ears. He wasn't Zack, but something about Cole felt kind of nice.

I had a really good feeling about this new arrangement.

CHAPTER THREE

I took a sip of my iced tea and hoisted my feet up into the chair across from me. I tipped my head back, turning my face to the sun, and took a deep breath, then let it out in one big half-gust, half-yawn.

Bethany's fingers were tapping her laptop keys, stopping every so often while she sipped her Dr Pepper. Intermittently, she made little "hmmm" noises over what she was reading, as if Colorado was the most fascinating subject on the planet.

"So, check it," she said, just as I was dozing off. "We could totally pool our money and rent an RV. We'll get my dad to do the driving, and we could do stuff like play games, watch movies, eat. It'd be like a party bus."

"Your dad? No way. No dads. Besides, it sounds expensive," I said, keeping my eyes closed. I'd rolled up my Bread Bowl uniform pants as far as they would go, and I could feel the September sun baking into my shins. After an early Saturday morning shift working the register and filling drink orders, the sun felt delicious. "I'm not made of money, you know. An RV sounds like a whole lotta early shifts." I yawned.

"Have you ever driven across Kansas?" she said, her fingers tapping again. She turned the computer around, a photo of a field pulled up on the screen. "You'd work round the clock to get an RV—it's that boring. Imagine how annoying Zack can be in an enclosed backseat, with eight hours of soy fields being his only distraction."

"Says the girl whose parents are paying for her trip. I'll be lucky to afford the gas to ride in Zack's crapmobile. Besides, never underestimate his ability to be annoying in the back of an RV. Or in a hotel, or on a gigantic mountain for that matter."

"Okay, okay," she said, holding her palms up, surrender-style. "The money thing. I get it. But I'm going to check out RVs anyway. If I find something really cheap, will you at least consider it?"

"No," I mumbled. The sun felt so good that I didn't even want to move my lips anymore.

"Thank you," she said. "Your open-mindedness is staggering. You should work for the UN someday." We both snorted. "I'll let you know what I decide to rent." That was Beth—she knew exactly when and how hard she could push me and still get her way.

She scooted her chair back, the metal legs making a

scraping noise on the patio. It was the midafternoon lull at The Bread Bowl, and we were the only two outside. She kicked her legs up onto the chair mine were resting on, and our ankles bumped against each other. I opened one eye and then closed it again. We rested there for a while, our legs pressed together, the sun on our faces, as Bethany rattled off various bits of news and gossip she'd heard over the week.

"Omigod," she said. "There's this new kid in my government class. Gor-to-the-geous."

"Really?" I asked. "What's his name?"

"I just know him as Hot Guy. But I think I heard Mr. Clairfield call him Mr. Cousin or something," she said. "He's from Pine Gate, I think. Let me tell you, girl, if that guy's any indication, they have some fine men at Pine Gate."

I opened my eyes and turned to her, fully awake now.

"What?" she said, looking around self-consciously. She pushed her glasses up on her nose, her eyes widening. "Is it a bee?"

I shook my head. "Cozen? Cole Cozen? He's the new guy I'm tutoring."

"Get *out*!" she said, a smile spreading across her face. "You're tutoring Hot Guy?"

I nodded. "Just started, like, two weeks ago. He's trying to get on the basketball team."

She leaned across the table conspiratorially. "Is he stupid? I knew it. Someone that hot has to have some flaw."

I shook my head. "No, he seems smart enough."

"Then he must have a girlfriend," she said.

I shrugged. "I don't know. I mean, I don't think so. It didn't come up. He's really nice. But kind of old-fashioned or something. He, like, shook my hand and called Mrs. Moody 'ma'am,' and if he's already in the lab when I get there, he stands up until I sit down. So different from the other cavemen at our school, you know? When I come into a room that Zack is in, instead of standing up, he always goes, 'Thought I smelled you coming.'"

Bethany giggled. "At least he doesn't call you Cowboy Ugly, like he does me. Wear cowboy boots to school one day in sixth grade, and Zack will never let it go."

I giggled, too, turning my arms over so my forearms could get some sun. "Well, Cole would never call you Cowboy Ugly. He's not a Neanderthal like Zack."

Bethany narrowed her eyes at me. "You totally have a crush on Hot Guy."

I felt my face flush. Sometimes I hated the way Bethany and Zack could see through me. "No, I don't. I was just telling you how different he is from Zack. And his name is Cole."

She picked up her Dr Pepper, studying me. She pointed at me while she sucked down some soda, her wooden beaded bracelet clicking, and then said, "You do too. I can tell. You're into him."

My face was practically burning now. "I just met him two weeks ago."

"Not a denial," she singsonged. "Alex is in lo-o-ove!"

"Very mature," I said, kicking at her foot. But I couldn't help smiling. True, I'd found myself thinking about Cole a couple times when we weren't together. About his dimple and the way he joked with me and the way he held my backpack for me and how I was both nervous and excited at the thought of letting him see my poem, which I still hadn't shown him. But none of that meant anything. "I'm just tutoring the guy," I said, pushing my sunglasses back up onto my face, closing my eyes, and tilting my head back again. "He's nice is all."

"And gorgeous."

"I thought you wanted to map our route to Colorado."

"It's a straight line. There's no mapping to it," she said. "I'm done."

"Well, let's talk about the hotel some more, then." I could feel a bead of sweat roll down my back.

"There's nothing more to talk about," she said. "I practically have the amenities list memorized by now." But I could feel Bethany's feet lift off the chair and heard the scraping of metal against concrete as she pulled close to the computer again. "So we arrive on day one, check in, eat somewhere fast, and sit in the lobby looking amazing in our new road trip wardrobe...."

"I can't afford a new road trip wardrobe," I intoned for the thousandth time.

"You can borrow," she said in the same tone, also for the thousandth time.

The door to the patio swished open, and Georgia

plowed outside, holding a plastic tray in one hand and a wet rag in the other.

"Never mind me, sun goddesses," she said, wiping down a table. "I'm just cleaning up because *somebody* didn't think to do it before she clocked out."

I smiled. "Sorry, Gee. Guess you just can't get good help these days."

"Don't I know it," she said. "Too busy working on their tans so boys like the one inside will notice them."

I stretched a leg up luxuriously and gazed at it, rotating my foot in the air. "It's tough being beautiful." I giggled. "But so worth it."

She flicked her towel softly at the top of my head. "Ha-ha-ha. I'm busting a gut over here." But I could see the amused grin on her face as she worked. She brushed the crumbs onto the tray in her hand. Georgia acted tough, but she was a pushover on the inside. After closing, she would turn up the music and we'd sing while we wiped down the kitchen. She called me her older daughter, and I called her the mom I always wanted. She'd been there for me more times than I could count. But if people were around, we acted really put out by each other. It was our little game.

"Go ahead, laugh it up," Georgia said. "I'll do your job for you, ya lazy good-for-nothin'."

Bethany turned and glanced over her shoulder, then turned sharply and looked again. "Alex," she hissed. "She's not kidding."

"What?" I let my leg plop back down onto the chair.

"Half the basketball team is in there," Bethany said. "And isn't that Hot Guy with them?"

My heart skipped a beat and I sat bolt upright, my head whipping toward the window. Inside The Bread Bowl, right on the other side of the window, sat a group of the most gorgeous guys in our school—with Cole Cozen right in the middle of them, eating a bagel.

"Oh, that one," Georgia said. "Yeah, he was asking about you, Alex." She set the tray on our table and followed my gaze to the window.

"He was? About me? What'd he say?"

"I knew you were into him," Bethany crowed, turning back to the computer and using the screen as a mirror. She pushed her glasses back up on her nose and pulled the elastic out of her hair, then re-slicked her ponytail.

"Shut up!" I hissed at her. "I'm not!" Then I looked at Georgia, who'd picked up her tray and gone back to wiping tables. "What'd he say?"

"Oh, just asking if you were working is all," she said. Yesterday, after I'd mentioned my job, he'd asked me where I worked. The conversation had seemed so offhand, though. I was surprised that he even remembered, much less showed up at The Bread Bowl asking about me. Georgia moved to the next table. I followed her.

"And...?" I prodded.

"And I told him you were outside with your girlfriend, and he ordered a bagel and sat down by the window with all the others."

"And that's it?"

"And that's it. Goodness, girl, you're acting like it's some big emergency."

"It's not," I said, feeling my face flush.

Bethany snapped her computer shut and crammed it into her giganto-purse. "Well, I hate to break up this party, you guys, but I've got to go. I promised my mom I'd babysit tonight. Alex, coming with?"

"Yeah," I said, pushing in my chair and bending to unroll my pant legs. My skin felt electric at the thought of passing all those guys—especially Cole—as we walked through.

"Hold it," Georgia said. I could tell by the way her mouth was set that she was trying to hold in a laugh. She reached up and pulled my visor—left over from work—off my head. Then she reached behind me and tugged the elastic out of my hair, letting it drop in waves around my shoulders. Lightly, she used her fingers to fluff and tame my hair. She stood back and assessed me for a second, then sniffed. "Well, you still smell like potato soup, but you look beautiful."

I smiled. Sometimes Georgia really was the mom I wished I had. Sometimes, when she got soft and took care of me, I imagined that's how a mom would've acted with me. Sometimes, like a mom, Georgia just instinctively knew all the right things to say and do. Sometimes I couldn't tell if she made the sting of missing my mom feel better...or worse.

If I were to write a poem about Georgia, I'd definitely

use the word *succor*, which means "comfort." Mrs. Moody would love that word.

"Okay. Come on," I said, grabbing Bethany's arm with both of my hands and leading her to the door. "We'll just casually say hi on our way out."

"Whatever, Miss Not-Into-Him," she mumbled, tossing her Dr Pepper into the trash.

The air inside The Bread Bowl was about fifteen degrees colder than it was outside, and almost immediately my skin crawled with a smattering of goose bumps. My teeth even chattered a couple of times.

Bethany and I burst through the dining area as if we didn't even notice anyone sitting there. I hated when guys from school came in when I was working. I always felt ridiculous in my high-waisted navy uniform pants and tucked-in polo shirt.

I put my head down and kept walking forward, tugging Bethany along with me.

Suddenly, Bethany stopped and turned around, forcing me to stop, too.

"Hey, I know you," she said, and even before I turned around, I knew who she was talking to. I was going to have to kill her. That was all there was to it. Sure enough, she said, "You're the new guy in gov. Cole, right? Alex was just talking about you."

"Hi," I said, giving an embarrassed little wave, imagining all the ways I would totally get Bethany back for this.

Kill a tree, maybe? Refuse to recycle my water bottle? Tell Zack she's hot for him?

"Hey, Alex," he said, swallowing a bite of bagel. "Just get off work?"

I glanced down at my uniform. "No, I just wore this outfit because I love polyester mom pants."

I was going for funny, but nobody laughed. But Cole smiled, that dimple popping up right over the corner of his mouth. At least he got my joke, which made me feel a little bit better.

"Dude, I gotta blow," Steve Shunk said to nobody in particular, scrunching up his sandwich papers in one hand. All the guys started moving then, pushing back their chairs and loudly wadding up wrappers.

"Yeah, we should go, too," I said, pulling on Bethany's arm. "See you in lab on Monday?"

"Yeah. I'll be there."

"Cool," I said, then turned and practically sprinted to get out of there before the guys jammed up the doorway.

Once outside, I wrapped my arm around Bethany's shoulder. "So, Cowboy Ugly, what shall your punishment be?"

She rolled her eyes and shrugged me off. "Please. Watching you two pretend you weren't making goo-goo eyes at each other was punishment enough."

I grinned, despite myself. She may have been right about that. I thought he had been looking at me a little differently lately, too.

Suddenly I couldn't wait to get to lab on Monday.

CHAPTER FOUR

Celia was with Bethany and Zack, waiting for me at my locker before final period. I took a deep breath. I knew this was going to be a hard year, with my baby sister roaming the halls. Not that I didn't love her or anything but, well, let's just say if they gave awards for being loud, mean, and completely immature, Celia would need a trophy case.

My grandma used to say it was because Celia grew up without a woman in the house. That she learned with my dad that if she just howled and stomped her feet she'd get whatever she wanted. *A spoilt baby, that one,* Grandma used to say, lifting her chin at Celia.

Grandma was right—Celia was difficult to take. And she howled and stomped her feet a lot. But it wasn't because Dad gave in to her; it was because it was sometimes the only way to get Dad to pay attention. Shannin and I had a way of just giving up on Dad and taking care of business ourselves. Or sometimes just giving up. But Celia figured she needed to squawk louder. And usually it worked.

Celia was spoiled. You'd have thought we'd have been closer, since we were only three years apart. But Celia was just too much sometimes. She was rude and abrupt and jaded and cynical. She skipped through life as if everything was hers and everyone should bow down to give it to her. She never smiled unless she wanted something. Sometimes I felt sorry for Celia because she never seemed happy, but usually that sentiment was short-lived because she would undoubtedly say or do something nasty and ruin any sympathy anyone could ever have for her.

Well, except Zack. Zack liked Celia in a big-brother sort of way. He thought she was "fragile" and would humor her, leaving Bethany and me shaking our heads and rolling our eyes.

"I need a ride home," Celia barked, before I even got to my locker. "I'm not going to Yearbook Club today."

"Okay," I said. "Just meet me outside the tutor lab."

"Can't you come down to the freshman hall and pick me up there? I don't want to have to walk all the way up here."

"You just walked all the way up here right now."

"Exactly. And I have a lot of homework. I don't want to have to drag my backpack up. It'll be too heavy."

I stuck out my bottom lip. "Poor baby. Think you'll live?"

"God, Alex," she said, tossing her ringlets over one shoulder. "Why can't you ever just be nice?"

I opened my locker, blocking out her face. I caught Bethany's eye — she was making a give-me-a-break face. If Celia were Bethany's sister, she'd probably be walking home today. Bethany didn't put up with much from her younger siblings. "I'm giving you a ride, aren't I?" I said wearily as I pulled a couple Starbursts out of the bag on my second shelf.

"You're such a bitch."

"Fine, Celia," I said, sticking my head around the locker door to scowl at her. "If I'm such a bitch, you can get a ride with someone else."

"Dad said you could take me home, and if you don't—"

"Ladies," Zack said, stepping in between us, "I think you're missing the bigger picture here." He reached into my locker and grabbed a handful of Starbursts. He held up a yellow one. "Alex has been hiding candy from us." He turned and fake-glared at me. "You know," he said, "one of the first signs that there's a problem is you start hiding the evidence from your friends."

I shoved him with my hip. "Get out of my way, you thief," I said, slamming my locker door. "I have them counted, just so you know." But I knew by the end of the next day they would be gone. Zack and Bethany and I knew one another's locker combinations. We each had free rein. He would eat them all. Knowing Zack, I figured he would probably replace them with condoms, just for a laugh.

Bethany and I started walking toward the tutor lab. Zack put his arm around Celia's shoulder and followed us. "Tell you what," he said around a mouthful of Starburst. "I'll meet you in the freshman hall and walk you up here myself. I'll carry your heavy backpack for you. I'll even give you a piggyback ride if your legs give out, m'lady," he said to Celia.

I glanced over my shoulder. She was beaming, leaning her head back against Zack's arm. Sometimes I thought maybe her damsel-in-distress act wasn't so much of an act around Zack. Sometimes I thought she really liked him. "Deal," she said. "Good to know *one* of you can be nice."

"Take that back," he said, brandishing a Starburst at her face.

"Fine. You're a jerk, and I hate you," she said, snatching the candy away from him.

"That's more like it," he said.

The warning bell rang and Celia gave out a little *eep*, ducked out from under Zack's arm, and then scurried away to get back to the freshman hall for her last class. Zack got caught up talking to some guy by the water fountain.

"You going to the soccer game tonight?" I asked Bethany, who'd had the biggest crush on Randy Weston, the team's star striker, pretty much since birth. He didn't know she existed.

She shrugged and pushed up her glasses. "Can't," she said. "Enviro Club." Bethany was one of those superbrain types who spent most of her time studying for math tests, even when she didn't have one coming up anytime soon, and in her "spare time" was busy "saving the world, one plastic bottle at a time." She wore bamboo T-shirts and hemp jewelry and generally made her parents' lives miserable with trash-can hypervigilance. And she was just smart enough to have every dreadful and depressing statistic about how humanity is ruining the Earth permanently etched in her memory bank. "But I saw Randy this morning in the caf, and he looked amazing. All dressed up."

"Did you say anything to him?"

She blew out a puff of air, looking miserable. "God, no. Plus, I don't know, I'm not sure I'm all that into him anymore."

I gasped. "You've been into him since kindergarten."

We reached the locker room and stopped; Bethany had Everyday Sports for seventh period, which was the PE class that all the kids who hate PE take in their senior year. She shrugged again. "And he has totally ignored me since kindergarten. It's probably time to give up on him. Go after someone more attainable."

"Maybe you should just tell him how you feel. See for sure if he's interested." This was rich, coming from me. If either of us was going to be the type to lay all of her cards on the table, it was so much more likely to be Bethany than me.

"Tell who how you feel?" Zack asked, coming up beside us. He leaned his elbow on my shoulder, a toothpick dangling from the corner of his mouth.

"You," I said. "Of course."

Bethany's grin widened. "Yeah. We feel that you smell like armpits."

We cracked up, bumping shoulders, while Zack pretended to pull a knife out of his chest.

"Is that so?" he said, then grabbed Bethany's head with one hand and lifted his other hand high over his head. "You asked for it!" he said, smashing her face into his armpit. She was squealing and smacking his chest, but when he let her go, she looked flushed and happy.

"Go away, you nasty!" she said, pushing his chest and ducking into her classroom.

"Not without Alex," Zack said, grabbing my hand and pulling me down the hall behind him. "Come on," he said. "I'll walk to the tutor lab with you. Celia wants some of my nice to rub off on you." He half-dragged me down the halls toward the lab, giving me "Nice 101" in a goofy falsetto voice, until Mrs. Moody ushered him into Amanda's room, saying something about him needing to put as much effort into his grammar as he does his humor.

I walked through my lab room door just after the final bell rang. Cole stood up, just as he almost always did when I came into a room. It was hard not to feel a little gushy inside when he did it.

"Sorry I'm late," I said.

His face was all smiles. "No problem. Guess what."

"What?" I said, plopping my backpack on my chair and unzipping it. He sat at his desk again.

"I got an A on my essay test. Ninety-seven percent."

"Hey, that's awesome!" I cried, and before I even knew

what I was doing, leaned forward and gave him a big hug. "Congratulations!"

"Thanks. I did everything you told me to do. Totally worked."

I pulled back, breathless and feeling a little awkward, but it was a good awkward.

"So," I said, slithering into my seat, pushing out of my mind how good he smelled up close. "I have a surprise for you, too."

He sat in the seat facing me, leaning forward on his elbows. The leather sleeves of his Pine Gate jacket creaked underneath him. "Yeah? What?"

I dug around in my backpack for a few minutes and then pulled out an old sheet of notebook paper. I handed it to him without saying anything. Truth was, I was so nervous I didn't know what to say. I wasn't exactly used to letting anyone other than teachers look at my writing. And Cole wasn't just anyone, either. For some reason, I wanted to impress him.

He gazed at the paper for a while, a crease between his eyebrows. "Oh," he said, finally, his eyes lighting up. "This is your poem! The one that won you an award, right?"

I nodded, my eyes feeling like they would burn right out of their sockets. "You don't have to read it, though."

"I want to," he said, and he read aloud:

"I cannot swallow your hardened eyes
Sightless of my shrinking heart

My caving chest
Shoulders to the polished floor

"I cannot swallow your bound arms
My throat the leg of a drowned man
Rubber of a smoldering tire
Your pointed elbows stabbing my temples

"I cannot swallow your cool tongue
Clicking behind your teeth as you
List my failures
I can only cry a dusty tumbleweed
A weathered fence post
A handful of rusted nails
Rolling out of me like marbles"

For a long time after he finished, he didn't say a word. Just sat there and stared at the paper. My face started to feel hot, and I felt a tug in my rib cage, embarrassment welling up inside me.

I hadn't ever shown anyone that poem, except Mrs. Moody. When I finally let her read it, she took off her reading glasses and rubbed the imprints left on the bridge of her nose, then told me she knew exactly what I needed to do with it. She'd given me a printout the next day of the guidelines for a youth poetry contest held by some college writing group. She told me she thought I really had a chance. Two months later, when I found out I'd won first place, I was ecstatic. But still embarrassed. That poem was like a part of my soul. My thoughts. My private feelings. Showing them around would have felt like going to class in my underwear.

"There probably weren't very many entries," I said at last, my voice sounding electric and crackly in the silent room. I reached for the paper in Cole's hand. He snatched it away.

"Are you kidding?" he said. "It's really good. I mean *really* good."

I felt my cheeks pull up into a smile, even though the embarrassment was still so intense I squirmed. "Yeah?" I said.

He finally looked up, his lips parted. "Oh, yeah. Definitely. I don't read a lot of poetry, but this..." He gazed at the paper again. "Wow. You're like...Emily Dickinson or something."

"Ha! Thanks," I said.

He looked at me, and our eyes locked. If I didn't know better, I'd have sworn he looked...moved.

Finally, I broke eye contact and busied myself pulling my notebook out of my backpack and slapping it down on the desk between us industriously. "So what do you have to work on today?" I asked.

But he was still staring at me, only now the dimple was there, perched above the corner of his lip. "Does it have a title?" he asked.

I thought about it, feeling really self-conscious now. In a good way, but still. I cleared my throat and grinned.

"Yes," I said. "It's called 'My Sparkling Personality and Unforgettable Good Looks.'" Our inside joke.

He smiled for real this time, and held it for a few seconds before cracking up. He handed me back my poem, and I stuffed it into my backpack, feeling the unease and self-consciousness melt away.

"Can we get to work now?" I asked, glancing at the clock. "Mrs. Moody would kill me if she knew I was wasting lab time showing you my poems."

"Okay, okay," he said, reaching to the desk behind him to pick up his English textbook. He plopped it on the table next to my notebook and started flipping through the pages. "If you insist. But personally, I don't think it was a waste of time at all."

He continued flipping the pages of his book, but when I glanced up at him, he was looking straight at me. I looked down again quickly, blushing and telling myself that his look was nothing. He was just impressed by the poem was all.

Still. Whatever the stare was about, there was no denying, I could feel its intensity right down to my toes.

CHAPTER FIVE

I barreled through Bethany's front door without even knocking. We'd been friends long enough that her parents just expected it. When we were little, Bethany lived right across the street from Zack and me. We barged in and out of one another's houses so freely nobody even seemed to notice anymore. By the time Bethany moved to the other side of town, in sixth grade, the habit was so ingrained in me, I still did it anyway.

Bethany's mom was sitting on the couch, holding Bethany's little brother's head in her lap, a pair of tweezers poised over one ear. He was squirming and ranting, his glossy red hair flouncing up against her arm.

"Hi, Alex," she said when I came through the door. "Don't suppose you've got an extra hand?"

"Sure," I said. I was already late as it was. Zack had probably already eaten all the pizza, and he and Bethany were probably cooking up a "punishment" for me. Last time Bethany was late to a Vacay Day, Zack made her let us videotape her while she sang "I'm Too Sexy" and then upload it on her Facebook page. But Bethany's mom was so nice and always so frazzled watching after Bethany's four insane little brothers, I kind of felt sorry for her.

"He stuck a raisin in there," she said, handing me the tweezers and pointing to his ear. "I can see it, but he won't stay still long enough for me to get it."

I hesitated. "You want me to get it?"

She nodded. "I've done it a million times before. Trust me, as long as you don't push it farther down in there, it'll be no problem. You'd think they'd learn. Stop, Ryan," she hissed at Bethany's brother, clamping his legs under her now-free arm.

"I don't know if I..."

Ryan let out another wail and a new series of kicks with even more vigor than before, almost freeing his head from under his mom's arm. "Ryan! No!" she said, and swatted his bottom. Now he was screeching as well as wiggling. "You'll be fine, Alex. Just do it fast."

I bent over and held my breath, hoping against hope that Bethany's little brother didn't suddenly break loose and get an eardrum full of tweezer. My face was right next to Bethany's mom's. It was lined and looked weary. She smelled like macaroni and cheese. Quickly, before thinking about it too much, I stuck the tweezers into Ryan's ear and plucked out the raisin, which—thank God—came out in one piece. Bethany's mom let go of Ryan and he bolted out the front door, screaming and holding his ear as if I'd punctured it.

I handed Bethany's mom the tweezers, and the raisin dropped into her lap. She let out a deep breath and ran her free hand through her tangled strawberry blond hair.

"Boys," she said, and then chuckled. "Thanks for the help, honey."

"No problem," I said, but before I could say anything else, there was a crash from the kitchen, followed by rapid-fire barking issued by Bethany's dog, Perry, and another of her brothers shouting "*Mom!*" Bethany's mom gritted her teeth, slapped her palms on her thighs a few times, and got up.

Sometimes I wasn't sure if I'd trade my so-silent-it-hurts life with Bethany's wild and crazy one if you paid me a million dollars. Her house was in constant chaos, and her brothers destroyed everything. Her dad worked some weird night shift and was never home and awake when everyone else was, so studious and obedient Bethany often stepped in as second mother to the boys. No doubt, she wanted to save the Earth because it seemed so much more savable than her own household.

I picked up my purse and scurried to Bethany's bedroom, where she and Zack were already sitting on her bed with the laptop open. A box of pizza lay next to them, and Zack was chewing and laughing at the same time, his eyes glued to the laptop screen.

"Sorry I'm late," I said, tossing my purse on Bethany's dresser and grabbing a slice of pizza. I took a bite. "I was on the phone." As I said it, I felt my face redden and suddenly wasn't sure if, no matter how long I chewed the pizza, I'd be able to swallow it.

This was new, but I was starting to feel it more and more often whenever I thought of or talked to or saw Cole. After I'd shown him my poem on Monday, he'd seemed to be around more often, tossing a shy "Hi, Alex" my way or waving at me from across the parking lot or whatever. I was starting to get a vibe off him that there was more to it than coincidence.

And tonight he'd called my cell just as I was getting ready to walk out the door.

"Hey, Emily Dickinson," he'd said, and immediately I felt as if I was trying to breathe on the top of a mountain. The air felt thin around me.

"No biggie," Bethany said, reaching under her bed and pulling out the green binder we'd all started calling the Obsessive Files. It was crammed beyond capacity with everything about Colorado she could get her hands on. There were itineraries and computer printouts, coupons, guidebooks, even ancient, crayon-written lists we'd once made of which celebrities we would be on the lookout for (Ricky Martin and the Spice Girls were at the top of the list). "We haven't started yet."

"But you will be punished," Zack said in his game show announcer voice.

Bethany rolled her eyes. "He has an Oreo in his sock," she said.

"Ew," I said, flopping on the bed next to Zack. "I'm not eating it if that's what you're thinking."

"Nice, Spoiler Sally," he said to Bethany. "You got any soda?"

"In the fridge," Bethany said absently, flipping through a stack of maps. "Bring me one."

"Me too," I added.

"Oh, well, I do live to serve, after all," he said, hopping off the bed. "Hey, Mrs. M!" I heard him bellow when he left the room.

I took my chance while he was gone.

"Beth," I hissed.

"Hmm?" she responded, scratching her chin and studying the map. "Hey, you know, I think there's this dinosaur museum or something on the way there."

"Bethany!" I said again, louder this time. "Quick, while Zack's not in here." I motioned for her to sit on the bed next to me.

She looked up and shut the notebook, then sat next to me. "What?" she said, pushing a lock of hair behind her ear, and resting the notebook in her lap.

"Guess who called me."

"Who?"

"Cole."

Her eyes widened. "Seriously? Hot Guy Cole?"

I nodded, unable to keep my smile at bay.

"What did he want?"

I shook my head. "English class. He had a question about this Ray Bradbury novel they're reading. But then we talked about stupid stuff, too. You know, like that assembly we had last week. That kind of thing."

Bethany looked confused. "So why is this a big deal?"

I flopped back against her pillow and groaned. "I don't know," I said. "I just... it's not, is it?"

"Not unless you like him."

I giggled and smacked her with a Dr Pepper pillow. "Shut up; you know I kind of do," I said.

Her eyes got big. "You're finally admitting it?"

Holding back a huge laugh that wanted, for some reason I didn't even understand, to burst out of me, I nodded slowly. "Yeah," I said.

"And you think he likes you, too?"

Again, I nodded, feeling like a big happy dork with my smile.

"That's awesome," she said. "He's really cute, Alex. You should make your move."

"No way," I said, hitting her with the pillow again. Pieces of her hair floofed up, and she had to wrangle them down again. "And don't tell Zack. You know how he gets. The whole world would know tomorrow."

"Oh, please, Zack is the last person I would tell," she said. But then we could hear Zack coming down the hall, talking to one of Bethany's little brothers. Bethany opened the notebook again just in time for Zack to open the door, carrying the entire twelve-pack of Dr Pepper.

He stood in the doorway eyeing us. "Okay, I missed something," he said.

Bethany and I hovered over the notebook as if it was the most absorbing thing we'd ever seen in our lives.

"Uh-huh. Just so you know," he said, shutting the door with his foot and digging cans of soda out of the box, "I'm not going to any girly spa and wearing a short robe and cucumbers on my eyes while we're out there, if that's what you're planning."

Bethany and I glanced at each other and cracked up.

"But you can get massages at those places," I said.

"Yeah," Bethany agreed. "With lots of oil and maybe a hot masseuse walking on your back. Topless."

Zack tossed Dr Peppers onto the bed and flopped down next to them. "Alex," he said, smacking the back of my head as if he'd just had a brilliant idea, "I think I just thought of your punishment!"

"Ew!" I said, rolling away from him. "I am not coming near you with my bare feet. Or bare anything else, for that matter."

"Come on, Alex," he teased. "Best friends share everything. It's in the rule book. Rule number seventy-seven: Best friends don't keep things from each other."

Bethany and I locked eyes over his head and then giggled. For now, Zack didn't need to know that I was totally crushing on Cole.

I was still glowing from the phone call and Bethany's excitement for me when I got to school on Monday. Something about saying it out loud made my crush on Cole seem more real. I found myself looking around everywhere I went, hoping I'd see him and we'd get a chance to wave at each other. Maybe say hi. Maybe lock eyes. Which all seemed kind of goofy and oh-so-middle-school, but that was the way I'd started feeling when I was around Cole—like crushes were new to me.

But by seventh period, when he didn't show at tutoring, it was obvious that he was absent, and I felt a little deflated. By Tuesday, when he still wasn't back, I started to get anxious, and by Wednesday I was trying hard not to take it personally. I sat in the lab by myself, writing poems and wondering where Cole was.

It's not like it was a huge deal, of course. It's not like we were a couple, or even that I knew for sure he was into me. It was hardly the end of my world, not seeing him.

But when I got to The Bread Bowl Wednesday night and he was sitting in a booth in the corner, all by himself, that wave of crush rolled up over me again. I tried not to look too excited when I saw him. He waved. I waved back. I clocked in and took my place at the register and tried not to look up at him too often.

He had the Ray Bradbury book with him and was slowly sipping a cup of coffee with the book propped open in front of him, but I tried not to get too excited when I realized that every time I looked up, he was looking at me, too, instead of at the book.

After the dinner rush, Georgia sent me on break, and I decided to casually stop by Cole's table.

"Hey," I said, trying not to look too awkward. "Where've you been?"

He hesitated, glancing down at his book. "Family stuff," he said. "I'll be back tomorrow, I promise. That's why I'm trying to get caught up tonight."

"Oh," I said. "How far behind are you?"

He grimaced. "Really far. You on break or you off?"

"On break," I said. "I don't get off until eight." My turn to grimace.

"So you've got a few minutes?" he asked. Again with that smile. I nodded, feeling goose bumps rise on my arms. Something about that smile. It occurred to me that the tenderness I felt when Cole smiled at me was something I'd never really felt before. Dad never smiled, and Celia only frowned. Beth and Zack smiled at me all the time, but their smiles didn't feel like this. Their smiles felt like laughter. Cole's smile felt like warmth. And like it was meant for only me.

There were a few moments of awkward silence between us, during which time I mostly focused on the sweat that I could feel trickling down my back. Suddenly I was afraid that if I were to look down, I'd have giant pit stains and would die of embarrassment right on the spot. I cleared my throat. My fingers drifted to the dream catcher and pushed on the beads.

Then finally he shut the book and slid out of the booth. "Come with me," he said. "I have something to show you."

He brushed his hand up against mine as he walked past me, digging his keys out of his jacket. I followed him out to the parking lot.

He led me to an old blue muscle car — one I'd seen in the school parking lot without even registering whose it might be — and popped the trunk.

"You showed me your poem," he said over his shoulder as he walked, "so I figured it's my turn."

He reached into the trunk and pulled out a guitar case.

"Sit down," he said, motioning to the curb. I sat, wrapping my arms around my knees.

"You play guitar?" I asked.

"A little," he admitted. He laid the guitar case on the sidewalk behind me and thumbed open the clasp. He pulled out a gleaming acoustic and sat down next to me, laying it across his lap. "I taught myself how to play, so I'm not great or anything. It's just a hobby."

"Cool hobby," I said, running my finger down the strings. I could feel his shoulder, warm against mine. "I can't play anything."

"But you can write killer songs," he said. "Check it out."

He propped the guitar up against his chest and started strumming. His fingers moved along the strings like it was nothing. Like everyone could do this. After a few bars, he started humming, and then pretty soon he sang, softly, "I cannot swallow your hardened eyes..."

My mouth dropped open. My poem. He was singing the words of my poem. I honestly didn't know what to think. I was still self-conscious hearing my words out loud, and Cole looked so vulnerable, sitting on the sidewalk singing and playing guitar. Hearing my feelings out loud like that, I could almost feel them all over again—the night when the hole where my family should be had swallowed me so completely I could do nothing but write about it. It was such a raw moment—so exposed—it felt almost too intimate to handle. I dropped my forehead to my knees and listened, clenching my eyes tight. When he finished, I turned my head to face him, resting my cheek on my knees where my forehead had just been.

"That. Was so awesome," I said. "I can't believe you memorized my poem."

He plucked at a few random strings. "I didn't have all the words exactly right," he said. "But I tried to remember most of them. It was the first thing I thought about when I read it—wow, this would make a good song."

I reached out and strummed the guitar softly with my free hand. "I always wished I played an instrument."

"Really?" He moved so he could sit up straighter. "Maybe I'll teach you sometime. It's not that hard." He hovered his hand over mine and strummed the strings with more confidence. The vibration under my fingertips seemed to move down my entire body. I curled my toes up inside my shoes.

Suddenly, there was a knock on the front window. Georgia was standing there, fiddling with the blinds. She raised her eyebrows at me.

"Shoot," I said. "I've gotta get back."

Cole stood, holding his guitar by the neck. "Yeah," he said.

And there was that awkwardness between us again. On my end, the awkwardness was filled with the vibration of the guitar strings, which I still felt in the arches of my feet.

Just as I started to make a move for the door, he reached out and touched my wrist, very lightly and very quickly, as though he were afraid I might burn him.

"So maybe I can teach you a little this weekend?"

At first, I was confused. What was going on this weekend? And then, with a *thunk* of my heartbeat, I realized what he was really saying.

"I'm working Friday, but I'm off Saturday."

He smiled. "Okay. We can go to the lake or something. Bring food. I'll teach you 'Yesterday.' That was the first song I learned. It's pretty easy."

"Yeah, sounds great. You want to meet there?"

"No," he said. "I'll swing by your house and get you." We sat there nodding at each other, and then Georgia knocked on the window again.

We both turned our heads this time. Georgia raised her eyebrows even higher. Cole chuckled.

"I guess I should get back now," I said. "I'll see you in lab tomorrow?"

"Yeah," he said, bending over his open trunk and laying the guitar inside. "I'll be caught up, I promise."

I pointed at him. "You better be!"

"See ya, Emily Dickinson."

I forced myself to turn around and open the door.

I watched him shut his trunk, get into the driver's seat, and take off, then practically hopped, giggling and making little squealy noises, all the way to Georgia, who was now messing with the blinds in the back of the dining room.

"Long break," she said, without looking at me.

"He asked me out," I said, putting my hands on Georgia's shoulder. "We're going to the lake on Saturday."

"Ooh la la, the lake," Georgia said in a droll voice. "Sounds like trouble waiting to happen."

"Oh, please," I said, moving to the blinds next to her. I twirled them closed much more quickly than she had done.

"I'm a good girl. I don't know the first thing about trouble." I batted my eyes at her dramatically.

Georgia turned away, swishing her towel at me. "Oh, lordy, don't let me hear things like that."

I reached over and hugged Georgia from the side, barely able to contain my excitement.

If I had to sum up today in one word? *Finally.*

CHAPTER SEVEN

Celia was following me as I practically sprinted through the living room, tossing discarded dirty socks and old wet towels into a laundry basket. I straightened up the throw pillows on the couch and folded a blanket that had been lying crumpled in a corner for about a week, and draped it over our ugly couch.

You could definitely tell the place was kept by a family who'd given up. Normally that wouldn't have bothered me. It was depressing, but I was used to it. But with Cole coming over, I was suddenly embarrassed about everything that was my life.

The drapes were heavy with dust, the couch wearing through on the outside edges of the cushions, the carpet filthy and flattened. Everywhere were dirty glasses and plates and laundry. Bottles of fingernail polish were permanently stuck to the coffee table, which was sticky on one end from God-knows-what. I couldn't remember the last time I saw anyone vacuum. It was amazing what kind of mess you can get used to. It was amazing what kind of life you can get used to.

"So when are you going to have time then?" Celia said for the thousandth time. "We have to plan this out. It's not every day Shannin comes home."

This was definitely true. Shannin hardly ever came home to visit. It was going to be a huge surprise to Dad to see her show up, especially given that she was coming to help us throw a big surprise party for Dad's birthday, not that Dad ever celebrated anything. A surprise this big needed months of planning, or at least Celia thought it did. Dad's birthday wasn't until April, and it was just barely October. I thought six months was way more time than we needed to put this together. Celia thought it was nowhere near enough time. Shannin just tried to keep Celia happy, but that was easy to do from hundreds of miles away. Shannin didn't have to live with Celia's nagging. "Plus," Celia continued, "you told Shannin you'd do it, Alex."

"I will, okay? Just not today," I answered. "We've got time." She sighed and flopped down on the couch, knocking the blanket off. "Watch it," I said, bending over and picking it up. I spread it over the cushion to hide the stains again.

"What's the big deal about this guy anyway?" Celia asked. "You're acting like he's royalty or something. I saw him in the library the other day. I don't think he's all that."

"Of course you don't," I said. "Because if you liked a guy I liked, the world might reverse its spin on its axis or something. I just like him, okay? And I want him to like me. So I don't want this place to look so…"

"So like our house? Maybe I should get Zack's mom to come over here and be a mom stand-in. Then maybe you wouldn't have to be worried about how our family isn't good enough."

I glared at my sister. Celia never saw any reason to care about what had happened to our mother. She saw it the way Shannin did—Mom's death was what it was, and Dad's life was what it was, and none of it had anything to do with her. Celia and Shannin didn't seem to feel anything when a kid would ask how come our dad never said anything or when another adult would ask us where our mom was. My sisters didn't seem to care that they couldn't answer any questions about our mom because those questions had never been answered for us.

"It's not like that," I snapped. "I just want this place to look decent. You're just jealous." Usually Celia was the one with boys coming in and out of the house. For once, it felt good to have someone over for me. Someone better than any of the greasy boys she liked.

The doorbell rang. Celia made a mock surprised face and pulled herself off the couch as I scrambled to take an armful of dishes to the kitchen. "Yeah," she said. "I'm so jealous of you going out with a guy who still wears his old school's letter jacket to his new school so everyone can see how amazing he is." She reached to open the door as I scurried into the kitchen and dumped the dishes in the sink.

I stood by the kitchen counter and took a few breaths, trying to clear my head. My hand drifted to the dream catcher necklace hanging beneath my shirt.

I wasn't embarrassed of my family; I just wanted to impress Cole. In a way, I felt the same as when I'd shown him my poem—nervous and afraid to show my real self to him. Afraid that he wouldn't like what he saw.

I heard the front door open and could hear Celia talking. Quickly I ran my fingers through my hair and stepped out into the living room.

Instead of Cole, Zack was sitting on my couch, his foot up on our coffee table, the remote already in his hand. Celia was sitting next to him, blabbing on about something unimportant. Zack didn't even look up when I came into the room. I walked over and smacked at his leg.

"I just cleaned that," I said. "Move your foot."

He wiggled his foot back and forth on the table, eyes still glued to the TV. "Moving it," he said.

"Ha-ha-ha," I said. "You're so funny." I pushed his foot and it flopped to the floor.

He finally glanced at me. "What? Why do you care so much about where my foot is all of a sudden?"

"Ever since the Prince of Pine Gate is coming to pick her up," Celia said.

Zack settled on a channel and dropped the remote in his lap. "Who? You mean that new guy in the tutor lab?" He leaned over and pulled a bent toothpick out of his front pocket, straightened it, and popped it into his mouth.

I nodded. "We're going out tonight."

Zack shook his head. "Guy's in my gym class. He's kind of a tool. Thinks he's a badass. Got a big mouth."

I picked up the laundry basket and held it against my hip. "That's rich coming from you." I started toward the basement. "Bethany thinks he's hot," I yelled over my shoulder. "She's happy for me."

"Bethany thinks everybody's hot," Zack yelled back as I tromped down the stairs. I set the basket on the floor next to the washing machine. Just as I was heading back up the stairs, the doorbell rang again.

"I'll get it!" I hollered, and raced up the stairs. I needn't have rushed—Celia and Zack were into the show they were watching and weren't making a move toward the door at all. "It's probably Cole," I said, catching my breath.

"Be still, my heart," Zack cooed in a falsetto voice. Celia giggled.

I pulled open the door and there was Cole, wearing a black T-shirt and jeans, his shirt tight across his chest, showing off the muscles underneath. He looked so strong and confident standing there. Like he could protect me from anything.

"Hey," I said, trying not to sound all crushy and breathless and like I was just checking out his pecs. "Come on in."

Cole stepped through the door. I could swear I saw his smile fade just a bit when he looked over at the couch. *God,* I thought, assessing the dusty room, *it's still a disaster in here*. But just as quickly his smile returned. "Hey," he said in the general direction of the couch. "How's it goin'?"

Celia twiddled her fingers in Cole's direction without even looking up, but Zack got off the couch and walked over to us.

"Hey," Zack said, stepping up to my side and leaning against me with his elbow on my shoulder, just like he always did. It had never bothered me before, but when he did it this time I suddenly wanted to shove him away. It felt too much like... ownership. Zack was my best friend, but sometimes he needed a reminder that I didn't belong to him. "You're in my weight lifting class."

Cole's eyes drifted to Zack's elbow. "Yeah, I guess I am."

I shimmied out from under Zack's arm. "This is Zack," I said. "He's my next-door neighbor. We've been friends since we were both in diapers," I added, then felt myself blush after saying. God, who talks about diapers on their first date?

"Oh, so you're sort of like a brother then?" Cole said.

Zack squinted at him, chomped on his toothpick for a moment, and then said, "I guess you could say something like that." Something in his voice was sharp enough to make Celia look over at us, curious.

I clenched my jaw and glared at Zack. He was acting like a jerk. But he didn't see me. His eyes were locked with Cole's, and the air in the room suddenly turned very uncomfortable.

It was weird, really. Zack definitely had his opinions

about people, but he was the kind of guy who almost always liked everyone. I could tell he definitely didn't like Cole, and I wondered what had gone on between them in gym class.

I tried to give Zack the benefit of the doubt—maybe he was just in a bad mood—but it pissed me off that he couldn't take his mood out on someone else.

"Cool," Cole said at last, and just like that the weird feeling in the room evaporated. Then he turned to me. "You ready to go?"

"Yeah," I said, grabbing my keys and my cell phone. "Definitely."

We both turned toward the door, Cole's hand on the small of my back, sending a shock of electricity all over my body.

"Hey, I thought we had plans tonight," Zack said at our backs. "It's Saturday." Just like that the electric feeling was gone and was replaced by annoyance. Whatever Zack's deal was, this was completely uncool. He was making it sound like we had a date or something.

"Nope," I said. "Bethany already knows. I texted her this morning. She was supposed to call you. We'll get together later."

"Whatever," Zack said. "But you know how she gets when you miss one of her Vacay Days. Tonight we were gonna work out, you know, sleeping arrangements and stuff for the trip." He got a cocky little grin when he said the words "sleeping arrangements," and I wanted to punch him for it. I was so going to make him regret this.

"Okay," I said, through clenched teeth, looking back at him as I opened the door. "Later."

Zack shrugged and pulled the toothpick out of his mouth. "Cool. Have fun, kids."

Cole turned and flashed a look at Zack. "See you in the gym," he said.

Zack lifted his chin slightly but didn't answer, and Cole and I plunged outside and shut the door behind us.

"Whoa," Cole said once we were on the front porch. "He always so protective?"

I thought it over and, you know, yeah, ever since I could remember, Zack had been so protective of me and Bethany it sometimes bordered on irritating. And whatever that little standoff was with Cole in my living room just now went beyond irritating and straight into obnoxious.

"Yeah," I said, stepping off the porch. "I'm sorry. I'll talk to him. He'll calm down."

We walked toward Cole's car. "He's intense," Cole said, pulling open the car door for me. "Your parents really letting you go on a trip with him?"

All I could hear were the words "your parents," and my face burned. I was definitely not ready to have the so-tell-me-about-your-parents discussion with Cole yet. I could never just say "my mom died" and leave it at that. Everyone always wanted to know how, and I hated answering that question. It was way too complicated. Usually I lied about what happened to her. But I didn't want to lie to Cole. I also didn't want to tell him that my mom was "crazy as goosehouse shit" on our first date together. I wanted this to be a fun night.

I forced a chuckle. "Actually, he'll be fine," I said. "Bethany and I wouldn't dream of going without him."

The idea that I wouldn't take Zack with me on the trip seemed almost laughable. Zack had been there from day one. He knew about the photos under my bed. He saw me cry when Bethany spent that Saturday shopping in St. Louis with her mom. He witnessed the embarrassed look on my face when I had to sit with him and his mom at the fifth-grade Mother's Day Tea. He backed me up when I told people that my mom died of cancer, and never made me act as though she was anything other than perfect and amazing. He understood how important this was to me. Plus, without Zack, we wouldn't be the Terrible Three. And, for all his faults, he did have a way of making things fun. "It's kind of a special trip. For all three of us."

"Well then," Cole said as I sat down in the passenger seat. He placed his hands on the roof of the car and peered down at me, his body blocking the whole doorframe, his face in shadows. "I'd apologize for keeping you from going to your friend's house tonight, but I guess I'm kind of selfish. I want you all to myself, Emily Dickinson."

He paused, then squatted down next to me. At last I was able to see his face, which was soft, friendly, just like it was every day in the tutor lab. I didn't know what Zack's problem with Cole was, but at the moment I didn't really care. This may be our first official date, but I'd been tutoring the guy for weeks. I knew him better than Zack did. I knew how nice he was. Whatever had happened between the two of them, Zack was wrong about him.

"I didn't get to tell you," Cole said, running his finger along my forearm. I got chills, but they felt warm and tingly. "You look gorgeous."

I smiled. "So do you."

He gazed at me another long minute and then slowly got up and shut my door. Sitting in his car, which smelled like cologne and leather, watching him walk around to the driver's door, I couldn't help but get an excited flutter in my stomach. Cole was so amazing.

I was totally going to have to have a chat with Zack later. His personal problems with Cole were *not* going to screw this up for me.

CHAPTER EIGHT

Cole had asked me out for our second date before we were even finished with our first.

"Hey," he'd said, sitting next to me on top of the shelter picnic table, both of us staring off into the dark woods that separated the picnic area from the lake. We could hear the water off in the distance, every so often lapping up against the rocks on the shore, just loud enough to drown out the rumbling car engines on the highway, which wound around behind us. He was leaning back on his hands casually, his legs stretched out and crossed on the bench beneath us. I could feel his forearm against my back if I leaned backward just the slightest bit. The sensation made me feel full of nervous energy, like I could jump up and dash through the woods, dive right into the water on the other side, and swim for miles on one breath. "You hear about the new *House of Horrors* movie?"

"Yeah," I said. "It looks really scary. I'm dying to see

it." I leaned back gently, felt his arm, then bent forward again, rubbing the goose bumps on my shins.

"Cold?" he asked. I nodded, and he took off his letter jacket and draped it over my shoulders.

I dipped my head, stealing secretive sniffs. It smelled like him—cologne, leather, something else kind of earthy and sweet—and it was warm. The goose bumps on my legs rose up even farther.

"Did you see the second one?" I asked. "The one where that really nasty-looking dead girl comes out of the closet? Scared the crap out of me."

He laughed. "Yeah, that was awesome! And the guy with the machete in the barn?"

I nodded. "Totally gross."

We both laughed, and once again I felt his hand snake behind me, only closer this time. I didn't need to lean back to feel his arm against me anymore. It was just there. Now the goose bumps had spread to my arms, even though I was warm under his jacket.

"So you wanna go next weekend?" he'd asked, and when I nodded, he'd pulled his arm around me even closer.

"Just a warning, though. I may have my hands over my eyes the whole time," I said.

He nudged me with his arm. "Chicken."

We sat and listened to the water through the trees for a while, Cole telling me about Pine Gate and me griping about my sisters. I slipped my arms into the sleeves of his jacket, looking at the patches.

"So you played football at Pine Gate, too?" I asked.

He nodded, dragging a leaf up the length of his thigh and back down again. "Yeah. And baseball. Pretty much every sport. Been playing since I was six."

"Six? Wow, you must be really athletic."

He shrugged, tossed the leaf to the ground. "Okay, I guess. I'm sick of it. Don't really want to play anymore."

"Then why don't you quit? Just not try out."

He let out a bark of laughter and hopped off the table, bending and stretching his legs one at a time. My side, where he'd just been sitting, felt drafty. "I'm just considering myself lucky that moving got me out of football this year. My dad would kill me if I didn't try out for basketball," he said.

"Why?" I asked. "It's your life. He can't force you to play if you don't want to." I wondered what it must be like to have parents who cared enough to force you to do things you didn't want to do. Would I hate it? Or would I just be glad for the attention?

Cole kicked at the foot of the table a few times, then all of a sudden brightened. "Hey, hang on," he said. He jogged out of the shelter to his car and rummaged around in the backseat. He jogged back to the shelter holding a worn football. "Think fast," he said, tossing it to me. I caught it just in time. "C'mon, I'll show you a play," he said, grabbing my free hand and pulling me off the table.

I couldn't help giggling. "I can't play football," I said, tripping after him into the grass.

"Sure you can," Cole said. "Watch." He grabbed my

shoulders and squared them up so that my back was facing him. "Okay, now you hike it to me on three, and then you run like a bat out of hell that way. We're gonna call the area past the water pump the end zone, so right before you get to the pump, start looking back. I'll throw it to you for the TD."

I laughed, shaking my head. "I can't do all that...."

He pushed my shoulders down toward the ground, leading me to a snap position. "Sure you can. Just do it."

I bent over. Cole yelled, "Thirty-seven...ninety-two... three!"

I didn't even look back. I shoved the ball backward between my legs and took off running through the grass, laughing the whole way. The air, just a few minutes ago making me shiver, now slid across my skin, giving me energy. As soon as I got to the water pump, I looked back. Cole pulled his arm back and launched the ball to me.

It was hard to see the ball in the dark, and I stumbled backward a little bit, squinting into the sky. In a flash, there it was, coming right at my chest. I reached out with both arms, maybe even closed my eyes a little bit, and, miraculously, caught it.

I squealed, pausing only long enough for it to register that I was holding the ball, and turned and ran past the water pump. "Touchdown!" I yelled, then did a goofy little dance, spiking the ball, then pointing my fingers in the air above my head and wiggling my hips. "She scores!"

Cole was practically doubled over, he was laughing so hard. "Throw it back," he yelled.

I bent over and picked up the ball, then lobbed it as hard as I could toward Cole, trying to remember Coach Hennessee's instructions from freshman PE—fingers on laces, snap the wrist. The ball soared almost past Cole. He had to jump to catch it, pulling it out of the night sky like a lightning bug.

"Hey!" His eyes lit up. "She's gorgeous, writes poetry, and can throw a tight spiral. She's perfect!"

I tossed my hair. "You should see me tackle," I teased, then crouched in a sumo pose, flexing my arms out on each side menacingly.

"Oh yeah?" Cole asked.

"Bring it, Nancy," I growled in a deep voice, cracking up.

"Let's see you try, baby," he said, and then started running toward me, narrating in a breathless commentator voice. "Cozen finds a hole in the defense. He's at the fifty, the forty, the thirty...looks like nobody will stop him now...."

I adopted my own commentator voice. "What's this? A defender on the ten-yard line...there's no way he'll get through...."

I ran at him full-tilt, my arms outstretched, but a few feet before I reached him, Cole tossed the ball over his shoulder. It bounced on the grass behind him. He took two long steps toward me, wrapped his arms around my waist, and pulled me down, swiveling so we both landed on our sides, his shoulder absorbing the fall.

"Hey," I squealed, "I was supposed to tackle you!"

"You never stood a chance," he said.

We both rolled onto our backs, half-laughing, half-gasping for breath. One of his arms was still underneath me, feeling comfortable under my waist.

After a while, he turned his head toward me, the grass poking shallow little indentations in his cheek. "You are full of surprises," he said.

I shrugged. "Trust me, I didn't know I could throw a football like that. I didn't even think I was going to pass PE freshman year."

He sat up, wiggling his arm out from under me and crossing his legs beneath himself. He pulled a blade of grass and fiddled with it. "It's not just that," he said. "You write, you plan graduation trips, you make a mean cup of coffee, and you aren't afraid to stand in the way of someone who's running at you full-tilt and could probably cream you. You're really amazing."

I was expecting to feel myself blush. Or feel that awkward feeling. Or embarrassment. But I didn't. I felt comfortable, lying in the grass, looking up at Cole and the stars beyond him. Something about him felt comfortable. "Thanks," I said, and for the first time, I didn't feel like I really needed to say any more.

He tossed the piece of grass to the side and plucked another one, running his fingers along it. "How come you didn't title your poem?" he asked me.

I rolled over onto one elbow and plucked my own piece

of grass, my belly pressing up against Cole's knee. "I don't know," I said. "I guess I didn't think about it."

"What title would you give it now?" he asked.

I thought about it. Plucked another piece of grass and rolled it into a ball between my thumb and forefinger. After a while, I said, "Maybe I'd just call it 'A Poem Without a Name.' Could be kind of symbolic. Like, the relationship described in the poem is over. It's done. It's no longer got a name. I don't know. That's cliché." I wrinkled my nose.

"Was it about you?" he asked. "Like, a breakup or something?"

For a split second, I considered just getting it over with and telling Cole about my mom. And not the edited version, either—not the one in which she died and is now an angel looking down at me and we'll someday be reunited, but the real version. The version that's ugly and embarrassing. But the moment passed, and I shook my head.

"Nah, I just wrote it," I said.

"I like it. You know what I would title it?" He pitched another piece of grass and leaned back on his hands, stretching his legs out in front of him. "I would call it 'Bitter End.' Because maybe it's not over, you know? Like they're sticking it out until..." He held up his hands, a cocky grin on his face.

"The bitter end," I finished for him, nodding my head. I pursed my lips. "Hmmm."

He poked me in the ribs with his finger. "What do you mean, hmmm? Come on, you have to admit that's a pretty good title."

"I don't know," I said, giggling and curling away from his finger. "How about this—if your song ever makes it big and, like, wins a Grammy or something, I'll let you title it."

"Deal," he said. "Hey, speaking of. Weren't we gonna teach you a song tonight?"

I brightened. "Yeah!"

He stood and reached down to pull me up, and then held my hand all the way to the car, loosely, as if we'd done it a million times before. "Get in," he said. "I've got the perfect place for guitar lessons."

CHAPTER NINE

We both slid into Cole's car and he took off, pulling out of the shelter and winding through the park, past all the other shelters, where other cars sat, dark and foggy, in the parking lots. Some of the shelters had fires smoldering in their shelter pits, just begging for the park rangers to show up and make everyone leave. The park was supposed to close at dusk, but nobody ever paid attention to that rule—not even the park rangers, as long as nobody ran the risk of burning the woods down.

We bumped along the lake road, past the closed swimming beach and the boat rental dock, and then pulled onto a grassy, gated road. Cole pulled up to the gate, put his car in park, and reached down below the dash to pop the trunk.

"Here?" I asked.

He nodded. "Well, not *here*, here. In there. The spillway." He pointed at the gate. A rusted red-and-white sign hung from the middle of it: DANGER: NO TRESPASSING. DROWNING RISK.

The sign needn't have hung there. Everybody already knew the risk of hanging out at the top of the spillway. There to drain excess water and keep the lake from flooding during rainy periods, the spillway gates could open at any time, releasing a rush of water down the thirty-foot concrete drop into the pool below.

Legend had it that sometime in the seventies, a drunk girl had climbed over the gate and immediately fallen to her death, going head over heels down the steep concrete slab and drowning at the bottom. Shannin always claimed it was just urban legend, and nobody ever seemed to know who the "drunk girl" was, only that she'd gasped and cried for help and there was nothing her friends could do but watch from the top of the spillway and call out her name.

The only kids who crossed the spillway gate were the kids with a death wish. One wrong step and you could tumble one way down the concrete or the other way into the lake itself. Or if a gate opened, the rush of water would take you down into the water below whether you wanted to go or not.

And if a park ranger caught you up there, you'd be in huge trouble.

"Cole, I don't think…" I started, but Cole had already gotten out and was banging the trunk shut, his guitar case in one hand. He came around to my side and pulled open the door.

"Come on," he said, holding out his other hand. When I hesitated, he bent to look me in the eye. "I'm not going to let anything happen to you," he said. He slid his finger down my cheek, and I got butterflies. "Besides, it hasn't rained in weeks. The spillway isn't going to open up anytime soon. Worrywart."

He winked at me, and suddenly I was overcome with a surge of boldness. *This is what life is about, right?* I told myself. Taking risks. Going for it. Not being like Dad—a husk of a person shifting this way and that in the wind, with no real place to land. Life was about staring down a tackle. Standing at the top of the spillway. Climbing gates with danger signs. I grabbed his hand and got out.

"Who you calling worrywart?" I teased, shutting the car door with my hip and darting to the gate. In three pulls, I was straddling the top of it, looking down at Cole. "What's taking you so long?" I said, and swung my leg over the top, pushing off from the fence and letting myself fall to my feet on the other side, barely able to believe I had just climbed that gate. I brushed my hands off and planted them on my hips. "Well?"

Cole's face split into such a wide smile, even his dimple disappeared into a deep groove. "Here," he said, and pushed the guitar case to the top of the gate, where it balanced and then slowly tipped in my direction. I stretched until my hands were around the neck, then pulled it down. Cole took the fence in two pulls and landed within inches of me, our faces so close our noses could touch. "Let's go," he said, his hand snaking over mine to take the case. I felt numb, but deep down my whole body was buzzing with adrenaline.

We high-stepped through the tall weeds, ducking under low branches in the grove of trees that separated us from the concrete ledge at the top of the spillway. When we came out on the other side, I held my breath, both hands pressed against my stomach, my heart pounding.

From the top, it looked as if the concrete went down forever, a straight drop into a pool of green, mossy water at its base. At that moment, I was sure the urban legend was correct about one thing—if something went wrong, you would die and there would be nothing anyone could do about it other than call your name and cry.

Cole stepped over a disintegrating Styrofoam cooler and planted a foot on the ledge. He noticed me frozen, half in the trees, and chuckled. "Eyes open or closed?" he asked, raising his foot to take another step.

"Cole, I don't think—"

"Closed?" he interrupted. "Okay, but that seems kind of dangerous." He closed his eyes and put his raised foot down, taking a step forward.

"Cole, don't, you could..." He took another step, holding his arms out to his sides, the guitar case dangling over the edge of the spillway dramatically as he walked along the ledge. My heart beat so hard it brought tears to my eyes. "Open!" I shouted. "Open!"

He stopped and doubled over, laughing. He sat the guitar case on the ground and came back to where I was standing. He held out both hands. "It's okay," he said. "I was looking. Come here."

His eyes, searching deep into mine, felt like danger and safety all rolled into one. My hands shook as I pulled them from my belly and placed them gently in his hands. He snaked them up to my elbows and gently tugged me through the grass. He walked backward, guiding my shaking legs and unwilling feet over the discarded cooler and onto the concrete. I could barely believe this was me, doing this.

"See?" he said softly, pulling me to the middle of the spillway. "You're safe, Emily Dickinson."

He let go of my arms, and we both turned to look out over the spillway. I let out the lungful of air I hadn't realized I'd been holding. I felt like I might throw up. But at the same time, I felt exhilarated, as if I was just now waking up. Just now feeling alive. As if Cole had brought me back from the depressing silence I was used to living in. Here, there were no brains being washed off anything. Here, there was just . . . life.

We stood there for a while, pointing out things — a hawk's nest in a tree below us, smoke rising from one of the shelter houses — the headlights of oncoming traffic washing over us. Finally, Cole sat down, his legs hanging over the lip of the spillway, turned, and opened his guitar case. He shuffled backward a few inches, then patted the concrete in front of him.

"Sit down," he said, and I did, lowering myself shakily into the U made by his legs, leaning my body back against his and feeling the concrete, still warm from soaking up the day's sun, underneath us.

He lowered his guitar into my lap, carefully winding the strap around my shoulders, then grabbed my hands with his and positioned them on the strings. I could feel his breath against my ear, his biceps pulling taut against the backs of my arms, his legs curled around mine. Slowly, he guided my hands with his, humming and naming chords into my neck.

We sat there like that for hours, the stars blazing above us—just the two of us, alone in a place that was so frightening and wonderful.

I was so scared and so exhilarated I didn't know where one feeling stopped and the other began. All I knew was I loved the feeling. And I never wanted it to end.

CHAPTER TEN

I sprawled upside down over the couch, my legs snaking up over the pillows and my head hanging limply toward the floor. I could feel all the blood rushing to my temples. When I talked, I sounded like I had a bad cold.

"We could whitewater raft," I said. "Watch out, Beth!"

There was a boom, followed by a groan of frustration. Zack burst into hysterical laughter. "You totally walked right into it," he said, crazily punching buttons on a video game controller.

"Go ahead, laugh it up, Zackhole," Bethany said, reverting to our seventh-grade nickname for Zack. There was another explosion, and this time Bethany laughed, shoving Zack with her shoulder and jostling the couch so that the top of my head grazed the floor.

Last weekend, while I'd been at the lake with Cole, Bethany and Zack had a Vacay Day at Zack's house without me.

Somewhere between Bethany beating Zack at *Holy Rollers 5* and Zack devouring an entire plateful of chocolate chip cookies, Zack's mom had pointed out to them that we probably wouldn't be doing much skiing if we were planning on going to Colorado in July.

"I can't believe I didn't think of that before," Bethany said, flopping back on my couch. "I guess I just assumed that you could ski any time of the year in the mountains."

"No problem," Zack said, plugging in a controller while Bethany and I picked at the tacos I'd made for tonight's Vacay Day. It was my turn to host, but I didn't have the money for pizza. Not if I was going to actually get to Colorado and do anything fun. "We'll just go in the winter."

"Hell-o, college," Bethany said, pushing her glasses back up on her nose.

"Hell-o, winter break," Zack countered, tossing her a controller.

He held a controller up at me. I shook my head, and he backed up to the couch and sat between us, holding a controller in his lap. I'd shoved my plate of tacos on the coffee table and flipped myself upside down so my feet were by Zack's head and my head was by his feet. They continued to bicker while my mind drifted to Cole.

The week in the tutor lab had been way tense between the two of us, in a good way. It was tough to focus on noun and verb placement when all I could think about, sitting across from him and staring into his eyes, was being alone with him again. Having his arm resting against my back, brushing up against me, coaxing out the goose bumps on my legs. Sitting on the top of the world, feeling puffs of air against my cheek while we brushed our fingers over the guitar strings.

We were supposed to go see the *House of Horrors* movie that night, but after Bethany burst into American lit class Monday morning in full vacation panic mode, I knew there was no way I could ditch our planning session two Saturdays in a row. I begged off my date with Cole, made tacos, and sighed as I tried to come up with things we could do in the summer instead of ski.

"We could, uh...go on a hike in the mountains," I said.

"Um, isn't that the first thing we're going to do?" Zack asked. "It's a given. And you can hike up a mountain in December, just so you...ha-HA! I just blew your arm off!"

"Gah!" Bethany roared, punching him in the shoulder. "Yeah, I think one hike is enough."

"We could ride horses," I suggested.

"You can ride a horse in Dec—dammit!"

"Take that, Zackhole!" Bethany screeched.

"Take that, Zackhole," Zack mimicked. "Bethroom," he said, pulling out his old elementary school nickname for her. This conversation was only going downhill, and I started to get annoyed. I'd missed a date for this?

"Zackass!" Bethany retorted.

"What about bike riding?" I said irritably, but they kept arguing, as if I wasn't even in the room with them.

"Cowboy Ugly!"

I tried again. "I think you can mountain-bike down Pike's Peak."

"Zackwad!"

"You guys," I said, but they kept horsing around. "You guys," I said again. Someone's controller cord knocked a taco off the table onto the floor by my head. "Stop it! God!" I shouted.

The couch went still.

"I'm trying to actually be productive," I said, my tone sharp. I could feel my pulse in my forehead. "You're acting like little kids!"

There was a beat of silence—the only thing I could hear was the ominous video game background music—and then suddenly both Zack and Bethany cracked up.

"She's right," Bethany said. "You're acting like a real Zack-off!" She burst into giggles, and there was more jostling.

The doorbell rang, and I struggled to get upright so I could answer it. But I'd been upside down too long, and Zack was too quick. He tossed his controller into Bethany's lap and leaped so he was sitting on my stomach, facing the back of the couch, where my feet were.

"Little kid, huh? I'll show you little kid." He wrapped his arm around my calves, locking my feet into place, and started tickling them, which he knew I hated more than anything in the world.

"Stop!" I squealed and laughed, pounding on his back,

trying to pull my feet out of his grasp. All hell broke loose on the couch as Bethany came to my aid, lunging into Zack's side over and over again, trying to knock him off me. I writhed, laughing until I could see spots in front of my eyes, like I was going to pass out, and continued smacking his back. I couldn't breathe.

Zack ate it up, just like Zack always did. If I said, "Don't. Stop," he would say, "Don't stop? Well, if you insist..." If I begged, "Get off," he would respond, "Well, I'll try, but I really just think of you as a friend, Alex."

He was impossible, but at least I wasn't mad anymore.

Celia stomped in from the kitchen, chewing. "There's someone at the door," she said accusingly.

"I can't get up," I said, between laughs. "This idiot is on top of me!" I banged on his back like I was banging on a door. Celia rolled her eyes at me and reached for the doorknob.

"Idiot, huh?" Zack said, and started tickling me again, sending me into a new gale of laughter and squeals.

I didn't see who had come through the door until Zack stopped abruptly. I pounded on his back with the flat of my hand a few more times and then opened my eyes. Cole was standing just inside the front door, peering at us over the couch. He had his hands pushed down in his jeans pockets, his shoulders slumped.

I felt even more blood rush to my face, and all of a sudden the room got very serious. I planted both palms on Zack's back and pushed. "Get. Up," I said through clenched teeth.

He raised himself up so he was kneeling on the couch

cushion and I *thunk*ed, headfirst, onto the floor, my legs slithering out from under Zack as I tried to right myself, pulling my shirt down and smoothing my hair with my hands. Bethany was still on her knees at Zack's side. She snickered and shoved him with her shoulder.

"Hey," I said, ignoring the head rush I was getting from being upright. I walked around the couch. "I wasn't expecting you. We were trip-planning." Even as I said it, I knew how it sounded. Of course we weren't trip-planning. That much Cole could see with his own eyes.

"No problem," he said, grinning. "I just thought I'd stop by."

Celia had moved over to the couch and sat where I'd just been sitting, picking up a taco. "Add me in," she said to Zack.

Zack walked across the room and bent over the game console, plugging in another controller. He didn't say a word, but he looked extremely put out.

"Hey, Cole," Bethany said, turning around and lowering herself back into playing position. "Taco? We can add you in, too."

Zack aimed a look at Bethany, and she shrugged like, *What am I supposed to do?* I didn't think I was supposed to see that and wondered what Bethany knew that I didn't know.

"Ah, no. Thanks," Cole said. "I'm not staying." He reached out and touched the back of my hand with his fingertips. "Can I talk to you for a second? Alone?"

86

"Um, yeah," I said. "Of course."

I stepped around him and took my jacket off the hook by the door. "Be right back, guys," I said, then opened the front door and stepped outside, pulling Cole behind me. They'd already started calling names again. I don't think they even heard me.

Outside, the air was crisp and not quite fall-like. Another clear night when the dew comes early and clings to your ankles as you walk through the grass. I turned to face Cole on the front porch, but right away there was a burst of laughter from inside. Cole's face twitched toward the front window. I could tell what he was thinking—this still didn't feel like we were alone.

I stepped off the front porch, grabbing Cole's hand, and walked down the driveway, then turned left on the sidewalk toward the neighborhood playground where Zack and Bethany and I used to play when we were little kids.

Cole and I said nothing. Just walked. My forehead was still pounding, and I was embarrassed and unsure what Cole was thinking. Our shoes made scuffling noises against the sidewalk as we plodded along, the laughter from my living room disappearing.

When we got to the park, the sounds of our footsteps changed as the pea gravel shifted under our feet. I slogged through the gravel to the jungle gym, climbing up a ladder and crawling into a tunnel at the top. Halfway through, I stopped and peeked out at Cole, motioning for him to join me.

The tunnel was where Zack and Bethany and I used to go in middle school when we wanted to be alone but weren't old enough yet to really go anywhere.

I settled myself right in the middle of the tunnel, where it's darkest, and sat, curving my back along the wall. Cole crawled in after me and then stopped awkwardly on his knees when he reached me.

"Hi," I whispered in the familiar dark, barely able to make out his facial features.

"Hey," he said, his voice flat.

"You wanted alone," I said, forcing a breathy laugh, trying to break the ice. I bit my bottom lip, waiting.

After a beat, I heard him chuckle, too, and could feel him shift his weight so he was off his knees, his back curved along the side of the tunnel opposite me, so we were facing each other. "We're definitely alone," he agreed.

We were both silent for a minute, as I replayed the scene Cole had walked in on in my head. Even though I knew it was innocent, how would it have felt to Cole? How would I have felt if I'd walked in on him with a girl sitting on top of him and tickling him?

"Don't be mad," I said. "Zack was just being a goof. It's what he does. There's nothing behind it."

Cole let out a little gust of air. I felt my hair move gently against my shoulder. "I'm not mad," he said. But his voice sounded very flat, and something about the feeling in the air between us made me think he was angry. "I just..." He stopped and shifted position again, the tunnel jiggling.

I waited. He didn't go on.

"They were acting like jerks," I said, rolling my eyes and feeling flushed. "I was trying to get them…I should have gone out with you tonight instead." I reached out and touched his leg with the tip of my finger. Out of the darkness his finger pressed down on mine, holding it against his leg.

"I just need to know," he said. "Do you like him?"

I laughed. "Zack? No."

He let up on my finger, and started rubbing it with his. "I just…I really like you, Alex. But I can't share you." There was something very raw in his voice.

I picked up his hand with both of mine, then pressed my palm against his. "You don't have to," I said. "I like you. Nobody else."

I felt another gust of air. "He wants you, you know."

I shook my head, even though he couldn't see it. The thought of Zack "wanting" me seemed almost laughable. It would be like Bethany "wanting" me. "He doesn't," I said. "You just don't understand our relationship."

"No," he said. "I guess I don't. But what you don't understand is that I want to explode every time I see him, because he's always got his hands all over you."

I pressed my palm against his even harder. "Then I'll make him stop."

He sighed, long and hard this time. "My Alex," he whispered, curling his fingers around mine, our palms still matched. "My little Emily Dickinson."

We stayed that way for a long time, talking about poetry

and football and the spillway and movies and English class. Anything but Zack and Bethany.

By the time we got back to my house and Cole drove away, Bethany and Zack were no longer in my living room. I could hear them talking on the steps of Zack's front porch. I walked across the grass, feeling an irritated scowl stretch my whole face downward.

"Ah, how's Big C?" Zack asked. "So hot he's positively melty?"

"Shut up," I said.

"Ouch," Zack said. "Someone's touchy. Don't make me start tickling you again."

"No," I said. "You have to stop doing that. Especially if Cole's around, okay?"

Zack's eyes widened. He glanced at Bethany, and then issued a bark of laughter. "Are you being serious right now?"

For some reason his laughter stirred up even more annoyance in me. "Yes, I'm being totally serious right now," I said. "He walked into my house and saw another guy sitting on top of me. Can you really blame him for being a little weirded out by it?"

Zack's face twisted with annoyance. Zack was the kind of guy who rarely got irritated, but when he did, it sometimes got ugly. "Uh, yeah, actually. I can," he said. "This guy's known you, like, five minutes. You've gone out what? Once?" He stood up and dug around in his jeans pocket, fishing out his plastic tube of toothpicks. He popped it open and slid a toothpick out, gesturing with it. "Is this why he came by? To bust us doing something bad?"

"No," I said, crossing my arms. "He was stopping by to say hi. Not that I need to justify anything to you. You're my best friend, not my dad."

"Exactly. Your best friend. So he needs to deal."

"No, you need to stop acting like I'm your girlfriend."

Zack's eyes narrowed and he stuck the toothpick into his mouth. He chomped on it angrily and then turned to Bethany. "Back me up here."

Bethany looked miserable. She cleared her throat and licked her lips, scuffed a pock in the concrete with her shoe, then shrugged. "Alex has a point. Just...don't tickle her so much when Cole's around. It's not that big a deal." She lifted her eyes to me. "But you did kind of ditch us," she said. "Again."

I put my hands on my hips. There were a million things I wanted to say. *No, I didn't ditch you. You weren't doing anything but playing video games anyway. Why do we need to have planning sessions every stinking weekend? And, um, yeah, by the way, you're making me choose between you and Cole, which I would never do to either of you.*

And when I thought about it that way, it seemed like they were the ones being very unfair.

"Next week we'll have to really nail some things down," she said, pulling her feet in closer to her chest, her flip-flops making a scratching sound against the concrete.

91

"I can't," I said. "I'm going out with Cole next Saturday. You'll have to play video games without me."

I turned on my heel and left, barely hearing the frustrated noise Zack made at my back, or the low murmuring between them as I stormed across the lawn.

Two hours later, when I was getting ready for bed, they were still out there. And I was still mad. I couldn't believe that, after all we'd been through as the Terrible Three, it looked more like they were two and I was one.

At least I had Cole.

CHAPTER ELEVEN

As it turned out, I wasn't going to miss anything anyway. Bethany's grandpa fell getting out of the bathtub, and the whole family was hanging out at the hospital, waiting for doctors to stitch up his forehead and patch his two broken ribs and sprained wrist.

Zack was going to a soccer game with some girl named Hannah from drama club.

Cole picked me up just as Zack was leaving to pick up his date, the two of them eyeing each other across the yard like stray dogs getting ready to fight.

"Come on," I murmured to Cole, pulling on his elbow to distract him. Zack and I had patched things up, and I didn't want him to think I was encouraging Cole to stare him down.

Cole shook his head and chuckled as he got into the car. "That guy definitely doesn't like me," he said. "In weight training, I refuse to let him spot me. I'm afraid he'd let a weight fall on me and choke me to death."

"He'll come around," I said, staring out my window at Zack's car backing out the driveway and zooming down the street. "He's got a date tonight," I added, hoping it would help put Cole's mind at ease about Zack and me. What I didn't tell him was that Zack thought Hannah was too loud and had a grating, nasally voice, and he was only going out with her as a favor to his mom, who was friends with her mom.

Cole put the car in reverse and started to back out of the driveway. But after a few feet he stopped suddenly. "I need to ask you something very important," he said.

I ducked my chin to my chest and tried to steel myself for it. Was this where he would ask me if I was into Zack... again? Or was this where he would ask why my house is such a wreck? Or maybe this is where he would ask why I don't ever talk about my family or why he never sees my mom or dad hanging around. I took a deep breath. "Okay."

"You eat butter on your popcorn?"

"The more the better," I answered, relief washing over me.

He pounded his fist on the steering wheel, then shouted into the closed car, "She's perfect, I tell you!"

Laughing, we pulled out of the driveway and headed to the theater, talking about, of all things, flavored popcorn and the merits of M&Ms as the perfect movie treat.

The theater was packed, so we had to park way out at the back of the parking lot.

"Stay there," he commanded, just as I reached for the door handle. "Don't get out."

My hand fell away and landed back in my lap. He turned the car off and jumped out, then jogged over to my side. He grinned as he opened my door with a flourish, bowing a little.

"My lady," he said in this phony British accent that had me giggling. He reached in and took my hand, tugging me gently out of the car, shutting the door behind me with his other hand.

I curtsied and adopted my own goofy British accent. "Why, thank you, sir," I said. But when I looked up from my curtsy, he wasn't smiling anymore. His face had taken on a totally serious look.

He stepped in toward me, resting both hands on my hips, which practically burned under his touch. "You look amazing tonight," he said, pulling me in until our bellies were touching.

I could feel my face get hot. "Thanks," I said. "You look great, too." I expected him to say something else but was surprised when instead he just reached up, buried his hands in my hair at the back of my head, and kissed me. It was a soft, slow, easy kiss. One of those first kisses where nobody gets adventurous and where it feels so good you think your toes might melt off, but you're so busy hoping your breath doesn't smell and your stomach is in such tight knots, it's over before it even really registers that it began.

But when he released me, I wasn't sure I could even walk

into the theater, which looked to be about a thousand miles away. My knees were shaking, and I couldn't believe what had just happened.

"Shall we go?" he asked finally, in that same British accent, and I nodded, pressing my lips together to smooth my lip gloss.

He wrapped his arm around my neck, and we walked into the theater, our hips bumping and me thinking that there might be other good days in my life, but there was no way any day could get better than this one.

We were early for the movie and walked into a mostly empty theater with our sodas and popcorn. A part of me hoped against hope that we would be the only two to show up, even though I knew from the looks of the parking lot it would be packed before the previews began.

Still. Maybe he'd kiss me again. The thought made me totally not hungry. I sipped my soda.

"You choose the seat," he said, gesturing with his soda.

I walked to the middle of the center row and we sat down.

"Perfect!" I said, settling my soda into the cup holder.

He sat next to me. "I'm surprised. I would've taken you for a front-row viewer for sure." He winked at me, positioning the popcorn in his lap and taking a big handful of it.

"Front row? Why?"

He shrugged. "I don't know. You just look like a woman who wants to be up close to the action."

I shook my head. "Uh-uh. Sitting in the front row gives me a headache. What about you? You a front-row guy?"

He shoveled the popcorn into his mouth, chewed for a minute, and then said, "Always."

"We can move," I said. "Really. I don't always get a headache. Besides, being in the front row for this movie might be really intense."

"Nah," he said. "My girl likes to be safe in the middle, we'll be safe in the middle."

"You sure?" I asked, but before he could answer, a group of girls wandered in, giggling. We both glanced up.

It may have been my imagination, but I could swear Cole stopped chewing for just a fraction of a second. But it was so subtle and brief, I felt myself doubting I saw him pause, even as I was thinking it.

But one thing wasn't subtle: One of the girls totally stopped laughing when she saw us. In fact, she stopped walking, her hands reaching out to her friends on either side of her, almost like she was startled.

They all hesitated and looked over at Cole, and then one of the girls whispered, "C'mon, Maria," and tugged at the girl's shirt. Finally, she stopped staring at Cole and followed them up the stairs behind us. Their giggles started up again after a few seconds, but when I glanced back at them, the girl was still just staring at Cole, her face stone cold.

I tried to read the reaction in Cole's face, but it was dark and shadowy, and he was chewing on the popcorn again. The light from the movie screen was flickering off his forehead.

"You know them?" I asked, trying to sound light and cheery. I didn't want to sound like a jealous girlfriend. But it was obvious that *something* was up between them.

"Yeah," he said, taking a sip of his soda. "They go to Pine Gate. Not exactly friends of mine, though."

I glanced back at the girl, who was now distracted by her friends. They were chatting, loudly, and passing a bag of candy back and forth. "I could tell," I whispered. "She looked ready to bolt when she saw you."

He made a snorting noise. "Nah, it's nothing like that. She's a junior. Her parents are friends with my parents. Used to be, I mean. They don't really hang together since we moved. Which is good 'cause Maria's kind of a psycho. Has to go to this therapist, like, three times a week. Nuts."

I glanced back again. It was true that the girl looked sort of disengaged, even sitting with her friends and talking. Every so often her eyes would go soft and blank, and she'd stare down into her lap with this really faraway expression on her face. And then someone would bump her, and you could almost see her snap out of it and start laughing again. But it was a fake laugh. A forced one. He was totally right. Something about that girl didn't look right.

I turned back and reached into the popcorn bucket. "So, how come you guys moved from Pine Gate anyway? It's so close."

He shrugged. "Who knows? My parents just decided to move. Wanted a bigger house and found one out here."

"Your senior year? I mean, couldn't you commute if you wanted to?"

He swallowed his popcorn and turned to me. "Are you trying to get rid of me?" he asked, his voice soft but ornery. He grinned, and his lips glistened in the blue light. "Already you're sick of me?" He turned toward the screen again, shaking his head in mock exasperation. "Dangit. Already blown it with the most gorgeous girl in school."

I giggled and then reached over and grabbed his chin, moving his face toward mine. "I'm glad you moved," I whispered.

"Good," he whispered back, and kissed me.

It was a lot easier to ignore the Pine Gate girls behind us after that. Cole and I held hands and tried to beat each other answering the movie trivia questions that were scrolling on the screen as the theater filled up.

After a while, a couple walked in and sat right in front of us.

Cole immediately leaned forward. "Hey, dude," he said. "My girlfriend can't see over you. Do you think you could maybe move to a different seat?"

Instantly my ears heard the word "girlfriend," and I didn't care if I ever saw a single scene in the movie after that. I, who'd never had a real boyfriend in my life, was somehow Cole Cozen's girlfriend. This guy who didn't even try to kiss me until our second date. Who was gorgeous and smart and talented and a sports star. This guy who taught me how to play guitar and was worried about some random stranger blocking my view of the movie screen without my saying a word. This guy who seemed to do little else but pay attention to me and work extra hard to make sure I felt like I mattered.

The guy in front of us shook his head. "Nowhere else to sit, man."

Cole leaned forward again. "Look, I just think maybe you should move to the back or something."

The guy in front of us shook his head again and turned back to the screen, clearly finished discussing this with Cole. His date turned around and glanced at Cole. "Why don't you switch places with her?" she asked. "If it's that big a problem to you."

I put my hand on Cole's arm. "Hey, it's no big deal," I said. "I can see if I lean to the side a little." I gave him a reassuring smile. "I'll be right back."

I shuffled out of the row and headed toward the ladies' room.

I could hear familiar laughter echoing out of it before I even got inside. I pushed open the door hesitantly, and there was the group of Pine Gate girls standing in front of the mirror, floofing their hair and slicking on lip gloss. Maria was washing her hands.

I squeezed through and pushed into a stall, trying to pretend I wasn't there. But their laughter had died into occasional eruptions of snickers, followed by prolonged periods of intense whispering.

After I was finished, I pushed my way to a sink on the far end of the wall. The Pine Gate girls were totally silent now, and I could feel them looking at me as I washed my hands.

Finally one of them—a heavily freckled girl with unruly curls—broke the silence. "Are you dating Cole Cozen?" she asked. I glanced at her as I pulled two paper towels out of the towel holder. They were all staring at me. All except Maria. She was staring at the floor.

"Yeah," I said, trying to sound defiant. "I'm his girlfriend." It felt weird saying those words, especially since I'd only known I was his girlfriend for about five minutes now, but I couldn't help smiling condescendingly when I said it.

They flicked sober looks at one another. "How long have you known him?" Freckles said.

I shrugged. "A little while," I said noncommittally. If Maria was kind of crazy, like Cole said—and I totally believed him, given how weird she was acting—chances were her friends were strange, too. I caught movement out of the corner of my eye. Maria had reached over and tugged on Freckles's sleeve, and they all started whispering again.

I threw away my paper towels and headed for the door, which meant I had to pass through their cluster. I could almost feel a drop in the temperature when I walked past them, rolling my eyes. Jealous, much?

The theater had darkened, and the previews were just starting as I got back to my seat.

"Sorry," I whispered. "I got trapped by your Pine Gate

friends. You're so right about…" but I trailed off as I noticed that the big guy in front of us was gone. I pointed to the empty seat in front of me. "Where'd they go?"

Cole grinned. "I convinced them to move," he said. "Now you can see."

This is it, I thought. *This is the part about relationships I always knew existed. The romantic part. The soul-mate part. This is what I saw in those photos of my parents— happiness, love, sacrifice. Real stuff. Here it is. It's mine.*

"I've got a better idea," I said, reaching down and grabbing his hand. "Come on."

We gathered up our sodas and popcorn, and I led him to the empty front row.

"But your headache!" Cole whispered, sliding into the seat next to me.

I shook my head. "Screw the headache. This is where all the action is."

CHAPTER TWELVE

"I'm really starting to freak out," Bethany said, sounding breathless on the phone. She'd been working out ever since our first Vacay Day, saying if she was going to be scouting for hotties, she couldn't be looking all flabby. I could hear the whir of her treadmill in the background. "I mean, I need to know if we're going to go in the summer or the winter, at least."

"I know," I said for about the billionth time.

"I have to think about college, you know?"

"I know," I said again.

"Because if we're going in the winter, I may not be able to go." There was a beeping noise, and her footsteps got louder. She was running.

"I know."

"But there's no good celeb-watching in the summer," she huffed. "And I think Zack really wants to go in the winter."

"Zack just wants some novice ski bunny to fall on him. I'm sure we could talk him into whitewater rafting with one word: bikinis."

Bethany chuckled, and I heard more beeping, and her footsteps got even louder and faster. "I've gotta...go," she said, sucking in air. "Can we...get together sometime... before Saturday?"

"Sure," I said. "How about tomorrow after school we'll go to Shubb's."

"Yeah," she said. "I'll text...Zack and...let him know." There was more beeping. "Shit." Bethany grunted and disconnected.

The next day went by slowly, pretty much like every day did now that Cole and I were official. It seemed as though the clock barely moved all day long until seventh period, and then it would fast-forward. Cole had been pulling As in his English class, so we mostly spent our lab time playing table football with a paper triangle, reading my old poems and trying to set them to song, or kissing in the corner between the supply cabinet and the wall, where Mrs. Moody couldn't see us if she looked in the door. Sometimes, if I didn't have to work, we'd go out to the spillway after school, and he'd play his guitar while I threw rocks down into the water.

But today Cole didn't seem to be in as playful a mood as usual. He slouched in and immediately started griping about Mr. Heldorf, his world history teacher.

"The guy's an idiot," he growled. "He's giving me a C

because I was absent on the day they took some stupid reading quiz and he wouldn't let me make it up. Moron."

I tried reaching over and holding his hands across the desk like always, but he slipped his hands down into his lap moodily.

"That guy couldn't teach lessons on how to wipe your ass," he continued.

After a while his phone buzzed, and he dug in his jacket pocket for it. He looked at the screen, rolled his eyes, and put it to his ear. "What?" he barked into the phone. There was a pause, during which his face slowly got redder and redder. "I don't care what you do with it. It's not my problem. No. No. Listen, don't call me with this shit, okay? I don't care what you do with it, just leave me the hell alone about it. Call someone who cares."

He snapped the phone shut and put it back in his jacket pocket. Immediately, it buzzed again, but he ignored it.

I sat up straight in my chair. I'd never seen Cole like this. His mood was so dark you could almost see it radiating off him. Usually he was happy and just excited to be around me. But not today. I didn't really know what to do with this Cole. I tried smiling, hoping it would help.

He rolled his eyes and shook his head. "That was my mom. She's always got some sort of problem that needs to be worked out. Always calling me or making me take her somewhere or some other shit. Never ends with her."

"She wanted you to take her somewhere?" I asked, trying again to trap his hands with mine. When I touched him, he seemed to snap out of a daze and see me for the first time.

He grabbed my hands with his and squeezed. "Nah. Just some bullshit. Listen, you don't want to hear about it." He stood up. "I'm gonna see if Mr. Heldorf has a second. I'll catch up with you later." He bent over and kissed my ear.

"Okay," I said. "I'll be home a little later, though. Bethany and Zack and I are going to Shubb's after school. Planning the trip, of course."

He stopped, wiping his forehead with three fingers. "Of course," he answered sarcastically. And he left.

I looked at the clock. Seventh period wasn't over for another twenty minutes. I gathered my things and slipped into Mrs. Moody's office. "Cole's mom called. He had to go," I said. "Is it okay if I go to the library?"

She checked her watch and nodded. "See you tomorrow."

But I didn't go to the library. Instead, I headed to Bethany's locker, where I waited until the bell rang, wondering what Cole's mom had wanted and why it had made him so angry. And why it had felt like he was angry with me.

We decided to ride to Shubb's in Zack's crapmobile. Zack was in rare form, telling us about his date with Hannah, and how the refs at the soccer game kept threatening to toss Hannah and Zack out if she didn't stop yelling. And how she'd almost gotten Zack in a fight with some big, burly college guy in the parking lot at El Manuel's afterward.

"And then, get this," he said, laughing. "She told her mom that she didn't feel any chemistry and didn't want to go out with me again. Can you believe that? I got dumped by Hannah Loudmouth! *That* is a new low. Even for me."

We got to Shubb's and slid into a curved corner booth. "Two orders of cheese breadsticks," Zack told the waitress, "and a pitcher of Coke." He patted his chest. "On me, ladies."

"Thanks," Bethany mumbled, rummaging through her giganto-purse and pulling out the Obsessive Files. "Okay, you guys..."

"No," Zack said, grabbing each of us around our necks. "I meant literally. On me." He pulled us toward his chest.

"Stop it," I squealed, pulling out from underneath his arm and punching him lightly on the chest. Bethany stayed there a little longer, laughing, but smacking at his arm.

"You wish," she said at last, squirming away. "Now, seriously, Zack. We can't get sidetracked. We need to decide what we want to do."

"I was trying to show you," he said, grabbing her head and pulling her close again.

Our drinks came, and Bethany used that as her chance to try to get us on track again. "I'm thinking summer would be better," she said, opening the notebook and turning to a tab marked OUTDOOR.

"I think summer would be better, too. I might take some classes at community college in the fall," I said, and as I said it, I was shocked that I really meant it. For my whole life, everything was leading up to this trip to Colorado. Everything. Never did I really consider what would happen afterward. Shannin went away to college on scholarships.

Bethany would go away to college, too. Zack would go to acting school. And I would...I'd never filled in the blank before. I'd always shrugged it off when people asked. It was as if I'd never considered that after I got to Colorado and solved the mystery of why my mother was so hell-bent on getting there that I'd have to go back to my own life. Or start my own life. Whichever it was.

"Since when?" Bethany asked, taking a sip of her drink.

I shrugged. "Since...I don't know...since now, I guess."

"Is Cole going to community college?" she asked, and even though she didn't mean anything by it, I still heard it as an accusation.

"I don't know," I said snippily. "We've never talked about it."

Bethany shrugged. "Cool," she said.

The waitress brought our breadsticks, and we ate silently. After a while, Zack started in with another Zack story—something about Celia asking him to sit with her and her freshman friends at lunch. Not surprisingly, he did it. Zack had more self-confidence than anyone I'd ever known. He could pull off sitting at a freshman table. Everyone else would rather die. Even most of the freshmen.

"Some of those frosh are built," he said, a string of cheese hanging from his bottom lip. "How come neither of you looked like that when you were freshmen?"

"Because we didn't get our parents to buy us water

bras," Bethany said. She slapped her palm against the open notebook. "Okay, so are we in agreement on…"

"Holy shit," Zack mumbled, and put down his bread-stick. "You've got to be kidding me."

Bethany and I looked up and followed his gaze through the front window of Shubb's. On the other side, shutting his car door, was Cole.

"Did you invite Cole here?" Bethany asked. Again, the tone of her voice sounded like she was accusing me of something, though I didn't know what exactly.

I shook my head. "Nope, he probably just wanted to say hi."

"Goody," Zack said sourly.

I shot Zack a look. He stretched his mouth in a wide fake smile.

"I'll be right back," I said, shimmying out of the booth.

By the time I got around the pinball machines, Cole was already inside, craning his neck to find me. I came up from the side and grabbed him around the waist.

"Hey!" I said. "What are you doing here?"

He jumped at first, but smiled when he turned toward me, and snaked his arms around my waist. "Looking for you," he said. "I got done with Heldorf faster than I thought."

"He change his mind about the C?"

He shook his head. "No. But it's no big deal. I can still try out for basketball." He pulled me in tighter. "Mmm, you feel good. But I don't want to interrupt you guys. I just wanted to see you." He was back to the Cole I was used to—happy and gentle.

"You're not interrupting anything," I said. Zack would just have to get used to it, and Bethany wouldn't care as long as we were still planning our trip. "Come on over."

I grabbed his hand and pulled him to our table, then slid into the booth beside Bethany, making Zack slide around to the other end of the curve. He had an irritated look on his face, but I didn't care. I wasn't going to sit next to him. God knew what he would do to egg on Cole and start a fight.

"Hey, Big C! What's up?" Zack said in a loud voice.

"Not much," Cole said tersely. "Just couldn't stay away from Alex."

"I'll bet," Zack said.

I glared across the booth at Zack, daring him to say any more. He must have gotten the hint because he shut up.

"So, Beth," he said, diverting his attention away from Cole, "what're we looking at here?"

"I think we're looking at summer," she said. "Agreed?"

"Agreed," I said.

"Nope," Zack said. "Not agreed. I want to ski."

"Maybe we can find some place to water-ski," I said. "Beth? Is there a lake somewhere?"

"Um," she said, flipping through the notebook. "I don't know...."

"No ski, no trip," Zack said. He stomped his foot under the table. "The man," he announced in a Ricky Ricardo voice, "has put his foot down, Lucy!"

"We could always tie you to the back of the RV on a pair of Rollerblades," I suggested.

Bethany laughed. "Yeah. I hear the skiing on I-70's great."

"Har-har, you guys are so funny," Zack said. "As it happens, I am a god on Rollerblades. I'd tear it up."

"Since when are you a god on Rollerblades?" I asked, while at the same time Bethany declared, "I've never seen you on Rollerblades in your life." And then we all started talking over one another. Zack threw a piece of breadstick at my hair. Bethany tossed a napkin in Zack's drink. The usual.

"Actually," Cole said, and everyone got quiet, "I don't know if they still do it, but there used to be some places out there where you can ride these slides down old ski runs in the summer. My uncle Ben took me once when I was a kid. It was a blast."

We all looked at one another.

"That sounds fun," Bethany said.

I nodded. "Definitely."

"You know, Big C," Zack said, "that's not such a bad idea. Alex, maybe you should keep this guy after all."

I felt Cole stiffen beside me, but I tried not to react. Zack was just being... Zack. And after a few seconds, I felt Cole relax. Maybe, I thought. Just maybe I could eventually get these two to get along.

"I plan to," I said, snuggling up under Cole's arm.

"So, this RV," Cole said. "How many does it sleep?"

Bethany's head whipped up. "We haven't really decided on an RV yet," she practically whispered.

Cole nodded.

"What're you thinking?" I asked, turning so I could see his face, but I was slouched too low.

He shrugged. "Not really thinking anything. Just curious. But...Bethany, would you mind passing on all the stuff you do know? A summer getaway might be kind of fun."

"Um, sure," Bethany said, her thumb picking at the corner of a piece of paper, bending it up. "I'll get it to you next time I see you."

By the time we left Shubb's, I was grinning so hard my cheeks hurt. The idea of Cole going to Colorado with us made me feel even more excited about the trip. Like he belonged there.

Better than that, it seemed like finally everyone was getting along. Maybe this would work out after all.

CHAPTER THIRTEEN

Cole was waiting for me in the back booth, like always. Ever since our date at the movies, every night that I worked, Cole would come in, order a coffee, scoot into the back booth, and do his homework while waiting for me. He sat there for hours. Sometimes he would just stare at me. Every now and then, when I looked up from the register, he would wink or blow a kiss at me. It was the most romantic thing I'd ever seen in my life.

"Doesn't he have any friends?" Georgia asked one night when Cole got up at closing and sauntered out to his car, where he would wait for me until I was finished with cleanup.

"Yeah, but they're all doing their own thing. He's new, remember? They've all known one another for years. Probably once basketball starts, he won't be here anymore. I think it's romantic."

Georgia nodded. "And creepy," she added.

I tossed a paper clip at her. "It's not creepy."

She shrugged and bent over to retrieve the clip. "All I know is if someone was just sitting there staring at me all night every night, I'd be a little creeped out."

"It's sweet," I said.

"I haven't seen those friends of yours around here much lately," she said.

"I know," I said. "We've all been busy." But the truth was, I was the only one too busy. Bethany and Zack were still hanging out like always, but I'd found myself begging off more and more often, hoping they understood and knowing they probably didn't. Cole kept me busy after work on the days I did work, all afternoon on the days I didn't, and pretty much every weekend. He had even started meeting me at my locker between most classes, which meant Bethany and Zack and I didn't even have that short time to catch up every day. And I couldn't be sure, but I thought maybe they were avoiding The Bread Bowl because they knew Cole would be there.

I'd begun to see Bethany's car at Zack's house pretty often. They'd text me and ask me to come over, but it was never a good time. I felt torn, but the fact was I wanted to be with Cole. I was really his only friend, and I could hardly complain that such an amazing guy was making me too much the center of his universe. Plus, even though we hadn't gotten to the "L" word yet, I'd begun to suspect I was falling in love with Cole. And when you fell in love with someone, wasn't that person supposed to be your best friend, too?

After Cole made the trip suggestion at Shubb's, I

thought we would all start hanging out together. And at first I really tried to make it happen. But it seemed like Cole irritated Zack just by being there, and Bethany, feeling caught in the middle, would uneasily just slip away. After a couple days of everyone feeling awkward, they began staying at my locker only until Cole got there. Then they stopped coming altogether.

"Well," Georgia said, "I miss that cute boy. He's always full of it when he comes in here."

"Zack? Yeah. He's always full of it, period." I smiled just thinking about it, all the crazy things Zack did over the years just to get a laugh out of Bethany and me. I kind of missed him. I made a mental note to go to his house and hang out for a few minutes.

"It's cool you have friends that close," Georgia said, closing up the safe. She sat up straight and then stretched way back over the top of her chair. "We're done, chickie," she said over a yawn. "Drive safe! And tell that Zack to come in sometime."

"Okay, Gee, I will," I said, clocking out and taking off my apron.

I pushed through the doors and looked down the parking lot. Cole was getting out of his car. I jogged to him and wrapped myself around him, breathing in his scent.

"Mmm, you smell good," I said. "I wish I didn't have to go."

He pulled me back to arm's length. "You don't," he said. "Get in. I have something for you."

"Okay," I said. "But just for a minute. You have to bring me back to my car. I need to stop by Zack's tonight."

Cole opened his door and I ducked in, crawling across to the passenger seat. He got in behind me and started the car.

"Why do you have to go to Zack's?" he asked.

I wadded up my apron and tossed it and my visor into the backseat. "Just to say hi," I said. "I kind of miss him."

Cole made a noncommittal humming noise and turned on the radio. We drove a few miles, jamming while I pulled out my hair tie and hung my arm out the open window, trying to blow away the scent of potato soup and yeast that always clung to me after a shift.

After a while, Cole pulled into a parking lot and turned off the car. I peered out the window. We were at McElhaney Park, the baseball diamonds where Zack played all of his Little League games and Bethany and I gossiped about who we had crushes on over by the tire swings.

Cole swung himself out of the car and loped over to the playground. He stood, looking out over the play equipment, kicking the railroad ties that fenced it in. I followed him curiously.

"The merry-go-round!" I exclaimed, jumping up over the railroad ties and rushing to it. I hopped up onto the rusty metal platform and stood in the middle, just the way Bethany and I used to do when we were feeling like daredevils. "Push me, Cole!"

He looked up. I motioned for him to come over. He

stepped up over the railroad ties and moved slowly toward me. I towered over him, my hands planted on my hips.

"Check it. No hands," I said.

He cocked his jaw to one side and leaned over, grabbing the metal bars and giving the merry-go-round a healthy shove. I squealed, the muscles in my legs and back tensing as I tried to keep my balance. The world began to spin away from me faster and faster, until everything was a blur, just like I remembered it. Bethany and I used to take turns, see who would wimp out and grab on to the bars first. I always won.

I laughed, straightening up and holding my arms up in a V toward the sky. "See? I told you, I'm the spinmaster!" I yelled.

"Really?" Cole said, somewhere near me. "How fast do you think you can take it, spinmaster?"

"Fast as you can give it, baby!" I laughed, and the merry-go-round lurched underneath me again. "Whoa!" I shouted, bending my knees again and holding my arms out in front of me for balance. "That's fast!"

The merry-go-round lurched again. And again. I could hear Cole letting out grunts of effort, he was pushing it so hard. And the world spun around me faster and faster, till everything was a dizzying darkness. I could no longer make out the lights of the parking lot, much less figure out where I was in relation to it.

Cole grunted and the merry-go-round spun faster. My right foot slipped a few inches toward the edge. My arms wheeled as I tried to keep my balance. I tried to look down, to find the handles, but I was too disoriented. The world started rocking up and down, as if I was on a ship in a storm.

"Cole," I said, my hands groping in front of me. "Stop. It's too fast."

But Cole only grunted and the merry-go-round lurched again. Again, my foot slipped and my arms spun wildly in front of me.

"Stop!" I said, louder this time. "Really! It's too fast!"

But if Cole heard me, he was ignoring me. My feet kept slipping backward, and I knew that soon they would have no purchase left.

"Cole, stop!" I yelled, the wind pulling tears from my eyes and across my temples. "I'm gonna fall!"

I felt a bar hit my hip. I was lurching side to side now. I tried to grab the bar with my hands, but I was too confused to find it, even though it had just been there.

"Cole," I whimpered. "Stop." But by then it was too late. My shoes were slipping across the slick metal, and I knew I had to do something if I wasn't going to get hurt.

I dropped down on my knees and groped with my arms until I found a bar, then wrapped them around the bar tightly and let my legs slip out behind me. Almost immediately, the toe of my shoe caught the playground wood chips and I dug in, crying out when my arms jerked hard to the crook at the end of the bar. The merry-go-round slowed down, and my legs collided with Cole's.

"You fell off, spinmaster," he teased, an edge in his voice. I'd stopped, but Cole didn't make any move to help me up. I bent my knees into the wood chips and slackened my grip on the handle, resting my forehead against the cool metal while I caught my breath.

"It's not funny, Cole," I snapped.

He laughed harder. "God, Alex. Don't be whiny," he said, jostling me with his knee. Then he clucked his tongue disgustedly. "Would it have been funny if it was Zack pushing you?"

I pulled up onto my elbows and wiped my eyes. "No," I fumed, looking up at him angrily. "I was yelling at you. Why didn't you stop?" I held myself from asking the next question: *Were you trying to get me hurt?*

"Oh, come on, Alex," he said. I felt the merry-go-round shift as he sat down on it in the slot next to me. He reached through the bars and pulled my hair out of my face. He put his hand under my chin and lifted it up so I was looking at him. "I wasn't going to let you get hurt."

I glared at him.

But the more I narrowed my eyes at him, the softer his face got. He stroked a thumb over my cheek. "I love you."

At that moment, it was like nothing else mattered. In an instant, all of my anger melted away under his touch. Cole's eyes had an intensity about them that I'd never seen before—as though he was admiring something precious, something he couldn't comprehend. His face was filled with tenderness and somehow managed to glow in the dusk. Had my heart not already been pumping furiously, it would have started just then. He'd never told me he loved me before.

Nobody had ever told me they loved me before.

I was struck with a memory of once when I was a little girl, asking my dad if he and Mom fell in "love at first sight." We were in the garage, where I'd been helping him fix the car. He had been twisting some car part around and around under a towel in his hands, and had stopped and kind of stared out into space for a second. Then he jerked back into motion really quickly and snapped, "Alex, I don't have time for...Hand me that wrench," and shoved his head back under the hood of the car he was working on, case closed.

So later, over the dishes, I'd asked Shannin if she believed in love at first sight, and she'd looked me right in the eye and said, "No. Because you only truly love your soul mate, and since your soul mate is the other half of you...you've seen 'em before, you know, in heaven."

I'd thought about what she said long and hard, trying to make sense of it all. Meeting up in heaven, as though heaven is one big junior high mixer or something. Shannin's explanation of love at first sight and soul mates and heaven made no sense to me whatsoever.

Until now.

Suddenly it didn't matter anymore that he didn't stop pushing me on the merry-go-round. It didn't matter that he was irritated about Zack. It didn't matter that he'd scared me and said I was whiny. He loved me. Now I knew that much for a fact. And I loved him, too.

For an agonizing few minutes, I wasn't sure I'd be able to answer him. I could smell his cologne. I could see the muscles in his jaw working anxiously, earnestly. I could feel his hand warm against my chin. *Pinch me*, I wanted to say. *Make sure I'm not dreaming this. Wake me up now before this goes any further.*

But instead, Cole's hand found mine and he pulled upward. I stood up, my eyes never leaving his. He scooted back on the merry-go-round and I sat on his lap, feeling tingly and like...well, like this kind of moment just doesn't happen in real life. Not to ordinary girls like me.

"I have something for you," he said. He reached into his pocket and pulled out a small stuffed bear, fuzzy and white, wearing a red shirt that said "I ♥ YOU." He handed it to me. "It's our one-month anniversary," he said.

"It's so cute," I whispered, finally finding my voice. I pressed the bear to my chin. "I love you, too," I said, wrapping my arms around his neck. A sentence I'd never uttered before, not to Dad or Celia or Shannin. Not to Aunt Jules. Not even to Zack and Bethany.

"Don't go to Zack's tonight," Cole whispered into my neck.

"No way," I whispered back. "It's our anniversary."

"Happy anniversary, spinmaster," Cole said.

"Happy anniversary," I said back.

We kissed, Cole's feet working the wood chips, pushing the merry-go-round, and spinning us lazily through the night air. And even though we'd kissed before, this one felt different somehow. There was something more behind it. He pushed a lock of my hair back behind my ear, and then we kissed some more, the little bear pressed between our hands, and I knew right then that this was what I'd been looking for my whole life. I wanted this. And I wanted it to be perfect. Untouchable. No fires, no cackling, no rushing off to the mountains.

What Cole and I had would be like the happy photos in that box under my bed. Only what we had would be so much better.

CHAPTER FOURTEEN

Celia and I sat at the kitchen table, papers spread out in front of us, the phone in the middle of the table set to "speaker." Dad was at work, and we made Shannin skip her afternoon sociology class so we could talk to her about the party.

"I'll be in charge of the cake," I said. "Chocolate on chocolate, with 'Happy Fiftieth Birthday, Michael,' right?"

"Yeah," Shannin's voice rang out over the speaker. "And, Celia, you're calling the grandmas, right?"

"Already did it," Celia said, leaning over the phone. "And Aunt Jules knows. She's doing some calling, too."

"What about food?" I asked, rubbing my temples. We'd been at this for an hour, and I was ready to be done with it. I had better parties to think about. Like the one at the lake shelter tonight that I'd gotten off work to go to, for instance. "How're we gonna get food here without Dad knowing it?"

"I'm still working on that," Shannin said. "But I'm pretty sure if Celia asks the grandmas, they'll take care of it. Grandma Shirley lives for that kind of thing."

"I'll ask," Celia said.

I rifled through some papers. "Well, then, I think we've talked about everything."

"Yeah," Shannin said over the phone. "I think we've got it all done. And with plenty of time to spare. We're in good shape."

I shot an I-told-you-so look at Celia, who glared at me. She leaned over the phone. "You sure you don't want to go over it again? Just, you know, in case?"

"No, I think I can still make my last class if I go now," Shannin answered. "We're good, Ceel. We'll talk again before I come home, okay? You can calm down about it now."

"Great," I answered, before Celia could say anything. "Talk to you later, Shan. Bye!"

Celia gave me a wounded look and snatched up the handset before Shannin could hang up. While she said her good-byes to Shannin, I gathered together the papers, took them to my room, and hid them in my desk drawer under my Colorado paperwork.

I felt a pang of guilt. It'd been weeks since our last Vacay Day, the one when Cole walked in on Zack tickling me. I knew Bethany and Zack were taking it personally, but it wasn't on purpose or anything. It was just that, between work and homework and making Celia happy with planning Dad's party, I barely had time to do anything else. Plus,

Cole had made the basketball team and was busy with practice almost every afternoon. I barely had time to talk to Cole, and they couldn't expect me to blow off my boyfriend just to talk to them, could they? It wasn't my fault Zack hated Cole for no reason. He shut himself out, if you asked me.

Besides, Cole was so amazing. Always so romantic. Always calling me "just to say I love you." Always bringing me things—a stuffed animal, a rose, a charm bracelet. Always waiting for me at work, at my car, at my locker. Always.

I tucked the birthday papers in securely and shut the drawer, pushing away my guilty feelings. I'd see Zack and Bethany at the party tonight. We'd talk then. Maybe I could even make Zack and Cole like each other. Maybe they'd become friends. I knew it was a long shot, but I had to keep trying.

My fingers idly found my collarbone and ran up and down the necklace as an idea formed. Yeah, that's exactly what I would do tonight. I'd bring everyone together, make us all friends, so I wouldn't feel so torn between them anymore.

Two hours later I was showered and dressed and standing on Zack's front porch. His mom answered the door.

"Hey, long time no see, stranger!" she said, hugging me and pulling me into their house simultaneously. "Where've you been these days, Miss Alexandra? Zack says you have a new boyfriend."

I nodded and followed her into their living room, which was bright and cheery and dusted and smelled faintly of lemon and pine. So different from our crappy living room. In a way, Celia hadn't been too far off that day when I was cleaning it up—I wouldn't mind borrowing Zack's mom just a little bit. If for no other reason than to make our living room smell so good.

"Is Zack here?"

"Sit down, sit down, yes, he is," she said. Zack's mom always had this way of running sentences together like that. She was sort of known for saying things like, *Why, yes—would you like a drink—I did in fact get new carpet in here—have a soda—thank you for noticing, do you like it?* Sometimes it was hard to follow her, and her habit of mushing sentences together really annoyed Zack, but I always found her to be an amazing, perfect mom. I always thought Zack was so lucky and he didn't even know it. "Getting ready for a party—this is a surprise—have a seat—he didn't say you were coming over."

"Yeah," I said, easing onto their couch. "He wasn't expecting me. But since we're going to the same party, I thought I'd see if he wanted to ride together."

She beamed. "I'm sure he'd love it—if you ask me—I'll get him for you—you kids are crazy for having an outdoor party in November!" She patted my knee and walked to the stairs and yelled up, "Zack, Alex is here!"

I heard footsteps upstairs, and a door opening. Then the footsteps got louder and faster as Zack came down the stairs, his hair still wet and sticking to his forehead. He got a curious expression when he saw me.

"Thought I smelled something," he said.

I stood up, shoving my hands into my back pockets. "Hey, you're going to the lake, right? I thought I'd see if you wanted to ride with."

He lifted his chin and scratched his neck, leaving red marks on his damp skin. His mom ducked away, touching me on the arm as she passed by.

"Uh, okay," he said finally. "I was gonna ride with Bethany, but I can call her."

"No," I said. "That's even better. We can all go together."

As if on cue, there were two raps on the front door and it opened. Bethany walked in. She saw me and almost stopped short, surprise registering on her face. "Alex," she said. "You coming with us?"

"Actually, I was just talking to Zack about all of us riding together," I said.

She pushed her glasses up on her nose and hoisted her giganto-purse higher on her shoulder. As usual, there were papers, notebooks, newspapers spilling out of the top of it. God only knew what Bethany kept in her purse. Maybe a whole library. "Okay, yeah," she said.

"Let me get my shoes," Zack said, and jogged upstairs again.

"We'll wait outside," I called, and Bethany and I headed out, walking across Zack's yard to my yard.

"God, I feel like I haven't seen you in forever," I said, stepping into the grass beside Bethany. "You got highlights."

I pulled up a few chunks of her hair and let them fall back to her shoulders. "They look really good on you."

"Thanks," she said. "I love your sweater." I looked down, and we both cracked up.

"Uh, maybe because I stole it from you?"

"Maybe," she said, laughing. "So how are things? With you, I mean."

I stopped, grabbed her wrist. "I didn't tell you. Cole told me he loves me."

Her eyes got wide. "He did?"

I nodded, beaming.

"Wow," she said to our feet. "Um, congratulations, I guess. Wow."

We walked a few more steps in silence, her giganto-purse bumping into my hip every so often.

"You know," Bethany said at last, "Zack really doesn't like Cole."

"I know." A few more steps. I stopped again. "Why not?"

She shrugged. "I'm not sure. But I think something went down between them in the locker room the other day."

"Really? Cole didn't say anything. What happened?"

Bethany shrugged again. "Are you really sure about this guy, Alex?" she asked. "I mean, because Zack makes him sound like a real jerk, you know?"

I felt a little crestfallen. Zack still hated Cole, which meant my idea of getting everyone to like each other tonight was an even longer shot than I'd originally thought. "I'm sure, Beth. Totally sure. I don't know what Zack's problem is, but Cole is amazing. I love him."

We kept walking. Bethany seemed to be really thinking about what I'd said.

As we walked across the lawns, Cole pulled into my driveway. I waved and kept walking, but I noticed after a few steps that Bethany had stopped short.

"Oh," she said when I looked back at her. "Cole's going?" I couldn't decipher the look on her face. Was it just surprise, or was there something else there as well? *Zack makes him sound like a real jerk.* Was Zack turning Bethany against Cole, too?

"Yeah," I said. "I just figured you knew that. I thought we'd all ride together. You guys haven't really had a chance to get to know him."

Zack had caught up with us and stood by Bethany's side. It wasn't difficult at all to tell what he was thinking by the look on his face. "I've met him," Zack said in a low voice. "No, thanks."

"Come on, Zack," I pleaded as Cole got out of the car, the look on his face a perfect mixture of the looks on both Bethany's and Zack's: surprise mingled with disgust. Cole hadn't said anything about getting into it in the locker room with Zack, but I could tell by looking at his face that something was up. I wondered if he could hear us. "You didn't even give him a chance. He's a really great guy, I swear."

They looked at each other dubiously. Bethany seemed really torn.

"Please?" I added. "I miss you guys."

Bethany took a deep breath and chewed her lip. "Okay," she said, letting the breath out in a gust. "Why not? A guy that hot can't be all bad, right?" She smiled.

I hugged her. "Thank you. I knew I could count on you, Beth." I looked up at Zack, my face pleading.

Zack looked from me to Bethany, then scratched the back of his neck uncomfortably and groaned. "Why the hell not?" he said. "Let's go."

"Thank you thank you thank you," I gushed, hugging him, too. "You won't regret it, I promise."

But when the three of us linked arms and started walking toward the driveway, I could have sworn I saw an icy look fall over Cole's face.

CHAPTER FIFTEEN

We drove most of the way without anyone speaking.

Back at the house, I'd skipped across the driveway to Cole, gotten up on my tiptoes, and kissed him lightly, but he'd made no move to kiss me back. Clearly, the tone was set. It seemed so ridiculous to me.

"Hey, baby," I said. "They're riding with, okay?"

His gaze turned slowly down to me, and I was actually so shocked by the hard look in his eyes that I stepped back. But he swallowed and his face softened just a little. "Sure," he said, an obviously forced smile stretching across his cheeks. "The more the merrier."

He stepped around me and pulled open the passenger door, reached down and pulled the lever to pop the front seat forward, then stood to the side, holding his arm out dramatically. "Any friend of Alex's is a friend of mine," he said.

Bethany glanced at Zack uneasily, but Zack's eyes wouldn't leave Cole's. Finally, she tugged on his shirtsleeve. "Come on," she said softly, and ducked into the backseat. Zack kept his face to Cole's the entire way to the car, and I knew Zack well enough to know that he was going to say something even before he did it. When he did speak, his voice was booming and dripping with mockery.

"How the hell are ya, Big C? Lookin' buff tonight," he said when he got right up in Cole's face. He slapped Cole's shoulder once, produced a toothpick out of nowhere, stuffed it into his mouth, and ducked into the backseat beside Bethany.

Cole turned and glared at me over the car door. I shrugged helplessly. "They're my friends," I whispered. "He's trying to lighten things up." But, really, I wasn't even convincing myself.

"Let's go," Cole answered, and walked around the back of the car and got in.

Riding along in the silence, I kept trying to think of something to say to get everyone talking, but every time I tried, I'd get a look at Cole's clenched jaw or hear Bethany clear her throat uneasily and would lose my nerve.

Finally, just as we were pulling onto Lake Road, I heard Bethany start digging through her purse.

"Oh, I almost forgot," she said. She pulled a sheaf of papers out and handed them up over the front seat. "The information you wanted about the Colorado trip, Cole."

"Oh, good," I said, taking the papers. I held them up

132

and shook them a little. "Your Colorado stuff," I said in a singsongy voice.

"Yeah, great," Cole said, his voice so chilly it was like nothing I'd ever heard come out of him before. "Look at that. The shit I asked for weeks ago. Real nice of you to get right on it, Bethany." He rolled down his window, grabbed the papers out of my hand, and flung them out onto the road.

I gasped. I turned and looked out the back window. The papers had scattered and were drifting into the weeds on the side of the road. Bethany and I exchanged glances. She looked as shocked as I felt. Her eyes were wide behind her glasses, her forehead crinkled, her mouth hanging open. Zack looked like he was fuming, his fists clenched in his lap.

"What the hell was that for?" I said, but surprise made my voice weak, and it sounded like a little squeak underneath the wind whipping through Cole's open window.

"Well, you know, Big C," Zack said, "you were the number one most important person on her list, but she was so overwhelmed by how amazing you are, she could never work up the courage to be in your presence."

"Zack! Don't make it worse," I hissed, but Cole put his hand on my leg, his fingers digging into my knee.

"No, Alex, let your girlfriends speak their minds. It's okay. Please, continue, ladies."

"Cole, stop," I said. I reached down and pushed his hand off my knee, feeling welts where his fingers had just been gouging me. I heard Zack laugh in the backseat, and Bethany shush him. "You guys," I said helplessly, but didn't know how to finish. Obviously, my idea of getting everyone together was going to end up a total disaster. I shrank back in my seat and closed my eyes. This was going all wrong.

"I'm really sorry," Bethany said, her voice thick with sarcasm. "Maybe it's just that I didn't have a chance to give it to you yet. I haven't seen Alex since she started going out with you." I could hear the blame in her voice. "Plus, we wanted to have a *good* time on that trip." She let the accusation hang in the air.

"Aw, but come on, Bethany," Zack said in this really fake sympathetic voice. "A trip wouldn't be a trip without Big C here. His middle name is fun."

"Zack," I snapped. "Stop it. You guys, please..."

Cole turned in to the shelter lot. He made a strange coughing sound in his throat and pulled into a parking spot under a tree. Night was just beginning to fall, and I couldn't really make out anyone inside the shelter, but it looked as if half the school was already there. Suddenly I didn't want to be one of them. I was in no partying mood.

Cole put the car into park and turned around. "Give me a fucking break. Alex may be too dumb to see what you guys are all about, but I'm not. You"—he pointed at Zack—"just want to get into my girlfriend's pants, and you"—he pointed at Bethany—"are too desperate to see that. It's obvious that you like this idiot. But you're never going to be good enough, because he wants Alex. Why don't the two of you take the trip all alone? Maybe you'll find a love connection. Be each other's consolation prize."

He turned back around with a smug look on his face. The car was totally silent, all of us too stunned to say anything. My ears rang. Cole knew nothing about our relationship. How dare he say those things? How dare he call me dumb?

"Alex," Bethany finally whispered, and gazed at me, her eyes watery, her chin trembling.

I opened my mouth to say something, but I honestly didn't know what to say. I was furious at Cole, furious at Zack, furious at myself, and so embarrassed. There were no right words.

Cole opened his door and got out. He popped the seat forward and bent down to peer into the backseat.

"Get the hell out of my car, big brother," he said in a voice that sounded more like a growl. "And take your number one fan with you." He turned and walked to my side of the car and yanked my door open.

Zack leaned forward. His face was inches from mine. "Yeah, Alex. He's real nice. Good choice of boyfriends, really."

Bethany wiped her cheeks and started to scoot toward the door. "We'll get a ride home with someone else," she said.

They both climbed out of the car, and I watched them walk toward the shelter, Zack's arm wrapped around Bethany's shoulder, Bethany's head leaning into Zack's side.

I felt lower than low, replaying the scene in my head. I tried to figure out where it had all gone wrong. It was almost unbelievable to me that only twenty minutes earlier I'd been walking between Zack and Bethany, linked arm in arm just like we'd been doing since we were little kids, convinced that tonight was going to be a perfect night and they'd fall in love with Cole just as I had. How could Cole throw those papers out the window? How could he treat Bethany like that? He might not like them, but he knew how important Bethany and Zack were to me. How could he do that?

I could've said something. I should've said something. They were my best friends. Bethany was just trying to be helpful. What a great best friend I was. I should've stuck up for them. Hell, I should've stuck up for myself.

After a few minutes, Cole crouched down and put his hand on mine. I yanked away angrily.

"Leave me alone!" I said, wiping my nose on the back of my hand. But he put his hand back on mine, gently rubbing it. I heard him take a deep breath and sigh.

"I'm sorry," he said softly, his entire demeanor changed. "But you know it's true. You know Zack is in love with you. He's always around you and touching you and...and I can't help it if I get jealous. I love you so much. I don't want anyone stealing you away."

I glared at him. "What about Bethany? You were so mean to her. She'll probably never speak to me again," I said, my tears slowing. "And you're wrong about Zack." I was sticking up for Zack out of best-friend habit. The truth was I was just as angry with him as I was with Cole. Zack did push it whenever Cole was around. Calling him Big C.

Really, in a way, Zack had started it, hadn't he? What kind of a friend does that?

"I did Bethany a favor," Cole said. "When Zack realizes you're mine and he can't have you, she'll have a shot with him."

I shook my head. "Bethany doesn't want Zack. You don't know about our friendship. I keep trying to explain it to you" — I thumped my finger against my temple angrily — "but you, for whatever reason, just can't seem to get it." But inside I wondered if that was true. Maybe Cole did understand, and *I* was the one who didn't get it. Maybe Cole saw something about our friendship that even I didn't see. Maybe we were all a little too close. Maybe he was right, and I was too dumb to see what this was really about.

"They'll get over it," he said, his hand moving up my arm to my shoulder. My leg felt tingly where his hand had gripped it earlier. I wondered if I'd have bruises there later. "Probably by the end of tonight they'll be over it." I shook my head doubtfully. "But I'd never get over it if Zack stole you away from me."

His hands found the sides of my head, and he slowly turned it. "I'd never get over it if anyone stole you away from me," he said.

He reached up with his thumbs and wiped the tears out from under my eyes, then kissed my cheeks where the teardrops had been. I leaned into him, feeling miserable and guilty as hell. I had done this. I had hurt everyone. This was all my fault. I should have never pushed my friends on him.

Bethany and Zack were my best friends, but I couldn't afford any weird love triangles right now. I couldn't afford them hating Cole for no real reason and pushing his buttons every time we got together.

They didn't understand about Cole. About the way I felt about him. About the way he touched me so gently and looked in my eyes so kindly. Those things didn't just go away because he got mad and lost his temper.

I would not let whatever weird stuff was happening between Bethany and Zack make things weird between Cole and me. We were so perfect together.

He leaned his forehead against mine. "I'm sorry," he whispered. "Forgive me?"

I closed my eyes and nodded, unsure what else to do.

The party wasn't fun, even though everybody was there, and people had brought everything from volleyballs to hot dogs. Even with the car doors swung open wide and music blaring, trunks popped and iced kegs flowing. This was going to be one of those epic parties that everyone talks about the entire year. The kind of party that goes down in school history. And it still wasn't fun.

Cole dove right into the crowd, clapping people on the shoulders and calling them "dude," as if they'd known each other their whole lives, his other hand clutching a beer. He was telling jokes and laughing and kicking a soccer ball someone had brought. It was as if nothing had ever happened in the car on the way over. As if he'd totally let it go.

Every so often he'd come over to the picnic table I was sitting on, squeeze my shoulder, and say, "Hey, babe, can I get you something?" and I'd just try to smile my "everything's okay" smile and shake my head.

But I couldn't help it. Everything was not okay. I'd nodded when he'd asked for forgiveness, but I was still mad.

Zack and Bethany were on the other side of the shelter, sitting on the ground next to the fireplace by themselves. Bethany's face was pink and sad, and every so often Zack would pick up a leaf or stick off the shelter floor and toss it into the fire. Neither of them would look at me. If they glanced up, they quickly looked away. It was as if I didn't exist.

I knew enough to know that Zack, usually the clown at an event like this, would normally be right in the center of the volleyball game, "accidentally" tripping and falling on one of the girls (preferably the one in the least amount of clothes), and at first everyone would laugh and think it was hilarious and then eventually the girls would get tired of being mauled and kick him out and he'd come over to where Bethany and I were and we'd play some dumbass game like Screw, Marry, Kill and he'd name all the girls he was just all over. Or maybe, if Bethany and I were feeling mean, we'd start up a game of Make Zack Do Stupid Stuff on a Dare, like eat bugs and climb trees in his underwear. Stuff we'd been making him do since we were seven. Stuff he never got tired of doing or got mad about.

Instead, I was sitting alone, Bethany was trying to look as if she hadn't been crying, and Zack was throwing leaves on a fire. But Cole was having a great time.

And I felt like it was all my fault.

After a while, darkness fell and it started to get cold, and Zack and Bethany took off with a couple of kids we'd hung out with a lot in elementary school, and then it was just me, sitting alone as the party got rowdier and rowdier, watching Cole, who'd organized a game of football so intense all the guys' shirts were plastered to them with sweat.

Cole's team was winning. Of course.

We didn't leave until the game was over.

In the car on the way home, Cole kept asking if I was okay, and I kept telling him yes, even though on the inside I wasn't sure what I was feeling, only that what I was feeling was definitely not "okay." I kissed him when we got to my house. I told him I loved him. And I went inside, not knowing what to think.

I didn't sleep much. I kept hearing Cole's words — *You just want to get in my girlfriend's pants, and you are too stupid to see that* — and seeing the hurt look on Bethany's face. I'd told Cole I'd forgiven him. And it was true that Zack was acting like a total jerk around Cole. It was true that he'd sort of brought it on himself with all his "Big C" talk and his "That guy's a tool" attitude since day one.

But still. Cole was way out of line. And I didn't understand how he could hurt me that way, just to rag on Zack. I didn't understand why he had to hurt Bethany. She was trying to be nice. Bethany didn't know how to be anything other than nice. I didn't understand why Cole couldn't just wait till we were alone and bring it up to me rather than blast them to their faces and ruin their night.

And I didn't understand how he could be having fun for the rest of the night, looking like he was on top of the world while the rest of us were miserable.

And I especially didn't understand why I'd let it go on.

As the night wore on and I thought things over, I'd started to forgive Cole less and less. It was easier to stay angry when he wasn't stroking my cheeks with his fingertips and telling me he loved me and was jealous. It was easier to be mad at him and think maybe Zack was right. Maybe Cole was a tool.

But then Zack wasn't there when Cole carried my backpack out to the car after the end-of-the-day bell rang. Zack wasn't there in the movie theater or at the mall, when I truly felt like Cole's queen. He didn't know how softly Cole could stroke my arm, or how that stroke made me feel inside or how cozy my neck felt when Cole walked next to me with his arm crooked around it.

Most of all, Zack didn't know how I finally felt as if...for the first time in my life...someone loved me. Someone could speak to me in longer than half-sentences. Someone could be more than a faded necklace and a bunch of old photos in a musty shoe box under my bed. Cole was real. His touch was real. His softness was real.

And real people made mistakes, didn't they?

When morning finally came, I was more confused than ever. I did love Cole—at least, I thought I did—but I'd never stuck up for anyone who'd hurt Bethany and Zack. And for the first time since we'd met, I was genuinely mad at Cole. And I was mad at Zack. Hell, I think I was mad at everyone.

Dad was in the kitchen, standing at the sink with a cup of coffee, when I came downstairs for breakfast. I sidled up to him, stood on my tiptoes, and kissed his cheek. As usual, he didn't say a word or make a move to kiss me back. Just sipped his coffee again, staring out into space.

"Morning, Dad," I said, reaching around him to pull a bowl out of the drying rack on the side of the sink.

"Alex," he said. Just one word. Typical.

"Sorry I got in so late last night," I said. "Cole was finishing a football game."

"Cole was getting wasted, is more like it," Celia said, coming in from the living room, carrying a bowl half-filled with milk. Her hair was standing up in greasy chunks around her head, and she was still wearing her pajama pants and tank top.

"He was not getting wasted," I said.

"That's not what Zack said," she countered. "You know, Zack? Your supposed best friend? He texted me last night. Told me about what happened." She walked lazily around me to the sink and set the bowl in it.

"Now, you know what I think about drinking…" Dad said, pointing at me around the handle of his coffee cup. But actually, no, I didn't know exactly what Dad thought about drinking, because that would require Dad to actually tell us what he thought about something. In fact, I'd love to know what Dad thought about drinking. Or what Dad thought about anything, for that matter. But I didn't say that out loud. No need to aggravate an already aggravated situation. Plus, I reminded myself, I wasn't mad at Dad. I was mad at Cole. And now Celia, too.

"I wasn't drinking. And Cole wasn't getting wasted, either," I said, glaring at Celia's back. I pulled the cereal box from the top of the refrigerator and shook some into my bowl. "Zack doesn't know what he's talking about. His mouth got him in trouble, and he's mad. That's all. He'll get over it. You shouldn't be texting my friends anyway, Celia."

"I didn't text him. He texted me. And Zack's my friend, too," she said. To Dad she added, "And he says Alex's new boyfriend is a total jerk."

I pulled the milk out of the refrigerator and poured some over my cereal, waiting for Dad to respond. He didn't. I grabbed a spoon out of the drawer.

"Zack doesn't know Cole," I said. "And neither do you."

Celia shrugged and sauntered out of the room, holding her palm out toward me, talk-to-the-hand-style, leaving me and Dad alone.

I waited for Dad to press me for details about Cole. A part of me wanted him to. Wanted him to ask me who this guy was and if what Celia was saying was true. I wanted to tell him that I was mad and that Zack was causing his own trouble and that I felt bad about Bethany but that I still loved Cole, and I wanted Dad to give me advice on what I was supposed to do now.

But he didn't. He finished his coffee, rinsed out the cup, and crammed it into the dishwasher, all in silence. I sat at the table eating my cereal, willing him to just say...something. Anything.

Instead, I heard his keys rattle.

"Going to work?" I asked around a mouthful of cereal. I could hear the sharpness in my voice.

Dad grunted.

"I have to work today, too, so I'll just see you..." I started, but he'd already left the room, a murmur I couldn't make out his acknowledgment that he'd heard me. I sighed. "Good-bye, Alex. Have a great day, sweetheart. I love you," I said softly into my bowl. Suddenly I had no appetite. I grabbed the bowl and tossed the cereal into the sink, listening to the front door close and Dad's car start up in the driveway. At the same time I heard the shower turn on upstairs and the echoey voices from Celia's stereo.

I sighed and leaned forward against the sink. I could see Zack in his driveway starting up the lawn mower. He glanced up, as if he knew he was being watched, but turned his gaze back to the mower before I could raise my hand in a wave. I knew by the way he paused before pulling the starter rope that he'd seen me and he was totally pretending that he hadn't.

I watched him press his earbuds into his ears, and he started walking, head down, behind the mower.

It was almost impossible to believe that just two days earlier I thought I had exactly what I'd always wanted. That one person who would make me his world. Who would tell me he loved me and mean it. Two best friends who were there for me, no matter what.

Today, everyone was off doing their own thing, and I was totally alone.

Only this time, it wasn't just my family that gave me the lonely feeling. With Zack and Bethany mad at me, alone really felt like alone.

SEVENTEEN

For the first time ever, I was late to work.

I had no good excuse. I'd stood by the window and watched Zack mow his lawn for a long time, waiting for him to turn and catch my eye, wave to me. Forgive me in the way only good-natured Zack could do. But he never did. Just mowed the side yard and moved around to the other side, where I couldn't see him.

I'd tidied up the kitchen a little. Stacked my bowl in the overflowing dishwasher and turned it on. Found an old rag under the sink and used it to wipe a sticky coffee cup ring off the counter. Stacked up the old newspapers and tossed them in the recycle bin in the mudroom. Put away the few groceries Dad had picked up at some point and left sitting, still in the bag, on the counter, as if the energy to put them in the pantry was more than he could muster. As if he were still leaving half his chores for a wife who wasn't there. And hadn't been there for a very long time. If she'd ever really been there at all.

Celia's shower turned off, and I headed upstairs to take my own. Halfway through washing my hair, I realized I'd been so distracted by Celia's accusations about Cole and by Dad leaving without a word and by Zack mowing without acknowledging me that I'd lost track of time.

I showed up fifteen minutes late, my hair still wet and hanging down, my makeup slapdash. And I'd forgotten my visor.

"I'm sorry, I'm sorry," I said, breathing heavily as I rushed past the managers' office to clock in. "I lost track of time."

Georgia was sitting in the office, separating coupons and rubber-banding them together. She shifted backward in her chair, which squeaked, and looked me up and down before saying anything.

"Where's your visor?" she asked. "Forget it. Here, put your hair up." She handed me a rubber band, and as I quickly gathered my hair into a ponytail, she leaned down and opened a drawer, then pulled out a smashed-looking visor and shook it to plump it up. "Have this one."

"Thanks," I said, taking the visor. "Just what I always wanted." But Georgia didn't respond with one of her usual smart remarks. I recognized the curt voice and pursed lips and blunt head nods. I'd seen her use them with other employees—always when she was mad. My stomach twisted as I realized that, for the first time ever, she was mad at me. God, was the whole world going to be mad at me now?

I slid the visor onto my head. "I'm really sorry..." I started, but Georgia cut me off with a nod of her head.

"You need to get out there," she said. "Greg stayed late to cover until you got here. Get on the register. Lunch rush'll be starting soon."

"Georgia, I'm really..."

She glanced up at me. "Later, okay? I need you on the register."

I nodded and left her to her coupons.

Lunch rush started early—almost immediately after I relieved Greg, in fact—and I was swamped. Flustered, I kept making mistakes—pressing the wrong buttons, forgetting to discount for coupons, giving out the wrong change and having to call for Georgia to come open my drawer with a key so I could make it right—and twice I got an earful from angry customers.

The upside was I was too busy and too worried about making up my lousy performance to Georgia (whose mood certainly did not improve with every mistake I made) to even think about Cole or Zack or Bethany.

After the rush was over, I felt a hand on my waist and heard Georgia's voice in my ear, softer now, more like the Georgia I was used to hearing.

"C'mon, let's talk," she said. Then, louder, toward the kitchen, "Jerry? Can you watch the register, please?"

I followed Georgia back to her office. She sat in her chair and I stood, my shoulder pressed against the doorway; the office was too small for two chairs.

At first she didn't say anything. Just bent down and opened the safe, tossed in an empty deposit bag, and closed the heavy door. I thought maybe she was still mad, and, more than that, thought I would go crazy if she didn't say something soon. Thought I would run down the street screaming if one more person gave me the silent treatment.

But after she shut the safe, she leaned back, pushed her fingers up under her glasses to rub her eyes, and then looked at me and smiled.

"Busy day," she said. "Been like this all week. Here, let me fix you."

She motioned for me to turn around and I did. Her chair squeaked, and then I felt the visor and rubber band being pulled out of my hair. My hair fell against my back again, and then Georgia's hands scooped it back up, deftly smoothing the sides and top.

"You're not yourself today, darlin'," she said, her voice muffled around what I guessed to be either the visor strap or the rubber band.

I shrugged. "I know. I had a really bad night last night. I'm sorry."

My hair pulled against my scalp as she wound the rubber band in it. I winced but didn't say anything.

"There," she said. I turned around and she handed me the visor again and sat back in her chair. "Don't worry about it," she said. "'Lot of them don't even show up at all and still expect to come back to work the next day. Greg was late this morning, too. He's late almost every morning, the lazy bum. You're not planning on becoming a lazy bum, are you?"

I shook my head as I tugged on the visor and worked my ponytail over the elastic strap. "It won't happen again, I promise."

She waved her hand at me. "Oh, honey, I was just kiddin' ya. Everybody has a bad day. But listen. Dave's been hanging around a lot lately. I heard from Nan over at the Clancy Avenue store that he's been on a rampage. Caught a manager stealing in the downtown store and is convinced that we're all out to get him now. Nan says he's firing people left and right, for the tiniest stuff, and that's why old Granite-Ass's been snoopin' around so much."

"Oh," I said. "He would've fired me today."

She nodded. "Maybe. And maybe me to go with you."

I leaned back against the door. The last thing I needed was to lose my job. I still had only about half of the money I'd need for Colorado, and that was if Bethany didn't plan any more add-ons like RVs and stargazing at mountain chalets. Thinking about Colorado gave me my usual pang of upset, and my fingers drifted to my necklace. But this time the upset wasn't because I knew I was getting closer every day to finally getting out there, but because of what had happened with Bethany the night before. I doubted Cole's outburst last night would have made her cancel the trip, but she was probably wondering if maybe I would cancel it. We'd been in arguments before, and we always made up. I just hoped this time would be no different.

I should have called her this morning. Should've apologized right off the bat. I made a mental note to call her as soon as my shift was over.

"Listen," Georgia said, leaning forward. "I'm still gonna tell you the same thing I tell everyone. Lily starts school this fall, and I don't need to tell you that it's gonna cost us a pretty penny to send her somewhere that can help her. Plus all the special supplies and equipment. So I can't afford to lose this job, and I need everybody's help with that, okay? You help me, I help you. You know I'm always going to bat for you guys."

The bell above the dining room door jangled, and we both leaned to see who was coming in. It was just an older couple, and Jerry seemed to have it under control. I could almost feel the tension radiating off Georgia as she leaned back into the office, her chair squeaking under her again. She was really worried about this Dave thing.

I guess I couldn't blame her. Georgia's daughter, Lily, had been in some sort of accident when she was a baby, causing her to have all sorts of physical problems and developmental delays. Georgia didn't talk about Lily's health much, and she brought Lily to the store only on very rare occasions. She and her husband worked hard to get their daughter the best of everything, but they didn't have much money, and Georgia was constantly worried about her job.

I nodded. "I totally get it. No problem. It won't happen again."

Georgia stood and put her hand on my arm. "I know it

won't," she said, reaching over and patting my elbow. "You're one of the few I can count on." She put her hands on my shoulders and spun me around, so I was facing out of the office. "Now get out there and get to work, you spoiled brat. You think the front line's gonna prep itself while you primp for a cotillion?"

I flicked her a salute. She had definitely forgiven me. All was back to normal.

I headed to the walk-in and grabbed a bag of lettuce, some tomatoes, and the pickle tub and stacked them high in my arms. I liked doing prep. It was easy and I got to move around, rather than stand at the cash register, filling green tea order after green tea order, not to mention I didn't have to pick up dining room trash. And I always found the rhythm of slicing vegetables to be soothing, sort of like listening to the radio.

The day stayed busy. Customers trickled in, a pretty constant stream. I kept having to abandon my prep work to ring someone up, which resulted in a lot of plastic gloves going in the trash, and it was getting closer and closer to dinner rush with the front line not prepped. That stressed Georgia out, so she abandoned paperwork in the office and came out to run the register while I feverishly chopped and diced and filled tubs and refilled tubs.

I was chopping so diligently I didn't even hear Cole's voice. Georgia cleared her throat meaningfully, and I glanced up. She had a warning look in her eyes. I knew what the look meant: *Don't stand around chatting all day. We've got work to do.*

"Hey," I said, turning to the counter and pressing my belly against it. I tried to smile, but it didn't feel right on my face. Suddenly I was so nervous. I still wanted to be mad at him for last night, but already last night seemed like a long time ago. He smiled that soft smile that always brings out the little dimple on one side, but something about it seemed wary, as if he knew he had some serious making up to do. And just the fact that he knew he was in the wrong and was going to make up for it made it easier to forgive him.

"Hey yourself," he said. Georgia handed him a coffee and he held it up. "Thirsty." Georgia took his money and handed him his change without a word, then flicked a sideways look at me again. I could almost hear her thoughts: *Think of Lily!*

Cole moved a couple of steps down the counter and stood right in front of me. I could smell his cologne. The smell made my hands shake, even though I wanted to stay mad at him.

"I can't talk," I whispered, not looking up. "I've got to get this done."

"I know," he said. "I was just going to chill until you got off."

I glanced at the clock behind me. "I don't get off till five." I continued chopping.

"I'll wait," he said.

"You're going to wait for two hours?" As if he hadn't already done that a hundred times before, but I was trying my best to seem irritated.

Suddenly I felt his hand touch my cheek. I looked up. He was stretched across the counter, gazing directly into my eyes. His hand caressed my cheek so softly I might have passed out right there on the floor.

"I'd wait for you forever if that's what it took," he said.

Despite myself, I smiled. Something about his touch was so much more real than the strange things he'd said and done last night. And I couldn't help it. I loved him.

Then Georgia's voice rang out from the office— "Alex, you get the eggs chopped yet?"—and just like that the spell was broken.

I went back to my prep work, but I was completely distracted and frazzled again. I kept glancing up at the dining room, and every time I did, Cole was looking right at me, leaning back in his chair, holding his drink in one hand. I felt a shot of electricity surge through me every time we connected, and it was like my brain kept getting short-circuited. I'd look back down at whatever I was doing, and it would all look so foreign to me. Had I really been slicing cucumbers? I didn't remember that.

Everybody has a bad day, Georgia had said. Everybody. Even Cole. Maybe that's all last night was—Cole's bad day. Colossally bad, but forgivable.

I spent so much time looking up, I wasn't caught by surprise when Bethany walked in.

She walked up to the counter, and I could see Georgia's shoulders slump after a second of talking in a low voice.

"Alex," she said. "Your friend needs to talk to you." She pursed her lips and then mouthed, *Make it quick.*

Unlike with Cole, when I saw Bethany my feelings weren't in the least mixed. I felt only one thing: guilt. So much so, in fact, that my feet didn't even want to walk toward her. My best friend for my whole life, and I was afraid to talk to her. I didn't know what to say.

"Hi," I said.

She wasn't smiling. She wasn't even really looking at me. Instead, her gaze fell on the countertop, somewhere around my hands. She pushed her glasses up. "When do you get off?" she asked.

"Five," I said.

"We'd like to talk to you," she said, sounding weirdly formal. "Zack and I. Can you come over?"

"Listen, about last night..." I said, but stopped short when her face snapped up to meet mine. Her eyes still looked really red.

"I don't want to talk about it here," she said. "I know he's sitting right over there, and I don't want to start anything. The thing is...well, the thing is, we need to talk. At Zack's. Will you come?"

I looked over her shoulder at Cole, whose face had gotten a very lined, flat look to it. He wasn't looking at me but seemed instead to be willing her to turn around and face him. I hesitated. Suddenly the silent treatment I'd been getting all day wasn't looking so bad. Everyone wanting to talk all of a sudden seemed way worse.

"Will you?" she prodded, snapping my attention back to her.

I took a deep breath. Basically there was no way I could win in this situation. I nodded. "I'll be home by six," I said. I didn't look back at Cole. But I didn't need to. I could feel him watching anyway.

EIGHTEEN

Even though Georgia had lightened up on me, by the time I got off, the dinner rush was really getting rolling, and her tension had made everyone grumpy. I'd found myself wishing that Granite-Ass would just show up and declare everything okay and put her out of her misery. Really, Georgia was an awesome manager, and she was as honest as the day is long. Dave had nothing to worry about with a store that she ran. I wished she could see that, too.

I was glad to get out of there. And glad I didn't have to work again for a few days. Maybe Dave would calm down and Georgia would be her old self again.

I stepped out into the dining room, where Cole was still sitting. He stood when I came in, and walked over toward me.

"My car's out back," he said. "Next to yours."

He put his hand on the small of my back and guided me

through the doors. I took off my visor as we walked, and pulled the rubber band, which kept snagging random hairs at the base of my neck, out of my hair.

"You're not really supposed to park back here," I said. "It's employee parking."

Cole made a gruff sound in his throat. "And how would anyone know I'm not an employee?"

"Well," I said, "I know."

But Cole didn't seem to care much about where he was parked. He coolly reached over and opened the passenger door.

"Something tells me you'll overlook my little infraction," he said, grabbing my belt loops with his fingers and pulling me toward him. "Don't write me a ticket, Officer Alex," he fake-whimpered. He kissed me on the forehead.

I smiled and leaned into him. He felt so good. Warm. Relaxed. Comfortable. And despite last night, he still felt... safe. If I closed my eyes and breathed him in, I could almost make myself believe that nothing had ever happened last night.

I tilted my face up to his, and he used his finger to push up one corner of my mouth and then the other. I rolled my eyes, but the smile stayed. He leaned down and kissed each corner of my mouth and then my nose and each eye. By the time he pulled me in closer to him, my eyes were closed and I was breathing in his scent and feeling the muscles of his arms around me, and suddenly I couldn't remember how I'd been so mad at him. The anger was just gone.

He took a step to the side and I slid into the car. He shut the door, walked around, and got in the driver's side. The seat made a leathery groan underneath him, and a whiff of leather puffed into the air, reminding me of our first date and giving me butterflies.

Once inside, he didn't move. Just sat there, his hands lying limp in his lap, staring straight ahead at the peeling paint on the back wall of The Bread Bowl. I watched him, then turned my head to the cars passing by, and at one point watched as the back door opened and Jerry hauled a trash bag out to the Dumpster, the whole time eyeing Cole's car suspiciously. I sank a little lower in the seat.

After several long minutes, Cole cleared his throat, tapped his thumbs on his thighs, and said, "About last night. With your friends. I'm sorry."

I blinked. "You already told me," I said, hoping I didn't sound accusatory.

He ran his finger along a ledge of his dash, swiping the dust off. "I know. But I wanted to tell you again today. You know, not in the heat of the moment. I could tell you were really mad all night."

I nodded, my fingers automatically lifting to the dream catcher. "They're my best friends," I said. "I don't even understand what happened. Bethany was trying to be nice. What you did was really...uncool."

He gazed at the peeling wall, his thumbs drumming on his thighs rhythmically. "She's controlling," he said. "She controls you. You know that, right? With all this Colorado shit…" He trailed off, shaking his head. "What's the deal with this trip anyway? You know, I would never ask you to be okay with me going on a trip out of town with another girl. A 'best friend.'" He made quotation marks in the air with his fingers as he said the last two words.

Suddenly it made sense to me. Yes, Cole was jealous of Zack. That much I knew. But he was jealous only because he didn't know everything. How could he? Every time we'd talked about our families, I'd changed the subject as quickly as I could. He had no idea what it meant to me to keep my best friends in my life. He had no idea how many times they'd been there for me, or how many times I'd been there for them. He wasn't there when we made the plan to go to Colorado to figure out the mystery of my life. He wasn't there when we vowed to take this trip together, the three of us, sitting on the woodpile in Bethany's backyard. He had no idea about any of it.

I bent one leg under me and turned to face him. I grabbed his hand, stopping the agitated drumming, and pulled it into my lap. His cheeks had flushed red circles high up on them. I reached over and touched one. It felt hot under my fingers.

"Colorado is everything to me," I said. "It has been since I was eight and my dad gave me this." I pulled the dream catcher necklace out from under my shirt and let it dangle between my finger and thumb.

He stared at the necklace, his face confused, then looked back into my eyes. He'd stopped drumming with his other hand now, and I knew that I would make him understand and everything would be good again.

I let the necklace fall against my chest and held his hand with both of mine, looking directly into his eyes. And I told him everything. I told him about Mom dying. I told him about the photos and how I used to obsess about them when I was little, and about Dad calling Mom crazy as goose-house shit. I told him about the nightmares and the therapy and the necklace that was supposed to bring me closure and how I'd never taken it off since, and about Shannin and Celia and how they never seemed to really care. I told him about how Dad could barely tie his shoes in the morning, much less do anything to take care of us, even all these years later.

And I told him about Colorado. About how it wasn't just that it sounded fun, but that I needed to go there. That sometimes I felt as though no matter what I said or how hard I tried, I'd never be able to put into words why I needed to go there. That it was like describing a hole to someone — other than deep and black and lonely, there was no description.

I told him that it wasn't about playing games and getting romantic or letting Zack and Bethany get so close to me there was no more room for him. It was about closure. It was about solving the mystery. Getting the answers Dad couldn't, or wouldn't, provide. It was about me getting where Mom wanted to go and putting her memory to rest. It was about me stepping up on a mountaintop and seeing if I could feel her there. It was about my life, and I couldn't just let it go because one of my best friends happened to be a boy. I needed to know that she wasn't just...abandoning me. That there was something better in Colorado. There had to be. I wasn't left behind because of...a whim. A stupid road trip.

I'd talked until the sun had gone completely down, and the lights had turned on, bathing us in an orangey glow. The cars whizzing past were using their headlights now, and I was glad for the feeling of privacy in the car.

At some point I'd started to cry. "You have to understand," I said, tracing the back of Cole's hand with my finger. "This is something I have to do. And I have to do it with my best friends, because they've been there through all of it. Both of them. Sometimes Zack even more than Bethany."

Cole had stayed silent through everything I said, and when I finished, he didn't move for a few minutes. Then, slowly, gently, he pulled his hand out from under mine. With one finger, he traced the strap of my necklace. "You've never taken it off?" he asked.

I shook my head.

"Why not?" he asked.

"Because," I said, making a fist over the necklace, my hand enclosing his. "Because it's all I have left of her."

He seemed to think about it for a while, then pulled his hand out of mine, straightened up just slightly, and dug his car key out of his front pocket. Then he started the car with a roar.

"I have to get home," I said. "I have to talk to..." I

paused at first, then sat up a little straighter and finished. "I have to talk to Bethany and Zack. About last night. I have to smooth things over with them."

"This won't take long," he said. "I just want to show you something."

He put the car in drive and headed out of the parking lot.

"I have to be home by seven," I said, curiosity winning out over my sense of urgency. I'd just have to tell Bethany and Zack that I'd had to work a little late is all. They'd understand. They always did.

Cole flicked on the radio and pulled into the street, hitting the gas pedal so hard I felt pressed back into my seat. He had that determined look on his face again. The same one he'd been wearing last night at the lake while playing football. The one that said he was going to get exactly what he wanted, no matter who or what got in the way. The one that said "winner."

After a few turns we were in a neighborhood, and Cole finally slowed down. A few more turns later, he parked in front of a gray house.

I peered out the windshield at the darkened house in front of me and then looked at Cole questioningly.

"C'mon," he said, opening his door. "I want you to see what you're missing out on." He stepped out and shut his door, but this time, rather than walk around and open mine for me, he just stood where he was. I opened my door and got out, looking at him over the top of his car.

"It doesn't look like anyone's home," I said.

"Oh, she's home," he said. "They both are."

He didn't say another word to me as I followed him inside, wondering why his voice sounded so bitter when he said the word "she."

NINETEEN

The house was completely dark when we walked in. Cave-like, almost. And had it not been for the echoing drone of sitcom dialogue off in the distance, followed by bouts of prerecorded laugh track, I'd have thought for sure Cole and I were alone.

Cole deposited his keys with a clatter on a little table next to the door, then strode through the front room so quickly I had to follow fast in order to keep up with him. I tried to take in as much as I could while we walked, but it was hard in the dark.

The house looked minimally decorated. No pictures on the walls. Only a couple knickknacks here and there on the sparse furniture, just blobby shapes in the dark. A basket on the floor with a blanket spilling out of it. A candle here. A book there. I wondered if the rest of their things were still in moving boxes, or if their house always looked so bare.

We walked through the front room and into a kitchen. Here the sound of garbled audience laughter got louder, and I noticed the blue-gray flickering of changing television images lighting up a short staircase on our right. Someone was downstairs watching TV.

"Want anything to drink?" Cole asked, opening the refrigerator. A yellow light patch cut across the linoleum and made me squint. Already my eyes had gotten used to the darkness.

I shook my head. He grabbed a can of something and popped it open, shutting the refrigerator and blanketing the room in what seemed like an even darker dark. Did Cole always live like this? Wandering around a shadowy house, listening to wisecracking and cheap laughter all night long?

"Cole," I said, but he'd already started toward the stairs.

"Come on. I want you to meet my parents." He stopped at the top of the stairs and held out an arm toward me. I couldn't see his face in the shadows and was suddenly glad of it. Something told me it was grim. Something told me the warmth of the guy caressing my cheek and telling me he'd wait for me until the end of time was missing at the moment. I walked toward him slowly, then grabbed his hand and held it as he led me down the stairs.

We ended up in a long, skinny living room that, had the TV been off, would've been darker than any room I'd ever seen in my life. The floor was tiled in a deep color—brown, maybe, or even black—and the walls were paneled. A sliding glass door was covered with a dark-colored curtain, and in front of it sat a large shadowy mass that I took to be a couch.

The television sat, facing us, on an old-fashioned aluminum stand at the other end of the room, by the fireplace. An old sitcom from the seventies was playing on it, the sound blaring. Directly in front of us, pointed toward the TV, was a set of recliners. One was in the reclined position, and a pair of bare feet—definitely male—stretched out on the footrest. The other chair, from the back, anyway, looked empty.

Cole pulled me between the chairs and into the room. "Hey, guys," he said in a flat voice. "I wanted you to meet my girlfriend, Alex."

I turned and saw the owner of the reclining feet. He was a large, gut-heavy man wearing boxers and a ribbed T-shirt. He held a beer against his stomach. He looked like Cole, only older and fatter. It was hard to believe that this was Cole's dad. I'd imagined someone handsome and successful. This guy almost looked like a caricature of the exact opposite of the way I would have pictured Cole's dad. Something you'd see on a cartoon—a spoof of a dad.

"Hi," I said, starting to raise my hand in a wave, but he cut me off.

"What the hell you doin', Cole? I can't see the TV, dammit!"

Cole and I shuffled a few inches to the side. "Dad. This is Alex," Cole tried again, and this time the man at least acknowledged that I was in the room, even if he didn't exactly look at me.

"'Lo," he said distractedly, waving his beer in my direction.

"Nice to meet you," I practically whispered.

"That's my dad," Cole said. "And this is my mom. Brenda, this is Alex."

I turned to the other recliner, where Cole was pointing, and almost jumped. I'd thought nobody was in the chair, but sitting, curled practically into a ball, was a wafer-thin woman with giant, vacant eyes. Her head laid against the armrest, her legs pulled up into the seat, her hands holding her shins tight. She looked like a toddler, hiding, frightened by a thunderstorm. She blinked slowly, taking us both in, but didn't say a word.

The TV switched over to a commercial, and Cole's dad shifted in his chair.

"So," he said. "Alex, you say? You a girl?" He laughed, like he'd made a particularly funny joke. "When I was your age, Alex was a boy's name. You not datin' a boy, are ya, Cole?" Again with the laughter. "Hell, I'd have to kick your ass if you were datin' a boy."

Embarrassment flooded my limbs, and I was actually glad for the dark. I opened my mouth to say something but wasn't sure how to respond.

Cole tugged on my hand a little.

"Just a joke," he said in a low voice. Correction: a defeated voice. "He doesn't mean anything."

The woman blinked her giant eyes and shifted them back to a space of linoleum about three feet in front of her.

I heard the other recliner shift again, and Cole's dad's voice boomed so loud I actually did jump this time. "Brenda, Cole's got company." He gave a bark of laughter that made me inch closer to Cole. "She's not so good with people. Woman's scared of her own shadow. Ain't that right, Brenda?"

The woman pulled herself up to sitting and peered over the arm of the recliner at her husband. She made a noise in the back of her throat and mumbled something I couldn't make out. I wasn't sure if she was talking to me or to Cole or to Cole's dad, and I shifted uneasily. Fortunately, the TV show came back on, and Cole's dad was engrossed once again.

"We're going upstairs," Cole announced, and began pulling me out of the room. I felt relief wash over me. Even in the dark, that room may have been the most uncomfortable room I've ever set foot in.

"You want me to bring you some sodas?" came a meek voice at our backs. So small and nasally it might have been mistaken for a meow or an electronic squeal. I saw a shadowy lump hanging over the side of Cole's mom's—er, Brenda's—chair that I took to be her head.

"Nope, Brenda, just stay there," Cole answered. I detected something in his voice. Annoyance, maybe? Embarrassment?

"For God's sake, Brenda, they're going upstairs. They can get their own sodas. They want to be alone," Cole's dad boomed again. And I could hear him continue as we climbed the stairs back to the kitchen. "Jesus, do you always have to smother people?...So what if they're up there alone?...Leave him alone, dammit....This is why you're always..."

Cole pulled me through the kitchen and back into the front room. But instead of heading for the front door, he turned and pulled me up another short staircase. We climbed the stairs into a hallway that was so dark I put my free hand on Cole's back to follow him.

We plunged into a bedroom, and Cole shut the door behind us. Up here, we couldn't hear the TV. It was like stepping into an isolation booth.

"Close your eyes," he said, and I did. I heard a *click* and saw light streaming in through my eyelids. "Okay, you can open them," he said. I opened my eyes and squinted. The lamp he'd turned on was low-light, but it still hurt, and I blinked a few times to get used to it. "Sorry," he mumbled. "This place is a mess. Brenda never cleans anything."

He bent and picked up some dirty clothes and then tossed them into a chair by the window. I studied the room while he tidied. An old wicker chair next to the window, a small amp and guitar on the floor in front of it. Shabby dresser on the far wall, the top of it a dense forest of trophies. Bed, unmade, facing the dresser. A modest nightstand next to the bed, holding a few empty glasses, a grungy-looking alarm clock, and a photo of me that I'd given Cole on our third date. I picked up the photo, feeling warm inside.

Nobody had ever kept a picture of me next to their bed before.

"Sit down, if you want," Cole said, motioning with his head toward the bed while he picked up a pair of shoes and tossed them in the closet. I thought about Bethany and Zack waiting for me at Zack's house. They were expecting me. I checked the clock—I was definitely late, but there was still time. I considered telling Cole that I needed to get to them. That I had to make it up to them, and the later it got, the harder it would be. But something about his face told me he'd be in no mood to discuss Bethany and Zack tonight. Something about the blackness that still rolled off him, even in the light, told me he needed me to stay. I sat on the edge of the bed and set the photo back on the nightstand, hoping Bethany and Zack would be understanding for a few more minutes.

"So," he said, scooping up a towel and hanging it over the back of the chair. "What'd you think of my mom and dad?"

I didn't know what to say. "Do you always call your mom Brenda?" I asked.

He shrugged. "Pretty much. You saw her. My dad says if she can't act like a mom, she shouldn't have the title. He started calling her Brenda around me as far back as I can remember. I guess I just picked it up." He kicked some books under his bed while he talked.

"Does she always, um..." I trailed off. How did I say what I was thinking? Does she always look like a zombie? Does she always talk in squeaks and lay curled up in her chair like she's trying to disappear?

172

But Cole finished for me. "Act like she belongs in a mental ward? No. Only when she's having one of her pity parties. Most of the time she's just really annoying. Always wanting to do stuff for me. Always wanting to be up in my business. Always being pathetic. My dad's no saint or anything, but at least he tells her when to leave me the hell alone. Don't worry. She won't bother us tonight. Not with him home."

I was silent. I'd never thought about it before, being annoyed by a mom who's "too there." Would I think it was irritating to always have someone prying into my personal life? I didn't know. One thing about my dad—I could have all the privacy in the world, if I wanted it.

Cole sat next to me on the bed and leaned forward, his elbows on his knees, his hands dangling between his legs. He let out a big sigh.

"I just...I wanted you to meet them," he said. "I wanted you to see that I understand what it's like to wish for a mother. To wish for a family. I always wanted it, too." He reached over and pushed my hair behind my ear. "I think this is what brought us together," he whispered. "We both need each other. We both get it."

I nodded. He was right. I knew at that moment, in every part of my body, that Cole was right. We were destined to be together. He understood. Just because there was a physical body of a mother in his house didn't mean he had a mom. He understood what it was like to wish for something perfect, a fairy tale. He understood what it was like to be lonely in your family. He understood me. And I understood him.

Bethany and Zack...they could say they understood. They could be there for me on the Meltdown Days. They could plan the trip to Colorado and say they would be there for me when I reached the mountaintop. They could appreciate the story of my family. But they'd never actually known what it felt like to be me. They had happy families. They had whole families. They never pined for love—it was always just there for them to take.

Cole knew. Cole was the only one who truly knew.

So when he leaned over and kissed me, I let myself forgive him for what happened the night before. Not just say it, but truly believe it. And when he pushed me back on the bed, whispering, "Alex. You're my soul mate," I felt it too. It felt like falling, only there was no landing to this fall.

And when he turned out the light and kissed my eyelids and bare shoulders and fingertips, I opened myself up to him completely. I was never wanted by anyone before. I never really belonged to anyone before, not in this way. Cole had me, heart, soul, body. And it felt right.

It almost felt like standing on a mountaintop.

Bethany and Zack were standing at my locker when I turned the corner after final period on Thursday. My stomach dropped when I saw them. I'd been dreading this all week. I felt so guilty for standing them up Saturday night, I'd been avoiding them since. But next week was Thanksgiving, and Dad and Celia and I always had dinner at Zack's house, and after dinner Zack and I always went to Bethany's to help decorate her Christmas tree, so I knew eventually I'd have to face them. I just wasn't sure yet what to say when I did.

Zack was looking ultracool, with his back pressed to the locker next to mine passively staring out the side doors of the school, where the stragglers were piling into their cars and screeching out of the parking lot. Bethany faced me, her arms crossed across her chest uncomfortably, her giganto-purse pulling one shoulder down a few inches lower than the other. A few wilting leaves poked out the top of the bag. Most likely Bethany rescuing a sapling from a sidewalk crack or something.

From the look on Zack's face, this wasn't going to be pretty. I didn't blame them for being pissed that I never showed up for our "meeting," but I also knew that they'd never understand why I couldn't just up and leave Cole after what had happened between us.

I wanted so badly to tell Bethany that I'd had a "first time" and that it felt amazing and surreal and that I was scared but so in love and so sure I'd done the right thing.

But I knew she wouldn't approve. I knew she'd not only still blame me for not showing up at Zack's like I'd promised, but would think I'd made a mistake, especially since it was with Cole. She wouldn't be happy for me.

And there was something else, too. Something that happened the very second I nodded when Cole asked if what he was doing was okay. I changed. I would never be "their Alex" again. They had to share me with Cole, because he now had a piece of me that they never had and I would never ever get back. And there was no way that Bethany or Zack, both virgins, despite Zack's repeated attempts to convince us that he'd "three-quarters done it" with Lynesia Mahan at the movie theater in seventh grade, could ever understand that.

I was different now.

But Cole hadn't come to school today—he'd texted me that he had "fam stuff" to take care of—and I was having to face them on my own.

"Hey," I said, trying to look and sound cheerful.

Zack didn't turn to face me.

"We missed you on Saturday," Bethany said. She uncrossed an arm long enough to push her glasses up on her nose, then tucked her hand back under her arm. She didn't look angry anymore, but she still had that red-eyed look, like she was upset. Maybe that look was permanent on her now.

"I know," I said, opening my locker, trying to be as nonchalant as possible. "I'm really sorry. I just...couldn't get away."

"From work? Or just too busy hanging out with Mr. Universe?" Zack said, finally turning to look at me. "Unlike you, we don't really travel in the same circles as the Big Shits."

"Zack," Bethany said, reaching out and touching his arm. He rolled his eyes, popped a toothpick into his mouth, and resumed his pose.

"We just...well, you didn't show up after you said you would," Bethany said.

I pulled my English book out of my locker and slipped it into my backpack, which was resting on the floor at my feet. "I'm sorry, guys. I just got busy with stuff."

"Stuff?" Bethany said, her face flushing. She pushed at her glasses again, even though they hadn't slid down her nose at all since the last time. "You mean Cole."

I paused and looked at her, my arm frozen in midreach to the top shelf of my locker. "Actually, yeah. Cole. He is my boyfriend, you know."

"Oh, we know!" Zack cried out in this sarcastic voice. He pushed away from the lockers and started down the hall. "We definitely know. But thanks for reminding us. Just in case we forgot," he spat over his shoulder. "Bethany, I'll wait for you in the car."

I watched him go, then whirled on Bethany. "What the hell? I said I was sorry. What's his problem?" I pulled out another book, shoved it into my backpack angrily, and slammed the locker door shut.

"Oh, I don't know," Bethany said. "Maybe it's because your boyfriend treated us like shit? Maybe it's because he probably treats you like shit, too? Or maybe it's because ever since you've been going out with him you've had nothing to do with us. Your *best* friends." The word "best" was dripping with sarcasm, and I think I actually winced when she said it that way.

I shook my head. "You're wrong," I said. "He treats me like I'm the best thing that's ever happened to him. And he understands me. Unlike my *best* friends." I tried to saturate "best" with sarcasm, too, but failed miserably. I only sounded needy. Because deep down I think I knew she was right.

Bethany set her jaw, then silently turned and started walking briskly the same way Zack went. Immediately I felt bad. I didn't mean to take this out on them. I was the one who should be sorry. I did blow them off. Even if I had good reason for it.

I went after her.

"Beth," I said, catching up to her and grabbing her

elbow. She stopped and turned, her eyes slits behind her glasses. "Beth, c'mon. I'm sorry. You're right. I've been a bad friend lately. It's just…it's just that Cole and I have gotten so close and you know how he feels about Zack and…I'll make it up to you. I promise."

She considered this for a second, her body slowly losing some of its rigidity. After a while she sighed, rolling her eyes dramatically, and then nodded. "Okay," she said. "I get it. I'm still mad, but…I know how I'd be if Randy knew I existed. I get it."

I smiled and hugged her. "That's why you're my best friend," I said.

"Zack used to be your best friend, too," she said into my hair. I noticed she wasn't hugging me back.

"He still is," I said, pulling away. "I just have to figure out how to have both of them in my life, you know?"

She nodded. "I know."

We started walking again. "He really does treat me like a queen," I said.

She nodded but didn't respond. Subject closed.

"Hey," she said after a while, "you know that RV we were talking about?"

I groaned. "Don't tell me…"

She grinned and nodded. "Zack's grandpa — you know, Grampy Big Bucks? — said he'd feel better about us in one of those than in the crapmobile, so he offered to pay for the whole thing. We're gonna be ridin' in style!" She snapped her fingers and did a funky little slide down the hall, leaves falling out of her bag and leaving a trail on the floor. I laughed.

"I can't believe you pulled it off," I said between chuckles.

She breathed on her fingertips and brushed them on her shoulder. "Baby, I can do anything." She got a serious look. "Cole isn't going to try to talk you out of going on this trip now, is he?"

"No way," I assured her. "He couldn't even if he tried. Don't worry about that. Okay?"

We plunged out into the parking lot. Zack was stretched out on the hood of his car, arms folded behind his head, toothpick in mouth, eyes shut. He looked like he was sleeping.

Bethany glanced at me deviously and put her finger over her lips. I nodded, turning my lips in on themselves to hold back a laugh. She snuck around the car, reached in the open window, and laid on the horn.

Zack looked like someone had Tasered him. He jumped, cursing, and rolled off the car.

Bethany had run back to my side, and we leaned into each other, holding our stomachs because we were laughing so hard.

"Oh, okay," Zack said, getting to his feet and bouncing over toward us, using his cocky walk. "Okay, girls. Go ahead. Laugh it up. Payback is a bee-yotch, just so's you knows."

Bethany sucked in a great gasp of air. "I'm sorry; I couldn't help myself. You looked so cozy."

"But too bad," I added between giggles. "I was hoping you'd pee your pants." I snapped my fingers in an aw-shucks move. "Maybe next time."

"Oh, really?" Zack said, launching at us suddenly. We squealed, trying to dodge him, but he got both of us, grabbing each of us under our arms, and was squeezing tight. "Let's see who tinkles. Won't be me."

We screeched and squealed and laughed until our stomachs hurt as he tickled both of us relentlessly. Soon we were all a heap on the asphalt of the parking lot, laughing and kicking at each other and wearing ourselves out.

Just like old times.

It almost surprised me how good it felt. I hadn't felt that light since before the lake party. It felt more than good. It felt necessary. I needed these guys, no matter who else was in my life.

Finally, Zack pulled himself out of the pile of legs and arms. "You ready to head out, Red?" he asked, tousling Bethany's hair.

She nodded, pulling herself up, too. "Yeah. My mom's going to wonder what happened to me."

Zack stood and then reached down with one hand. "What about you?" he asked.

I paused for just a second and then grabbed his hand and pulled myself to standing, next to him. I reached down and picked up my backpack. "I'm good," I said. "I'm parked over there." I pointed at my car a few spaces down.

"Cool," he said.

We smiled at one another. All forgiven. No big apologies needed. We were best friends. There was nothing we couldn't get past.

Zack and Bethany got into his car, and I headed for mine. Just as I was opening the passenger door to put my backpack in, Zack's car sidled up to me, and Bethany poked her head out of the window.

"You going home?" she asked.

"Yeah," I said. I didn't add that Cole had some family function to go to tonight and that was the only reason I wasn't going to be with him. "Catching up on homework tonight."

"Wanna come over to Zack's? We still need to talk about the trip," she said. "I mean, I told you about the RV, and there aren't a whole lot of other changes, but…hey, we're making cookies."

"Sounds great. I'll be there."

She smiled. "Cool. See ya!"

She pulled her head back in, and they roared out of the lot. I slid my backpack onto the floorboard and shut the door. There was a squeal at the entrance of the school as Zack peeled out, which was a practically a requirement at our school—everybody did it.

I glanced up just in time to see him take off.

Just after his car pulled out, though, another pulled out behind him, slowly, calmly.

And if I didn't know better, I'd have sworn it was Cole's car.

Everything was right again.

I drove home and rushed inside, heading straight upstairs to drop off my backpack. I changed into a pair of pajama pants and tossed my hair up into a messy ponytail, peeking out the window at Zack's driveway. His car was already there, which meant they were waiting for me.

The house was silent—Dad wouldn't bring Celia home from Yearbook Club until after six. I scrawled a quick note on the back of an envelope on the kitchen table, telling them I was next door, then stepped outside and shuffled through the grass in my socks, the cold quickly seeping into my toes.

When I walked in, Zack's mom was in the study, pulling dried flowers out from between the pages of a phone book and pasting them onto little note cards. Mrs. Clavinger was really crafty that way, always making things out of raffia and hand-embossing envelopes and stuff. She had her own scrapbooking business and would have meetings once a month. Zack always called them her "hen gatherings," and he always found somewhere else to be when the ladies were over.

"Hey, Mrs. C!" I called, shutting the door behind me.

She looked up, a piece of hair falling out of the bandanna over her forehead. "Alex!" she gushed. "What a — they're in the kitchen — wonderful surprise — they're making cookies."

"Great," I said, and headed for the kitchen.

Bethany was holding a metal bowl to her stomach and smacking Zack with a wooden spoon as he tried to stick his fingers into the dough.

"Hey," I said, sidling up to them. I waited for Bethany to swing at Zack again and swiped a fingerful of cookie dough while she was occupied.

"Hey!" she cried, and smacked my arm with the spoon, too, leaving a smear of dough. While she was concentrating on me, Zack stuck his hand in the bowl from the other side, coming out with a fistful of dough. "You guys!" she squealed, but she was laughing too hard now to keep either one of us out, and we ended up taking the bowl to the table and all sitting around it, eating it with our fingers.

It was just like we'd done a million times before, eating junk and talking about everyday stuff like our classes and which teachers we thought were secretly hooking up on the side and how Mia Libby's boobs had suddenly gotten way huger this year after she'd "gone to Europe for two weeks."

We talked about the Colorado trip, still arguing about the merits of summer over winter travel. Bethany showed us photos of our RV. She pulled up the Stanley Hotel on her laptop, and we read about all the hauntings that supposedly happened there. We decided that for sure we'd go to the natural history museum in Denver. Things were really coming together. All we needed to do was pick a date.

Nobody brought up the night of the lake party. Nobody brought up Cole.

This was what best friendship was about: forgiveness and unconditional love. And cookie dough.

Zack was just about to get up to get us some sodas, when his dad poked his head through the door that led into the garage.

"Hey, it's the three-headed monster," he said.

"Hi, Mr. C!" Bethany and I said together, our mouths full of cookie dough.

He nodded at us, then turned his attention to Zack. "Hey, buddy. Can you help me carry your mother's birdbath to the backyard? Thing weighs a ton."

Zack stood up and flexed his muscles, pro wrestler-style. He let out a long grunt. "Need a real man to do the job, eh?" he joked.

"Something like that," his dad said, chuckling and shaking his head. "Girls, I don't know how you put up with that one."

"Neither do we," Bethany said. "Mostly we just ignore him."

"Good plan," Mr. C said, then ducked back into the garage with Zack.

Bethany and I were alone. Zack's mom was still busy in the den, and Zack and his dad were fumbling around in the garage. It was just the two of us, and I couldn't remember the last time that had happened. Everything felt so right, except for one thing: There was something huge I hadn't told my best friend yet. As sure as I was just a few hours before that I shouldn't tell her, now I was just as sure that she had to know, because it would hurt her too much not to.

"Beth," I said. "I need to tell you something. But you have to swear you won't tell Zack."

Bethany swiped a fingerful of cookie dough and stuck it in her mouth. "Okay," she said, chewing.

I swallowed and rubbed my palms down the legs of my pajama pants, taking a deep breath. Suddenly I wasn't sure how to even say it, so I just took a deep breath and let it out. "I did it with Cole."

Bethany stopped chewing. She peered into the bowl like maybe what I'd just said had come out of there instead. A beat went by, and I thought maybe she hadn't heard me, or maybe I hadn't actually said it out loud like I thought I had. But then she started chewing again and swallowed, turning her head slowly toward me. Her eyes were huge behind her glasses. "You did?" she asked.

I nodded. "That's why I didn't make it over Saturday night. He took me to meet his parents. They were horrible. His dad was really mean, and his mom was like this zombie.

We went up to his room and..." I shrugged, my hands lying limp in my lap.

"Whoa," Bethany said. "I can't believe you did...you haven't been going out that long."

"Well, it's not like Cole and I just met yesterday, either," I said sharply.

"Don't get mad," she said defensively. "It's just...are you sure you're doing the right thing?" She pushed up her glasses, leaving a greasy cookie dough smudge on the bridge of her nose.

Now it was my turn to be defensive. "We used protection, if that's what you're asking."

She shook her head. "I mean, yeah, that's good, but... Well, it's just that he was so nice at Shubb's, and then at the lake party he was so..." Her voice trailed off.

This was not how this was supposed to go. Bethany was supposed to be excited for me and ask me for details. "He was having a bad night at the lake party, Beth," I said. "If you got to know the real Cole, you'd love him, too."

She got up. She didn't say anything as she walked to the sink and rinsed her fingers off. Then she went to the fridge and pulled out two sodas.

"Beth," I said, "I want you to be happy for me."

Her shoulders drooped, and she hesitated in the open refrigerator for just the tiniest second. When she turned toward me, she had a wobbly smile on her face, almost embarrassed. She sat down, pushing one of the sodas across the table at me.

"I am happy for you," she said. "But it's just...I don't want you to get hurt. Cole doesn't seem...all that nice."

"You don't know him," I said in a low voice. "Not like I do." I popped open my can of soda and gazed out the sliding glass door into the backyard, where Zack and his dad were standing next to the birdbath, hands on hips, chatting. It seemed so unfair that I had finally found someone who loved me, had finally fallen in love with someone enough to go all the way, and I had to defend him to my best friends like this.

"I know," she said. "But..." She leaned forward and peered into the cookie dough bowl again. "Remember when I told you that he and Zack got into that fight in the locker room a few weeks ago? Do you know why they were fighting?" she asked.

I shook my head.

"They got into a fight because Cole kept talking about how he wanted to get you into bed. He was being pretty gross about it, so Zack stepped in."

"Gross how?"

She shrugged. She leaned back and used her thumbnail to flick some cookie dough from the front of her jeans. Zack and his dad retreated from the backyard, coming back toward the house. "Just talking about your body, I guess. In a lot of detail."

I flushed. Cole was talking about me in the locker room. So much so that my "big brother" Zack had to step in. In front of everybody. How embarrassing. I stuck a dollop of cookie dough in my mouth, but suddenly it didn't taste good anymore.

We could hear Zack and his dad in the garage and could hear the big door rumbling to a close.

"Alex," Bethany said, putting her hand on my shoulder. "I know you love him, but he's just...he's not...just be careful, okay?"

I resisted the urge to roll my eyes. Something about the way she was talking to me felt so condescending. Like she was trying to be my mother.

Okay, so he was talking about me in the locker room. It was embarrassing, but it wasn't the end of the world. Maybe he wasn't trying to be "gross." Maybe he was just expressing desire. Cole wouldn't embarrass me on purpose.

Bethany just didn't know Cole like I did. Neither of them did. And if they never got to like Cole? Well, they'd have the choice to support me or not. That was up to them. I wasn't the only best friend in this scenario.

"I am being careful," I said around the dough in my mouth. "I promise."

CHAPTER
TWENTY-TWO

I didn't see Cole at all the next day.

Well, actually, I saw him a lot. But he never seemed to see me. He didn't come to my locker after second period like he usually did. And he walked through the halls looking the same as he'd looked at the lake party, the intensity giving his face an almost shiny sheen. The couple times I saw him through the crowd, he was hand-slapping and belly-laughing so hard it was as if he were putting on a show. As if he wanted everyone to see what a great time he was having.

Honestly, it was weird. At first I tried not to think too much about it. He'd had some family junk to take care of the day before. Knowing how he felt about his dad and Brenda, it wouldn't surprise me at all to find out that he was upset and just wanted to be left alone.

But it was one thing to be forgiving for the first couple

hours of the day. By lunch, I was starting to really feel stung. I was supposed to be his respite from the bad stuff. I was supposed to be his other half of "alone." I thought we'd opened up to each other about our family issues now.

Those times we'd spent wrapped around each other, talking about our parents, talking about loneliness and about desire for something different, something better. He'd said, *I've never told anyone but you this stuff, Alex.* Those times we promised each other we'd be there. We understood. Only now I wasn't needed. It just didn't make sense.

By the time sixth period ended and it was time to go to the tutor lab, I actually had butterflies in my stomach. I had stopped convincing myself that his distance from me was about his family problem. Something was wrong between us. I could feel it. I just didn't know what it was. I racked my brain over and over, trying to pinpoint something I'd said or done to make him mad. Sometimes Cole got moody for no reason, but usually that was aimed at Brenda. He always got grouchy when she'd call him. He'd yell at her without even saying hello, then hang up and turn off his phone. But he'd never gone a whole day without speaking to me.

He was late. Really late. I'd gotten out my homework but was feeling so lost and upset my eyes felt full and I couldn't concentrate on it. Finally, just before the bell rang, he burst through the door.

I froze. Watched him as he glided across the room and sat in his usual seat.

"You're late," I said, swallowing to keep the tears from

spilling over. I was trying to sound indignant, but my voice had a plaintive ring to it that made me sound desperate and frightened and whiny. I wanted to sound pissed.

He looked up at me sharply. "So?"

That was it? *So?*

"So," I said. "Where've you been today? You haven't even said hi to me. What was your family thing yesterday? Why didn't you call?"

"Wow," he said, leaning forward, an arrogant half-grin on his face. I was starting to really dislike the air in the room. Something about him felt more than moody. More than mad. "You've got a lot of questions."

Silence stretched between us. My eyes were practically stinging now, and it was all I could do to keep them dry. All I knew was I needed to get out of there immediately, before I cried or...before I figured out exactly why I felt so uncomfortable all of a sudden. I stood up, shoveling books and papers into my backpack as fast as I could.

"I think we'll just skip this today, okay?" I said, again mentally kicking myself for the wobble in my voice. I started to zip my backpack.

He reached up and grabbed my wrist. Hard. "I don't think so."

I was shocked at how tightly he was holding my wrist. I remembered the night of the lake party, when he grabbed my knee so hard it left faint little finger-shaped welts. I stared at him incredulously. I'd assumed those welts had been an accident. I'd figured it was just the heat of the moment and hadn't even thought about it again after we'd made up. But here he was grabbing my wrist, hard enough to leave welts again. And the way his lips pressed together in a thin pink line told me this was no accident. He was squeezing my wrist on purpose.

I tried to pull free of his grasp. "Let go of me, Cole. I'm leaving." He squeezed tighter, his fingers digging into my skin, and twisted just enough to make my wrist throb. "Ow," I hissed, bending at the knees and yanking backward. "That hurts. Let go. I'm serious, Cole."

He stood up, coming around the table and getting so close to me, our noses were practically touching. I could smell the gum on his breath. He stared at me, and whatever thoughts were in his head made his eyes grow darker. The smile had gone and been replaced by a snarl. I didn't think it was possible, but he gripped me even more fiercely. I felt something inside my wrist thump and strain. I sucked in air through my teeth, my knees buckling even further. There was nothing I could do about the tears now, and I blinked them away angrily.

It seemed like forever that he just glared at me like that. Then he got even closer and whispered, "What? Does Zack's touch feel so much softer?"

Surprise rocked me. I forgot about my arm for half a second, and looked up to him in confusion. Zack's touch? What did that even mean? "What're you . . . ouch! Cole, stop it! That hurts!"

But he squeezed with such force he was shaking now.

My fingers were turning purple, the circulation cut off so I couldn't bend them. "I saw you," he said, his face going red, his voice turning into this gruff bark that made goose bumps pop up on my arms. I reached down with my other hand and pulled at his fingers. They didn't budge—he was too strong. "I saw you groping each other in the parking lot yesterday. Looked like a real lovefest out there. Very cozy."

"Groping each other? We weren't...oh my God...are you spying on me now?" I thought of Georgia saying Cole was creepy, the way he was always hanging around, watching me. And I thought of the car that had slowly followed Zack's car out of the parking lot yesterday.

He yanked on my wrist, and the breath was sucked right out of me. "Don't lie to me, Alex!" he snarled in my face. "I saw you out there! And I saw you leave his house and walk back to yours last night, too."

At the word "too," he released my wrist by shoving it into my stomach and giving it a mighty push. The relief in my wrist was short-lived, as I stumbled from the force of his shove and fell backward, toppling over my chair and smacking my hip hard against the floor. I was so stunned, I couldn't move. My wrist and hip ached.

He stood over me, breathing hard through flared nostrils like an animal. I scrambled up to my knees, which wasn't easy one-handed, with a hip that didn't want to move. I couldn't say anything. And the tears were suddenly gone, too.

"It's not bad enough that I have to deal with Brenda's

shit, is it, Alex? It's not enough that I have to stay home to take care of that bullshit. But you take the first opportunity you get when I'm not around and you cheat on me with that idiot next door."

I was still trying to get my feet under me, when he suddenly grabbed my hair and yanked upward. I gave out a cry. Somehow I was standing, and not even feeling my hip or wrist because of this new pain at the side of my head. I felt a few hairs snap and pull out. I was shaking so hard I wasn't sure I'd be able to stay standing up if he let go. This was more than leaving a few finger marks on my knee. This was scary.

He pulled my face to his again. "You won't screw around on me, Alex," he growled in a voice I'd never heard out of him before. "You're not smart enough to pull it off anyway. I will catch you. Every. Single. Time."

"Okay," I whimpered, my hands hovering around his hand, standing on my tiptoes to keep him from pulling any more hairs out. I wanted to tell him that I hadn't been screwing around with Zack but had actually been trying to convince my friends that he was a nice guy. But I was afraid if I protested he would pull harder or do something else, so I just nodded, as much as his grip would let me, and agreed with him. "Okay."

He held me there for a few more seconds, then released me with a half-shove and moved back to his side of the table. He picked up his backpack and slung it over one shoulder, just as calmly as he'd do on any ordinary day. Meanwhile, I was rubbing the side of my head where he'd pulled my hair, just concentrating on staying upright, my knees were shaking so bad. Trying to make sense of everything that had just happened. It had all happened so quickly, it was almost as if I'd imagined it.

Backpack in place, he finally spoke. His voice was normal again, not that wired snarl he'd adopted just a few minutes before. Instead, he sounded spent, tired, calm.

"We'll talk more later," he said. He walked toward me, grabbed my chin gently between his thumb and forefinger, lifted up my face, and kissed me. "I love you," he said as he walked toward the door. "And I won't let you fuck me over."

He slipped out the door and let it shut behind him with a soft *shush*, and suddenly I was alone.

And that's when everything began to hurt.

My wrist.

My hip.

My head.

My neck.

And none of it hurt nearly as much as my heart.

How was it possible that this was the same guy who'd rested his hand so lightly over mine, strumming chords and putting my poetry to music? How was this the same person I'd trusted to keep me safe at the top of the spillway? Who'd kissed my eyelids in his bedroom?

I didn't know what to do, so I got busy. I spent a few minutes straightening the table and chairs, my whole body shaking. I couldn't really use my left hand—the one he'd grabbed — so I kind of half-pushed, half-pulled things back into place.

A part of me couldn't believe what had just happened. Most of me, really. Like maybe it was all just a dream and I would wake up from it, shaky and upset but so glad it was over. But a part of me knew that it was true, what I'd just experienced. Part of me had known it at the lake party. Part of me had sensed something dangerous about Cole even back then. But nothing like this. Never, not in a million years, would I have sensed this.

Slowly, shakily, I slid down into a chair. I turned my hand over and stared at my wrist, which was red with welts and would surely be bruising at that very minute. I leaned over and tugged down a small space of waistband on my jeans. My hip already sported a puffy bruise, so purple it almost looked red.

And then the tears started.

How could he? my mind raged. *How could he do this to me?*

My thoughts spun. What would I do?

I felt that I should tell someone about what had just happened to me. Run screaming it down the hall. Call the police. Tell Mr. Nagins, the school counselor. Do something. Call Bethany. Run next door and get Zack out of lab. Get someone's attention, and...

And what? Show them my bruises? Tell them about the lake party? About the merry-go-round when he scared me on purpose? Tell them that I'd had sex with him anyway, even after he'd already bruised me once? Tell them that I'd made excuses for him that night?

I was so embarrassed. I couldn't even imagine telling anyone those things. Those things made me look stupid and gullible and needy, and I knew I wasn't those things. I knew it was more complicated than that. But nobody else would understand.

Not to mention, I'd probably get enrolled in some schmucky battered women's workshop or something by Mr. Nagins. They'd call Dad. It would be a huge deal because it happened at school. And everyone would find out.

I knew how this school worked—if one person found out, everyone would know immediately. And I was so not ready to be the school's domestic violence example. *Did you hear what happened to Alex Bradford? God, I would never be so stupid. I'd kick his ass.*

They would probably pull me up to the front of the room in health class, make me tell my story so others could learn from it. All the while everyone in the classes would be thinking how I was such an idiot for not fighting back. They'd wonder how I could love a guy like that. They'd call me pathetic.

And, God, what about Bethany? *He doesn't seem that nice,* she'd said. *Be careful.* If I told her what he'd just done, she would think she was right about him. I would have proven her right.

And God only knows what Zack would do if he found out.

And the worst—and I couldn't even believe it myself, that I was thinking this—if I told everyone the truth, Cole would hate me. He would never forgive me.

And I hated myself for even thinking about Cole's feelings right now, but I just couldn't help it.

I crossed my arms on my desk and laid my head down on them and cried, thinking all these things and more. Thinking that this was not like Cole. He was stressed. He must have been, because normally he didn't do this. It was his family problems.

And thinking that maybe I pushed him into doing this. I pushed him by letting Zack tickle me in the parking lot and by not telling him that I was going to Zack's house that night, by not explaining to him that Bethany was there and we were eating cookie dough and talking RVs.

Maybe I should have even invited him to come along. Talked Bethany and Zack into letting him join us.

I should have made him see that it was completely innocent. That *I* was completely innocent.

What would I have thought if I were him? Of course I would've thought something was going on. I would have been angry, too, if I'd seen Cole leaving a girl's house at night. I would have been hurt. I would have been livid.

At some point my tears turned from tears of pain to tears of sadness and regret. We would break up now. It would all be over.

And somehow that turned out to be the worst thought of all. Even though I was hurt and embarrassed and ashamed and pissed that he'd done this to me, I still loved him. I still felt as though we were meant to be together. I still wanted him. And I ruined it.

The bell rang and I sat up, wiped my face on the backs of my hands, and finished putting papers into my backpack, wincing every now and then when I'd forget and use my left hand to move or lift something. I wondered if Amanda, in the next room, had heard what just happened. Probably not, or Zack would've stormed in. At least I thought he would. Nobody had heard anything. Nobody had seen anything. I was the only one who knew.

I stood and took some deep breaths as I slipped the backpack on my arms, and then walked out as if nothing had ever happened. As far as I was concerned, nothing had.

TWENTY-THREE

Celia noticed my wrist right away.

"Holy cow, what happened?" she breathed, scooting onto the edge of my bed, waking me up. I opened one eye to find her gaping at my wrist, which was lying on the pillow next to my head.

"Nothing," I mumbled, pulling it under the blankets. "What do you want?"

"No way," she said. "That's not nothing. That's disgusting." She threw back the blanket and tried to grab my hand.

I yanked it away and smacked it against my hip, and had to hold my breath to keep from crying out. Both hurt like hell. I sat up, annoyed, hiding my wrist in my lap. "I slammed it in a door at work, okay? It doesn't matter. What do you want, Celia?"

She made a face. "Good morning to you, too, Mary

Sunshine. I was just going to tell you that Shannin called, and the grandmas are totally all over the food for Dad's party. You ordered the cake, right?"

I rolled my eyes. Not with the party again. I swear, Celia was going to make some poor man completely miserable someday with her nagging. We still had months to put this together, yet Celia asked me pretty much every day if I'd ordered the cake, which I had not. I just had too many other things on my mind.

"I'll get to it," I said, sliding out of the other side of the bed and checking the clock. I had to work in an hour. Which meant I had to take a shower, get dressed, eat breakfast, and figure out how to hide these bruises, with not that much time. And I still hadn't heard from Cole since yesterday. Thinking about what happened made sadness and fear wash over me all anew. "Did Cole call this morning?"

"You still haven't ordered it? Alex, this is important."

"So is my job. And school. And…you know, it's not like you have to order a cake months in advance, Celia. I said I'd do it. I'll do it," I snapped, pulling my uniform out of my closet. "Did Cole call this morning or not?"

Celia glared at me, still sitting on the edge of my bed. "No. He did not. Not making phone calls must be one more fabulous thing you two have in common. I'm supposed to talk to Shannin today. She's going to be super-pissed if you don't order that cake, you know. You said you'd be in charge of it, so she's expecting you to do it."

"I will!" I practically shrieked, pulling underwear out

of my drawer and heading for the bathroom. "Just...God, Celia. You're such a..."

I let the sentence trail off as I shut the bathroom door. But I heard her on the other side calling out, "The whole world doesn't revolve around Cole, you know!" Her footsteps thudded down the hall toward her bedroom, and I turned on the shower as hot as it would go.

While I waited for the shower to heat up, I turned my hand over and stared at my wrist. It was mottled and dark purple. Almost yellow. Nasty. I pulled off my pajamas and looked at my hip, which didn't look any better than my wrist. I touched it gingerly, wincing at the little jolts of pain but feeling better. The bruises weren't as bad as I'd originally thought they were. This, I could cover. And, thankfully, it was the weekend. I had a couple days before I had to worry about keeping covered up at school. Maybe they would heal before Monday. I touched the side of my head where Cole had grabbed my hair. Nothing. At least I didn't have to worry about that.

After my shower, I dried my wrist carefully and thoroughly, then gently spread concealer all around it. I covered the concealer with a dollop of liquid foundation out of an old bottle I found pushed all the way back in the bathroom drawer. Probably one of Shannin's. I finished it with powder and held it out for inspection.

Not too bad. Much better than it was. Probably nobody would even notice it. You'd have to be really looking.

I guess I was half-expecting to see Cole's car waiting for

me in the employee parking lot at The Bread Bowl, but it wasn't. I was running too late to ruminate over it, though, so I just threw the car in park and went in. But just to be sure, I walked around to the front door to check out the parking lot up there.

Nope. No Cole.

I was so distracted coming through the front doors of The Bread Bowl, I almost ran smack into Dave's chest.

"Whoa," he said, a sincerely annoyed look crossing his face. He was holding a bowl of soup and raised it head-high to keep from spilling it. "Watch it, Anna."

"Alex," I corrected, then wished I hadn't when he glared at me over his shoulder.

He delivered the soup to a table, and I took that as my chance to scurry back to Georgia's office to clock in. She was sitting in there, craning her neck to look out into the dining room.

"Did you run into him?" she whispered.

I shook my head. "Close."

"Oh, girl. He's gonna be after you now. He's in a hell of a mood today. Here he comes. Get your visor on, quick."

I typed my ID number into the computer to clock in, plunged the visor down over my hair quickly, and then grabbed an apron off a peg next to the office door and tied it around me.

Georgia tapped a few numbers into the old adding machine that sat on her tiny desk, then wrote down a number on a form. "All this paperwork..." she muttered, then said in a louder voice, "There's a new batch of bagels ready to go up front. And see what else is ready to put up. Just keep busy and you'll be fine."

I nodded and started toward the kitchen.

"Everything okay with you, Alex?" Georgia asked.

I stopped, leaned back into the office, and nodded. "Yeah. I'm good," I lied. And for some reason I couldn't totally explain, tears welled up in my eyes. I turned my face down and acted like I was brushing something off my apron to keep Georgia from seeing. When I looked back up at her, she was squinting at me, head cocked to one side.

"You don't seem the same these days, girl. I hope you're taking care of yourself. Not doing anything stupid."

I thought about yesterday. About picking myself up off the floor of the tutor lab. Would Georgia think that was stupid? If I told her that I'd almost made Granite-Ass spill soup down the front of him because I was still hopefully looking for Cole's car after what had happened yesterday, would she think I was stupid then?

Instead of telling her anything, I just shook my head. "I'm not. I'm just…stressed, I guess. I don't want to get either one of us in trouble with you-know-who."

She squinted at me and then shook her head and went back to filling out the forms on her desk. "If you say so," she said. "I've got too much to do to argue with you. Just don't be doing anything stupid, or I'll come after you myself."

I rolled my eyes exaggeratedly. "Yes, Mom," I said. She wagged her pen in the air over her shoulder.

The day crept by, and trying to look constantly busy eventually made it so there was no work to do.

Zack came in with his parents for lunch. They brought Celia with them, who stared at me with an ultra-smug look on her face the entire time, no doubt telling them what an awful daughter I was for not ordering Dad's cake yet. Or maybe she just looked smug because she was Celia.

After a while, Zack got up to refill his soda, and stopped by the counter, where I was refilling the chocolate chip cookie case.

"*Psst!* Waitress! Can I get some service over here?" he hissed.

I glanced at him. "What do you need?" I asked, straining to hear if Dave was still in the kitchen with Jerry, fiddling with the new bread recipe corporate was making all the stores launch in two weeks.

He wiggled his eyebrows up and down at me suggestively. "Well, Doc, I have this pain in my..."

"Ha-ha-ha," I deadpanned. "I can't play around. The owner's here today."

"So?" he said, fishing in his pocket and coming out with his plastic tube of toothpicks. He opened the top of the tube, and I could smell cinnamon oil waft out. That was Zack's new favorite flavor—cinnamon so hot it made his lips swell. "I just wanted to say hi. And I'm a customer. You can't ignore the customers, you know. You have to fulfill our every need."

"I seriously doubt Dave would call jackassing with you filling the needs of my customers. Where's Bethany?"

He took a sip of his drink. "Home. Babysitting, I think. Trying to earn some cash for our trip. She keeps saying something about wanting to buy some real Native American leather or something. If I get bored enough, I'll go over and bug her. Let the kids tie me up or something. Unless you want to volunteer for the job…" Again with the suggestive eye thing.

Out of the corner of my eye, I saw Celia pull herself out of the booth and sidle across the restaurant, pretending she needed a refill of her drink, too, but keeping her eyes glued to us the entire time. "Looks like you're too busy with Miss Personality to go hang with anyone else."

Celia slid up next to Zack. He reached back and wrapped an arm around her shoulders.

"What? My girl?" Zack drawled. "She can go with me."

"Go where?" Celia asked. "To order a birthday cake?"

I made a face at her. "Listen, kids, I'd really love to chat, but need I remind you that I'm supposed to be working here? And if I lose my job, there is no Colorado."

Celia rolled her eyes. "You guys still talking about that stupid trip? God, when I graduate, I'm so going somewhere amazing. Like Beverly Hills or New York City. Totally not Colorado."

Instinctively, my hand drifted to my collarbone again and touched the necklace. How could Celia have no interest? Were we that far apart?

"Mmm, Beverly Hills," Zack said around his toothpick. "Home of hot blonds in short shorts."

Celia made a face and slapped at his chest, wriggling out from under his arm. "You're disgusting. Don't touch me."

He reached over and poked her in the side. "Touch," he said. Then he reached across the counter and did the same to me. "Touch."

Celia squealed when he touched her, and the faces of several customers turned toward the counter. She poked him back. "Touch!" she said. Loudly. And next thing I knew they were batting at each other's hands, Zack hopping around in a fencing pose, talking in a French accent.

"You zink you can tek me in a battle? En garde!"

"Guys!" I hissed. "Stop it! You're gonna get me in tr—"

I felt someone come up behind me. But they kept going at it, Celia crying out, "What, are you gonna touch me with your nasty wrist? Did you see it, Zack? It's gross. Touch! Ha-ha!"

My stomach dropped. I was afraid to look behind me, to see who had overheard Celia's remark. My guess was that everyone in the restaurant had heard it.

I quickly picked up the spatula again and started shoveling cookies into the cookie case, double-time, acting as if I hadn't heard a thing.

But then I heard another set of footsteps swishing up behind me, followed by Dave's unmistakable voice. "What's going on here? Anna?"

Immediately, Celia and Zack stopped their finger-sword fight and hustled back to their booth, where Zack's parents were gathering up their trash.

I turned around. "I'm sorry," I said. "That's my sister.

She's just..." I trailed off, not sure what to say that would not make Granite-Ass even angrier at me than he already was.

Georgia, who'd been the one standing behind me in the first place, didn't say a word. She just stared at my wrist, which I held out in front of me awkwardly, gripping the spatula in the air.

Dave's face went stony and red. It was like watching someone build a brick wall right in front of you. His jaw moved outward a few times, and he took a giant breath in. I almost expected him to let the air out in a gale of screaming, but instead he just said very calmly, "This is not a place for you and your friends—or siblings, whatever—to mess around. I can't have customers being bothered by a couple kids wrestling up front for the jollies of the cashier."

"I kept telling them..." I said, but he held out a hand to silence me. He turned to Georgia, who was still staring at my wrist. I laid the spatula down on the pan and sank my hand as far as it would go into my apron pocket.

"This go on all day?" he asked, gesturing at me. "Is that why this store is losing money? Are your employees' friends driving away all the paying customers while they drink free soda refills and act like this is their personal playground?"

"No," I said before Georgia could even open her mouth. "No. We don't play around here. Plus, my sister and her friend were here with his parents. They paid."

Georgia reached over and put her hand on my arm. She didn't need to speak for me to hear the message loud and clear: *Don't go to bat here. This is my fight to fight.*

"I try to discourage them from chatting when their friends are here. But with this store being so close to the high school, I can't keep the teenagers out. We'd go under. This," Georgia motioned toward the dining room, "is truly a one-time thing."

"Every time I'm here, Anna is gabbing with some friend or another," Dave countered.

"Alex," I mumbled, even though I knew he didn't hear me. And even if he did, he'd never care enough to get it right.

"Dave, I really think we should be concentrating on these fall promos..." Georgia answered, letting go of my arm and ushering him back into her office. My arm felt cool where her warm hand had just been resting. I shivered.

Zack waved good-bye as they left, mouthing the word *sorry* to me, and I was left balancing a half-filled cookie sheet on the counter against my side, my other hand stuffed in my apron pocket.

I pulled it out and gazed at it. I was stupid to think the concealer would cover up the finger-shaped bruises there. I could still see them, looking rotten and black under a film of beige.

And Georgia could definitely see them. She was staring right at them. Staring right through the concealer and the foundation and the powder at the ugly mess beneath.

The question was...could she see through me?

TWENTY-FOUR

For a while I considered just marching into Georgia's office and holding my wrist up and telling her everything.

After all, this was the sort of thing you would tell a mom, right? You'd show her the bruises and cry on her shirt and tell her you still love him and ask her what you're supposed to do now. And she would give you advice and say she understands and tell you that you're beautiful and this won't define you. That it can't, no matter what, ever define who you are.

But when I stepped into Georgia's office to time out at the end of my shift, she was sitting there with a wadded-up tissue in her hand, and her voice was scratchy and her nose was stuffy and I realized that I couldn't lean on her today because today just wasn't a good day for her to be my mom, and if she really was my mom it wouldn't matter because your mom is your mom no matter what kind of day she's having. And as much as Georgia was *like* a mom to me, she wasn't and never would be my mom, so she could have bad days off.

And then I thought of Brenda, and how it seemed as though she was always having bad days, and I felt sorry for Cole, despite everything, and could understand why he was so stressed and angry with nobody to lean on. And just like that, I realized that in a way, what happened yesterday had already started defining me anyway; I was making excuses for why he hurt me.

I'd heard the muffled shouts coming from behind the office door as I finished stocking the cookies. It went on for what seemed like forever. Dave's voice, on edge, rising, falling, rising, falling, then answered by Georgia's voice, steadily loud.

Then Dave stormed out, and a few seconds later I saw his silver Lexus squeal away at the stoplight, but before I could go back to the office, the dinner rush started and I was too busy to do anything but fill soup orders.

I heard a heavy clink as Georgia slammed the safe, and the creak of her office chair as she pulled herself out of it. And then she retreated into the kitchen, where she stayed until just a few minutes before my shift was over.

"I'm sorry," I said, while I typed in my ID number to clock out. "I really did tell them to cut it out. I hope I didn't get you into trouble."

She rested an elbow up on the desk and palmed her fore-head, then looked up at me, her red-rimmed eyes watery and weak behind her glasses. "You didn't," she said. "But I saved your ass. I probably won't be able to again."

"I'm sorry," I repeated. "I mean, thank you. I..."

"Don't," she interrupted. "He's just a fool. Don't give him the dignity of responding to that shit. He doesn't know the first thing about compassion."

A tear slipped out from under her glasses, and she wiped at it with a tissue.

"Georgia?" I said softly. "Everything okay?"

I could swear I saw her flick the tiniest of glances at my wrist. She stood up, took a deep breath, dabbed at her eyes again, and said, "You like hot chocolate?"

She didn't wait for me to respond. She pushed past me and I followed her out of the office and back up front, where she poured two cups of hot chocolate and carried them out through the dining room and outside to the empty patio.

"I'm taking a quick break," she called to Clay, the new hire, just before letting the door swish shut behind us.

It was getting dark on us already. The lights on the outside of the building were on, and moths fluttered around them manically, bumping into them repeatedly, as if they thought if they could fly hard enough into just the right spot, they might make it through that light after all.

It had finally started to get cold in the evenings, and I was wishing I'd brought a hoodie with me. The breeze seemed to whip right through my polo, and before I even sat down I was shivering.

Georgia set the mugs on a table and pulled out a chair—

the same one Bethany had been sitting in on the day we first saw Cole here. Georgia used her hand to wipe off a couple of stray leaves, then moved around to the other side, did the same, and sat down.

"Whoo, winter's gonna be here before we know it," she said, picking up her mug and blowing across the top. I thought maybe I could see steam float away when she did that, but probably that was just me feeling cold and thinking it was colder than it was.

"Feels like it's already here," I said, easing down into the chair and wrapping both hands around my mug. "Thanks for the hot chocolate."

She waved me away. "Lily loves the winter," she said, looking out over the highway at the rush-hour cars lined up at the stoplights, their headlights lit and their windows dark. "But, oh, it's such a pain, trying to get her from place to place in all that snow and slush and ice in a wheelchair. I'm not ready for it already."

"How's Lily doing in school?" I asked.

Georgia smiled. "Aw, she loves it this year. Has a great teacher. Just great." She was silent for a moment, sipping her hot chocolate. I followed her lead and took a drink of mine, too, and was instantly warmed. The shivering died down a little, and I took another.

"You know," Georgia said at last, "one thing about winter is you can hide a whole lot of flaws with all those big, bulky clothes."

I stopped in midsip and looked at her over the top of my

mug. She was still staring out over the highway, her forefinger wrapped in the handle of her mug.

Without thinking, I set my mug down and rested my hands in my lap. "Uh-huh." My voice was quiet and uncertain.

Finally she snapped out of her highway trance and leaned back in the chair, patting her neck. "I can wear turtlenecks and hide this damn turkey gobbler I've got going on."

I giggled. "You don't have a turkey gobbler," I said, even though, now that she said it, I could totally see that she did.

"Girl, just you wait. You're beautiful now, but eventually you'll turn forty, and next thing you know you'll be gobbling and hiding behind the couch come Thanksgiving."

We laughed, and I sipped my hot chocolate again, picturing Georgia with a big set of tail feathers.

"Just make sure," she said, interrupting my thoughts with a very serious tone, "that you're not hiding things that shouldn't be hidden."

The giggles rushed up on one another and died right there in my throat—a stagnant stockpile that created a lump so huge I thought for sure Georgia could see it on the outside.

"I don't know what..." I said, my voice sounding all strangly coming around that lump. "Like what?"

She reached over and grabbed my hand, which I'd absentmindedly rested on the table again. My wrist actually didn't look bruised under the concealer in the dark. It looked like a perfectly normal wrist, and had it not been for the way her eyes looked liquid and searching, I might have denied that anything was there. Instead, I just swallowed.

"Is he hurting you?" she said, her voice low and urgent.

And once again I had this thought that I'd finally been given my chance to come clean about what had happened between Cole and me. I finally had my chance to talk about it. To get my advice. To cry because I still loved him and was worried that he was so mad he'd never come back. And cry even harder because I knew how that made me sound and I so didn't want to be that girl, the one everyone pities because she is too stupid to stop loving an abuser.

But once again, saying those things felt like trouble. I knew that I was going to work harder than hell to keep this from ever happening again. And if I spilled it all out now, then when he came around, everyone would hate him and I'd lose him for sure. The lump surged forward—pulsating and begging to be let out—but I couldn't break it loose. I had to keep it down in there, undulating and safe.

I shook my head.

She closed her eyes briefly and took a deep breath. "You sure?" she asked. "Because that doesn't look like a door slam to me. That looks like fingerprints."

Once again, my wrist felt as if it were on fire, only this time the fire spread up my arm and into my face, and I was sure if I opened my mouth again, everything would spill out of me in a rush. I pulled my hand out of hers and stood up, the backs of my knees pushing the chair back on the patio with a loud grating sound.

"I've gotta go," I said. And before Georgia could so much as argue, I bolted back through the restaurant and out the doors I had come in through at the beginning of the day.

I was digging through my purse for my keys and concentrating so hard on getting out fast, before Georgia could come after me. I was almost all the way to my car before I saw Cole leaning against it.

In an instant, my fingers went numb and I dropped my keys on the ground. I bent over to pick them up, my heart beating so hard it felt as if it was going to pop right out of the top of my head. I was hit with a rush of emotions — so many of them, I wasn't sure what I was feeling at all.

"Hey," he said, pushing off from the side of the car as I stepped down off the sidewalk. "I've been waiting for you."

"I had a meeting with my manager," I said, stopping a good distance from him. I tried to pull off cool and uninterested, but I was certain he could see my chest heaving in and out under the force of my heartbeat.

"I know," he said. "I saw you."

Are you spying on me now? my mind echoed from our earlier argument, but I shooed the thought away. There was only one way in and out of The Bread Bowl employee parking lot, and that required you to drive past the store. He probably just drove past us when he got here.

Unsure of what to do next, I took an awkward step toward the driver's side door, punching the unlock button on my key. The blinkers flashed yellow against his forehead, making it look like the edges of my bruises. Again I pushed those thoughts away and tried, with whatever faltering grip I had left, to hold on to my take-you-or-leave-you attitude.

But finally, the leather of his jacket creaking, he moved forward, cupping my cheeks with his hands.

"Alex," he breathed, then pulled me into a hug. I tried not to react—to just stay stiff—but I could feel myself thawing. I couldn't get that hug from Georgia. I couldn't get it from anyone. Not Bethany or Zack or even my dad. But I could get it from Cole. And it didn't matter what he'd done—being enveloped felt so good, no matter who was giving it out.

I leaned into him. My body felt hungry up against his, and for the briefest second I could imagine that nothing had ever happened and that everything was good now. Everything was perfect. Even though I knew it wasn't.

He pulled away, his hands sliding down my arms. He stopped at my hands and pulled them up, turning them over to inspect my wrists. He stared at them, dropping my good hand and tracing my hurt wrist softly with his forefinger. He lifted it and kissed it, gently, tenderly, once, twice, three times.

"My Emily Dickinson," he whispered, and when he searched my face with his again, I could see sorrow in it, just like before at the lake. "I'm so sorry," he said. "My Alex, I'm so, so sorry."

I pulled my arms away from him and stepped back. "You should be," I said, my voice ragged. "You just assumed

I was screwing around on you. You didn't even let me explain."

He reached for me again, but again I stepped back, determined to let him know how I felt about everything that had happened. "I'm sorry," he said again. "I should have... you're right... it's just... God!" he turned and kicked the wall of The Bread Bowl, cramming his hands into his jacket pockets. "It's just my parents. Brenda's put herself in the hospital again. And my dad... you'd think the whole freaking world was basketball. And you told me you weren't going to let Zack touch you anymore. I just... I can't deal, Alex." He lurched toward me, grabbing my arms and pulling me into him. I could feel his frustration running tight through his body. He wrapped himself around me, burying his face in my neck. "You understand," he said. I could feel his breath on my neck, giving me goose bumps. "I know you understand. You're the only one who does. Please forgive me, Alex. Please. I don't know what I'd do without you."

Tears—of relief, sadness, understanding—started falling down my face, wetting both of our cheeks as they brushed together. "I swear to you, I'll never hurt you again," he said into my hair. And then he turned me so that my back was against the car, and he kissed me like I'd never been kissed before, his hands rushing all over me, like he was assessing that all the parts were present and accounted for, unbroken, undamaged.

After a long time, he pulled back. He ran his hands through his hair, then wiped them across his messy face, which was covered with streaks of my mascara. He used his thumb to wipe my cheeks, so gently I could barely feel them against my skin.

"I'll never hurt you again," he whispered, and I believed him.

This was nothing, I convinced myself. I could fix it. We could fix it together.

I was so glad I'd rushed out of The Bread Bowl before I told Georgia the truth.

I would tell nobody. What had happened would be our secret. He and I would share it alone. Another reason that he and I had to stay together. We already shared so much. This was just another piece of us that we—and only we—owned.

I could feel my body relaxing as he pulled me tighter against him, as if he were holding on to a life preserver, whispering and dropping kisses into the hairs at the nape of my neck. And more than anything, I was glad that I hadn't told anyone what had happened between us.

An hour later—my lips numb and sore from all the kissing, my eyes tired from all the crying—I knew I'd done the right thing by keeping this a secret. I was all Cole had. I understood him. And we would work through this together. I didn't feel guilty at all for leaving Georgia sitting on the patio alone.

It's just...I didn't expect her to still be sitting there when I drove by on my way home, her eyes on Cole's car following behind me.

CHAPTER

TWENTY-FIVE

I was still carrying the coffee that Cole had brought when he picked me up for school, and I almost spilled it on him when Bethany bounded up to me.

"Guess what?" she said, practically bubbling over. "Guess what?"

"What?" I said, jerking my arm away from her flailing hands to save my coffee.

"Watch it," Cole snapped, pulling back, like he was being hit by a scalding tidal wave or something. Funny how Bethany's presence could wind Cole tight like that. Just minutes ago he'd been standing at my door, grinning over a steaming coffee, kissing me after I sipped it, smacking his lips and saying, *Mmm, sweet! And the coffee's tasty, too!* and making me giggle. He'd just been joking with me in the car, squeezing my knee and putting my name into dirty limericks, making plans for all the things we'd do together over Christmas break. And now he was snapping at us like he'd woken up on the wrong side of the Earth this morning.

But his mood was going to do nothing to squelch Bethany's. "Zack got the lead in *The Moon for Me and You!*" she squealed. "Total upset. Mickey Hankins thought he had it in the bag. Mickey's, like, freaking out right now. Nurse's office, crying. Swear to God."

Mickey Hankins had good reason to think he'd get the lead in the musical. After all, he'd had the lead in All Things Theatrical since he was in the womb. But Zack had worked really hard over the summer at drama camp and had even taken private voice lessons from a college student, some girl he called Big Boobs Belinda. He was gunning to go out his senior year as a lead instead of chorus drone in just one production, and he was definitely out for Mickey Hankins's head.

In my opinion, Mickey never stood a chance. Zack had gotten amazingly good.

"Oh my God, I can't believe I forgot about tryouts last week. That's awesome!" I squealed. "Where is he?"

"Outside," she said, looking toward the double doors. "He wanted to call his mom and tell her. She was dying to know."

I turned to Cole, who was still scowling at my coffee. "Did you hear that?" I said excitedly, pulling on his arm. He'd acted so sorry in the couple weeks since the wrist incident. I was hoping he'd make another try at getting along with Zack. Or that he could at least pretend, for my sake. "Come on, let's go outside and congratulate him. He's gotta be so stoked."

"Pass," Cole said, pulling his arm out of my grasp.

I tried to ignore the look that flitted over Bethany's face. I was pretty sure she'd passed the stage of being afraid to dislike Cole in front of me. And I was pretty sure I couldn't blame her. Not that any of them seemed to care what kind of awkward position their little feud put me in every day.

Bethany continued. "We're going to celebrate after school at El Manuel's. Come with. All-you-can-eat salsa, extra hot, and virgin piña coladas, extra yum…"

"Okay. Yeah. Of course," I said. "I'm off tonight. We'll be there."

"No," Cole said next to me. "No, *we* won't."

"Cole," I said, turning and looping my arms through his. "Can't you try? Just this once? For me?" I batted my eyes, trying to make him laugh like he'd just been doing in the car.

He sighed and kissed me on the nose. "I can't," he said. "Basketball practice, remember?"

"Oh," I breathed. "I forgot about practice." I turned to Bethany. "I promised I'd come watch." Bethany visibly wilted, and I let out a deep sigh. "Cole…I mean, it's just practice, right? And Zack's worked really hard for this all summer. I'll leave Manuel's early and catch the end of basketball, okay? I'll do both."

I heard Bethany let out a frustrated grunt, but ignored

her. If she wanted me to suck down salsa and piña coladas with her, she was going to have to give a little, too.

Cole's face softened. "Okay," he said. "No problem. I'm just gonna head to class." He squeezed my hand, pecked me on the forehead, smiled at Bethany, and walked away.

I stared after him, my stomach getting an icky feeling— even though he'd agreed, it still felt like he was mad at me. It was that same weird feeling in the air that I got right before the wrist incident. Bethany grabbed my elbow and started to pull.

"Forget him," she said. "C'mon. There's Zack."

We caught up with Zack just as he was barreling in the double doors from outside. His face was lit up in a smile so wide I thought it must have hurt.

"Congratulations," I said, sidling up to him and patting him on the back. Bethany moved to the other side of him, tripping along with such short steps and gazing up at him so loyally she almost looked like a puppy.

"What'd your mom say?" she said. "I bet she bakes a cake today."

Zack wrapped his arms around our shoulders. "Ladies," he drawled elaborately, "today the Mexican feast is on me. Someday when you see me on TV accepting my Oscar, you can say"—his voice ratcheted up to a squeaky girl voice— "'Hey, that dude gave me a big burrito when he landed his first lead, and it was h-o-t, hawt!'"

"Ew!" we both squealed, smacking his chest and ducking out from under his arms.

He laughed, and then in the girl voice added, "And I ate it All. Night. Long."

We cracked up, the three of us laughing and bumping into people and saying stupid stuff on our way to first period.

Except.

Well, except I was guiltily looking over my shoulder and in every doorway and stairwell, hoping my boyfriend wasn't looking on, spying on me, thinking I was standing too close to my best friend.

When had my life turned into this? When had I started worrying that being happy for my best friend would be making someone else angry?

TWENTY-SIX

By the time we got to El Manuel's, basketball practice had already been going on for half an hour. Zack had had to stop in at Mr. Tucker's office to pick up the script for his part in the play.

Bethany and I waited outside Mr. Tucker's office for him, thinking it would only take a minute, but apparently Mr. Tucker had plans to explain the entire play to Zack while we sat in the hallway, where I grew increasingly agitated.

"What time do you think basketball is over?" I asked, chewing on the skin around my thumbnail.

Bethany made a soft, noncommittal noise, shrugging her shoulders as she bent over her homework, which I probably should have been doing, too, but I was too on edge to concentrate.

"You think we'll even *be* at Manuel's before it's over?" I asked, spitting a piece of skin onto the floor.

"I don't know," Bethany said, still not looking up from her homework.

I got up, paced the hall a few times, and then slid back down to the floor where I'd been sitting before. "God, what's taking him so long?" I said.

Bethany set her pencil down on her book. "Really, Alex," she said. "So what if you don't make it to Cole's practice on time? What's he gonna do? Break up with you?"

"It's just..." I motioned at Mr. Tucker's door. "I mean, he was going to be right back. But this is taking forever, and I did sort of have plans..."

"Fine," she said, picking up her pencil again. "Then go be with...your plans. I'm sure Zack will understand. Since your plans are so much more important."

"It's not like that," I said softly, stung. But before I could say any more, Mr. Tucker's office door, thankfully, opened, and Zack stepped out, carrying a script in his hand.

"Let's go," he said, rolling the script and stuffing it into his back pocket while Bethany shoveled her things into her backpack.

"Excellent!" she said, zipping her backpack and standing up. "The air in this hallway is stuffy. They need to add some ventilation in here. The same air is just circling and circling and getting really old."

I rolled my eyes but decided to let it go. I just didn't have the energy to play go-between for them and Cole anymore.

Once we stepped into El Manuel's, the tension between

Bethany and me lightened. Zack was so buoyant it was impossible to stay angry. He kept adding the word "el" to the beginning of everything and "o" to the end of it ("We'll have el table-o for el three-o, el please-o") and insisted on saying "Hakuna matata" to everyone who passed by. We were giggling before we even sat down.

"So opening night is March tenth," Zack said, pulling his script out of his pocket and spreading it out on the table in front of him. "You guys gonna come, right?"

"Of course," said Bethany. "There is no way I'd miss it. You could have a costume malfunction, and what kind of friend would I be if I wasn't there to laugh my ass off at you when it happens?" She gave him a wide, fake smile, all teeth.

"Plus," I added, stuffing a chip into my mouth, "I really need to work on my heckling skills." I cupped one hand around my mouth and mock-shouted, "You suck, mama's boy!"

"Har har, you guys are too funny. I'm gonna hire a bouncer to kick your asses out," he said, wiping a dropped dollop of cheese dip off his script with his thumb. "Hey, guys, listen to the lyrics of this song I have to sing. 'I have something in my hand, my love. I'm going to give it to you, my love. I live to hear you swoon. Tonight we two will spoon. For what I have in my hand is the gauzy, the shiny, the romantic December moon.' God, when was this written?"

Bethany and I took one look at each other and cracked

up. "I dare you to bend over and moon the audience when you sing it," I said, trying not to choke on my chip as I laughed.

"Oh my God," Bethany gasped between giggles. "What's the title of that song? 'The Creepy Exhibitionist Song'? I have something in my hand, my love..."

I laughed out loud, spitting chip crumbs across the table at Zack, who wiped his forehead dramatically, keeping his face straight as Bethany and I practically fell under the table, we were laughing so hard.

"Okay, okay," he said. "Laugh it up, you two. Go ahead. Har har. You're such cutups." But when that only made us laugh louder, he lost his straight face and struggled to keep himself from cracking up, too. "All right, that's it," he said, visibly trying to keep himself composed. "You two don't stop laughing and I'll have something in my hand for you." He held up a fist like he was going to knock us out.

And just like that, it wasn't funny anymore.

I stopped laughing and sat up, Bethany leaning against me, oblivious to my mood change. But Zack crinkled his eyebrows at me, unfurling his fist into an open palm, which he held up surrender-style. He stared at me a little too long, and I smoothed the napkin on my lap, clearing my throat to change the subject.

"You guys," I said, "we probably should order. I've got to at least try to get to Cole's practice." And then I hated myself a little for saying it, especially after Bethany groaned.

By the time we paid our bill, I knew there was no way practice was still going on. When I got in my car in the El Manuel parking lot, the sky had already started to darken, and a cold wind had worked up, whipping a plastic bag out of my car as soon as I opened the door.

I wasted no time getting out of the parking lot, though, just in case I could catch Cole, even at the last minute. It would be really nice if I could play it off as though I'd been there, watching, for a long time. Maybe then he'd never know the difference.

I waved at Bethany and Zack as I pulled past them in the parking lot. They were standing next to Zack's car, bent over the script, Bethany's cheeks puffed up with a smile, her fingers pushing her glasses back up on her nose every few seconds. Zack half-waved before sticking a toothpick in his mouth.

Basketball must have been over for a while, because the school parking lot was a ghost town. Totally empty. Even the coach's car was gone.

And, of course, Cole's car was gone.

I parked, got out, jogged to the side door by the gym, and pulled the handle. I don't know what I was hoping for—I guess maybe that I was wrong. That Cole was still here, still waiting for me. That his car wasn't gone and that he'd see me, wave, and jog over to hug me, his shoulder sweaty against my cheek.

But the door was locked.

I kicked it in frustration and walked back to the car,

where I sat, uncertainly, for a few minutes. I checked my phone. No messages. No texts.

I dialed his cell number. It rang. No answer.

"Hey, Cole," I said to the voice mail. "I'm at the school. Looks like I missed you. I'm..."

Sorry was about to come out of my mouth, but suddenly I was struck with such a certainty that this was it for us, I couldn't go on. I'd already put so much on the line for this relationship. I'd already lost so much to make it work with Cole. I was losing Bethany. I'd already lost Zack in a way; these days, he spent more time with my sister than with me. If I lost Cole, too, what exactly would I have left? Celia? She hated my guts. Shannin? Away at college. Georgia? She had her own kid to take care of, plus I'd already established with her what I wanted with her advice when I ran out on her the other day. Dad? He'd actually have to be there in order for me to lose him.

I hung up and chewed on my thumb again, thinking things over. If I went over to his house, chances were he'd be really pissed at me. But chances were he was really pissed at me anyway. And if I went to him tonight, maybe I could smooth things over. If I waited till school tomorrow, I'd only have a few minutes between classes to talk to him.

It was settled.

I put the car in drive and headed toward Cole's house.

TWENTY-SEVEN

Brenda answered the door. There were lights on in the kitchen behind her, and I got a good look at her for the first time.

Oddly, her skin had the same blue lit-by-TV-screen tinge to it that it had when I first met her in the darkened family room. Yet there was something warmer about her somehow.

"Alex," she said in that tiny mewl of hers, pulling open the door and moving to the side to let me in. "I didn't know Cole was expecting you. Come in."

"He's not," I said, stepping through the door. "I missed him at basketball. He's here, then?" I sounded so casual I almost believed myself that this was no big deal. That my palms weren't sweating and I wasn't imagining him breaking up with me in the next five minutes.

She nodded, turning and heading toward the kitchen. I followed her. "In his room," she said. "I'm making us some dinner."

I blinked at her. It was almost as if she was an entirely different woman. There was a pot of soup simmering on the stove behind her, and the oven light was on, illuminating a batch of muffins inside. There was music coming out of a radio sitting on top of the refrigerator, and she kind of swayed to it a little while she talked.

It was like when Cole's dad was around, Brenda was some sort of zombie. But when he was gone, she was alive.

Again, I was struck with sorrow for Cole and what he had to live with. Brenda was anything but the perfect mom, and his dad was so gruff and biting. Even though my family wasn't exactly sitcom-perfect, Cole's family seemed so… weird. Like his dad was the negative energy that beat the family down, yet the driving force that kept it going. Like for Cole's family to stay alive…it had to be mean and frightening. No wonder Cole liked to keep his cell phone turned off. No wonder he never wanted to hang out at his house. No wonder he was tense and unpredictable sometimes.

Brenda turned and stirred the soup, and I stood uncomfortably next to her, wondering if she was going to call Cole down or if I should just go upstairs to his room.

"Would you like to stay for dinner, Alex?" she said over her shoulder. "We'll have plenty."

I'll bet, I thought, eyeing her tiny birdlike wrists and spine, which poked out in knobby little juts, even through her turtleneck. She looked as if she hadn't eaten in months.

"Okay," I said, ignoring the protest of my stomach, still

full of guacamole and tortilla chips. This could be a great way to make up with Cole—dinner with him and his mom. The way she was acting tonight, we may even have a good time. "Can I go up?" I asked.

She glanced at me, and for just a split second I thought I saw those black holes behind her glasses again. But her tiny little child lips pulled up into a smile, and she nodded. "Of course."

I climbed the steps. Cole's door was open. I could hear soft tinny clangs coming out of the room and stepped up into the doorway to see him sitting on his amp, his back to the door, strumming his electric guitar, which was not plugged in. I lingered in the doorway, holding on to the frame lightly with my fingertips, and watched him.

He was wearing a pair of jeans and was barefoot and bare-chested. His hair was wet, a few rivulets of water running down the back of his neck. The air in the room smelled like body heat and soap, as if he'd just gotten out of the shower.

For a moment I was struck numb. He was so beautiful sitting there on his amp. And I felt like the worst girlfriend ever. I had ditched him, after I promised I'd be there for him. I'd had plans with him first, and I'd bumped them for Zack and Bethany, after he made the effort to be understanding about why I'd changed our plans.

My hand lingered at my collarbone, my fingers pressing into the tiny beads on the dream catcher.

"Shut the door," Cole said, making me jump. He hadn't

turned around, hadn't stopped strumming his guitar, but he knew I was there. "I said shut the door," he repeated when I didn't respond.

I stepped in and did what he'd asked, but stood just inside the doorway, unsure of what to do next. He didn't turn to look at me, didn't stop strumming. Was I supposed to go to him? Wait for him to come to me? This was the part of our relationship I was starting to really hate—the part where I had to try to guess what would make him happy. Or, more accurately, what would keep him from getting mad.

"I got out later than I thought," I said, trying to keep my voice as close to normal as possible. "I went to the school, but everyone was gone."

He finally turned. He had the look on his face that someone gives when you've said something so ridiculously stupid they can't believe you even opened your mouth. "Yeah. We were gone. That's what we do when practice is over for an hour."

He pulled the guitar strap over his head and laid the guitar on the floor beside him. He swiveled to face me, then leaned his back against the wall behind him and stretched out his legs, crossing his feet in front of him, lacing his hands together and resting them in his lap. As if he didn't have a care in the world. As if he wasn't furious with me.

The air in the room suddenly felt very cold. As if all happiness had been sucked out of it. Sort of like the tutor lab had felt right before he'd grabbed my wrist.

"Look," I said, trying to sound confident. Trying to

sound as if it really was no big deal. Trying to warm up the air around me. "I said I was sorry. I don't know..."

"You're sorry?" he said, his voice a boom in the quiet house. "You blew me off for another guy, Alex. Again. Same guy. Why don't you admit you want him, huh? He wants you. Why don't the two of you go off and be very happy together? I don't give a shit. Just go do it."

"I don't want him," I said, taking a step forward. "And he doesn't want me. I want you, Cole, in case you didn't notice."

"You know? I didn't notice. Because I was too busy noticing that my supposed girlfriend is a slut who can't seem to pry herself away from her next-door neighbor to come to my practice like she said she would. Oh, I mean *best friend*. *Neighbor* makes her sound like a total whore. *Best friend* is more just... slut."

I stiffened. "I'm not a slut, and I'm not doing anything with him. And he is my best friend," I said, my voice going high and shrieky. "It's not totally unheard of for a boy and a girl to be best friends without anything going on, you know."

He nodded his head sarcastically, looking as if he was barely holding in laughter. "Whatever, slut," he said. "Did you and Bethany give him a nice little congratulations gift for getting the big part in the play?"

Suddenly all those feelings of worry were gone, replaced with anger. He was going too far. What kind of boyfriend calls his girlfriend a slut to her face? Who acts like that? I loved Cole, but sometimes loving him just felt like I was on a roller coaster and I couldn't catch my breath between dips and turns. And sometimes I just wanted off.

"Stop calling me that, Cole. If you're too dense to see that..."

"Dense?" Anger flashed in his eyes and I saw the muscles in his stomach go taut, but I didn't care. I was pissed.

"Yeah, it's how you're acting. Dense and jealous and stupid and rude."

"Shut up, slut," he breathed, but I kept going.

"And if you weren't so stubborn and you actually tried to get along—"

But before I could so much as wrap my mouth around the next syllable, he was off the amp and across the room, one hand on my neck. I made a surprised little noise in the back of my throat, but he was squeezing too tightly for me to say anything. My hand reached up to his, but before I could pry his fingers off my neck, his other hand, curled in a tight fist, came down high on my cheek, twice, hard. I saw flashes of light with each blow, and pain flared through my face. I cried out for real this time.

"Don't ever tell me what to do," Cole said, so full of fury that foamy pieces of spit were gathering in the corners of his mouth. "Don't *ever* tell me what to do. I swear to God, Alex. Don't. Do. It." He shook me by my neck with every word, my head snapping back and forth like the floppy head of a rag doll.

Just like that, my anger was shaken right out of me.

Suddenly it didn't seem like such a huge deal to be called a slut. Suddenly all that mattered was the ringing in my ears and the fact that my eye felt like jelly and my knees wanted to buckle right out from underneath me.

"Okay," I cried, my voice rasping past his tight grip on my throat. I brought my hand up to my face, because I couldn't think of anything else to say or do other than cover and agree to whatever he said. Whatever it would take to make him stop. "Okay, okay, okay, okay, I'm sorry," I cried, tears pouring out of my eye in rivers, even though I had it squeezed shut. My stomach lurched, and I had to clench my teeth to keep the vomit back.

He let go of my neck and I crumpled to the floor, holding my face and sobbing. Too afraid to run. Too surprised to stand. Too hurt to be brave or indignant or anything other than broken. "I'm sorry," I whimpered, curling up over my knees and pressing my forehead into the carpet, willing my eye to stop watering. Willing my face and neck to stop hurting. "Oh my God, I'm so sorry..."

I heard Cole breathing hard and pacing. Heard a clang as his guitar met with something hard. Heard the bedsprings twang as he sat on it, heard them groan again a few seconds later as he got up. He was muttering things, how it was my own fault and that I should keep my promises and how nobody talks to him like that. "Why don't you write about it in one of your stupid little poems?" he said at one point, but I didn't answer. I was too afraid to lift my face, to look at him head-on.

None of this made sense. I still had the faint lines of bruises on the inside of my wrist. I'd been proud of myself for forgiving him that time. I'd convinced myself that it was a one-time thing. How could this have happened again?

He'd promised—stood there in the parking lot of The Bread Bowl, pressing up against me and kissing me, and promised—that he'd never touch me again. And this time he'd done more than grab my wrist. He'd hit me. Actually hit me. My whole head felt split open, like a hot, gaping cavern, and throbbed like it was alive. I couldn't stop crying. I couldn't breathe, I was crying so hard.

I cried so long that I almost forgot all about Cole. I definitely lost track of time. And when I felt his arms slide around my shoulders from behind, I jumped. Panic rocked me as I wondered what he would do to me this time. Would it be possible that he'd just kill me right here in his bedroom with his mom downstairs humming and stirring soup?

But it was the warm Cole who wrapped around me. The tension in his body was gone. The fury in his voice all drained out.

"My Alex," he breathed into the back of my neck. "Oh my God, my Alex." Just like before. "Forgive me. You have to forgive me. I didn't mean to...I didn't want to have to... I just get so jealous...Jesus, I don't want to lose you... please...please don't leave me...don't go...I'll make it better...God, I swear to you..."

I said nothing. Just cried harder, unsure how to move

after something like this had happened. Did I just get up and walk away as though my whole world hadn't just been destroyed? How? How did legs and feet and arms and lungs work after something like this? Was it even possible?

We stayed like that for a long time. He whispered things. Apologies. Excuses. Promises. They bounced off me, impossible to absorb. I believed him and I didn't. I hated him and I didn't. I loved him and I didn't. I hated me and I felt sorry for me. Words had no meaning. There was no past and no future. It was as if all I had to do was live through this moment and everything would be all right.

I kept my face down in the dark for so long that what had just happened began to feel like a dream. Like I was about to wake up into something better. Like I'd open my eyes and things would be bright and pretty.

Instead, when he finally turned me around and I blinked the real world in again, all I saw was blurriness in my right eye, and I felt an all-encompassing numbness.

My nose was running down into my mouth, and I was squinting against the light, my hair stuck to my face. And Cole looked pretty much the same. We were grieving together, and in some way that felt right. Felt better. At least if I was going to be miserable, I wasn't going to be alone. At least he'd hurt himself, too.

I watched his face contort and his mouth move as he apologized, but I didn't really hear his words. I watched him lean forward to kiss my cheeks, my hair, my eyes, which hurt, but there was such a disconnect between the hurt and my brain that I barely noticed. It was like the pain belonged to somebody else. Alex was there, but she wasn't me. She was someone else, shutting down, piece by piece.

I stopped crying.

I just watched.

Numb.

I watched myself slowly get up to leave. I watched myself start walking. I watched myself thump down the stairs and turn the handle of the front door, wiping my eyes with the backs of my hands. I watched myself get into my car and turn it on and back out of Cole's driveway and drive home. And I watched myself come home and go up to my bedroom and shut the door. I watched myself pull off my clothes and step into pajamas, all in the dark, and curl up in bed and stare at the ceiling, the tears leaking into my ears, the scene replaying on the blades of my ceiling fan.

But it was like watching myself from the end of a long, black tunnel. The poor girl on the other end—she was bruised and confused and beaten and I felt sorry for her. Whoever she was.

TWENTY-EIGHT

All it took was one look in the bathroom mirror the next morning to convince me that there was no way I could go anywhere.

My eye had a smudgy-looking purple line underneath it—probably something I could cover up with makeup pretty easily—but my cheekbone was a mess. It was puffy and bruised, and it hurt to look at, much less touch.

Walk out of this house looking like this, I told myself, *and you're going to have questions to answer. And are you prepared to answer them? No? I didn't think so.*

I tried washing my face in the coldest water that would come out of the sink, but it didn't help, except to soothe my eye, which felt like it had sandpaper under the top lid. It was still hard to open my eye fully, and it watered from the sunlight.

In the end, I crawled back into bed, flopped onto my

side, pressing my cheek into the pillow to hide it, and called Celia into the room.

"What's with you? Sick or something?" she asked, leaning in the doorway.

I nodded, gritting my teeth against the pain in my cheek, pushing up against the pillow like that. "Can you have Dad call school? I'm supposed to work tonight, too, so have him call both."

"Is it cramps?"

"No," I said. Why couldn't Celia make anything easy? "I think it's the flu."

She frowned. "You don't look like you have the flu."

I grunted exasperatedly. "Just...Celia, can you just do this one thing for me, please?"

"Whatever. But if you're lying so you can hang out and have sex with Cole all day, don't expect me to cover for you. Gross."

If I could have, I would have thrown something at her at that moment. But I couldn't let my cheek leave the pillow. Instead, I pasted on my best pathetic, miserable fever face and batted away thoughts of killing her.

She left the room, yelling for Dad, and not for the first time I wondered how my sisters and I had grown so far apart. When we were little and Dad was desperate and failing, we'd hung on to one another like lifelines. The sting of not having a mom fresh and raw, we became one another's mommy.

But after a while, it seemed like Shannin and Celia

just...forgot the sting. And because I didn't fit into their world, perfect despite everything that was missing, they started doing the stinging instead.

I knew Celia didn't really hate me. But most days it felt like she did.

After a few minutes I heard Dad's heavy boots scuffing down the hallway, and I checked my hair and pillows for maximum black-eye coverage. I pulled the quilt up to my good cheek and curled into a ball, grabbing my knees and trying to shiver without being obvious.

"Celia says you're sick," Dad said, standing in the doorway, hands hanging at his sides awkwardly.

I nodded. Gave a weak cough.

"I called school and work," he said.

"Thanks," I croaked.

"I can't stay," he said uncertainly. Not like I ever expected him to. Not since Shannin got old enough to babysit, anyway.

"'S okay," I said, keeping my voice weak.

"Okay," he said, squinting at me. I pushed my face harder into the pillow, just in case in my theatrics I'd started to show some cheek. "Well, if you need anything..." But his voice trailed off, and I wasn't sure if that was a question or a statement. He knocked twice on the doorframe with one knuckle and then started to leave but seemed to think better of it and turned back. "When I called...that lady you work with," he said. "She said I needed to look after you real close. Said she thought you might be in some trouble."

I almost forgot that I was trying to hide my cheek and

244

sat up. Georgia! She'd talked to my dad behind my back? How could she?

I shook my head slightly. "She must have meant that we're all in trouble with the owner right now, that's all. I'm not in any trouble."

"You sure?" he asked.

"I'm not pregnant. I've just got a bug, Dad."

He shuffled his boot against the hardwood floor, thankfully giving my face a rest. At least now the shivering I was doing wasn't an act. I was furious with Georgia for getting into my business. So mad I was shaking. If it wasn't for my face, I'd go up to The Bread Bowl and confront her right now. She had no right.

"You know what your mother would say about trouble," he said, and I nodded, even though I never knew what my mother would have said about anything. If she'd ever said anything to me, I didn't remember it. Just once I wished he would stop insisting that I knew what my mother would have said or done about something and acknowledge that I, truly, had no clue.

He tramped back down the hallway. A few minutes later I heard him and Celia talking as they headed out the front door, and at last I could relax.

I took a shower, and the warm water felt like heaven on my eye. Then I got dressed and grabbed a bag of frozen peas. For the rest of the day, I leaned back against my headboard as mindless talk shows and soap operas droned away on my TV, and held the peas against my cheek. My mind was racing, trying to understand what had happened the night before. Trying to understand what I'd done to set Cole off this time.

But I just couldn't understand any of it. I didn't understand why basketball was such a big deal in Cole's world. I didn't understand how his parents made him so tense. I didn't understand why he couldn't get over the Zack thing, and I didn't understand his mood swings or why he had to call me names and make me feel small. I didn't understand what made him snap.

I didn't understand how he could hit me. Not just a shove or a wrist-grab, but an actual hit. And I didn't understand how he could be punching my face one minute and telling me he loved me the next.

And I didn't understand how I could let him.

On the drive home the previous night, I'd thought about Shannin's story about the night Mom left. Shannin made Mom sound like a bad guy—like someone who could beat the person she loved one minute and hold him the next. Shannin made Mom sound like someone who could understand who Cole was.

Did that make me like Dad?

The thought made me sick to my stomach, and I started to wonder if maybe my lie about being sick hadn't had a little bit of truth in it. *Sorry, Dad, I lied about having a bug. Turns out, the illness I have is the same one you have: forever walking around like a whipped puppy, pining after someone who's as crazy as goosehouse shit.*

Twice during the day, I picked up the phone and started to dial The Bread Bowl — not to bawl Georgia out for going to my dad, but to tell her. Tell her everything. Stop this craziness and all this stuff I was living without understanding from seeping into my brain too far. *Help me, Georgia*, I would say. *Help me get out of this.*

But every time I started to punch in the numbers, I thought about what it would be like to be "the abused girl." I thought about people whispering at school. About Celia's smug look. About Bethany and Zack sadly shaking their heads and saying they tried to tell me. About counselors and "talking it out" and everyone saying it was shocking because Cole and I looked as though we had a perfect relationship.

And, yeah, as pissed as I was... I couldn't help thinking of Cole. The hell he would go through. The way he'd feel that I had betrayed him. I would miss him. As crazy as that sounds, I would miss him. The kisses. The little romantic gifts and calling me Emily Dickinson. The guitar lessons. The inside jokes. The spillway. They would all be gone, and I would miss him.

I texted Bethany and told her I was sick. She didn't answer. I texted Zack; he responded: "Gt wl sn."

With all that was going on between me and Cole and with Georgia and now Dad, too, I couldn't really deal with those two.

"Gt wl sn." Not best-friend wishes, really. Which hurt. But it didn't surprise me in the least.

Cole never called.

Before Celia came home, I put the bag of peas back in the freezer and sneaked another look in the bathroom mirror. The swelling was a lot better, but there was still a bruise. I was going to need another day before I'd be able to cover that with makeup.

By the time I heard Celia's key in the front door, I'd already gotten back in bed, bad cheek down, and adopted my sick look again. A few minutes later she appeared in my doorway.

"Better?" she asked, munching on a granola bar.

"Puked twice," I groaned, closing my eyes like she was interrupting my sleep.

"Uh-huh," she said. "I saw loverboy today. He didn't look very happy. Maybe he's getting sick, too."

"Well, at least you know he wasn't here all day," I said.

She chewed contemplatively, then rewrapped the granola bar and placed it on the edge of my dresser. She walked over to me and crossed her arms. Then, with a sigh, uncrossed them and sat on the edge of my bed.

"Something seems different about you," she said. "Is everything okay?"

I was so taken aback by Celia's sudden interest in someone other than herself, I almost gasped. But if I made a list of people I'd never be able to tell about what was going on with me, Celia would be at the top of the list. She had a big mouth, and she almost never liked me. She'd use it against me for sure. "I'm just sick," I said. "That's all."

She cocked her head to one side and squinted at me. I held her gaze. "It's just," she said. "It's just that your boss told Dad there might be something going on with you. Zack and Bethany were talking this morning about how your boyfriend is a total jerk, and on the same day you're sick he looks like shit. I just...well, if you needed to talk or something."

I closed my eyes. "I actually need to sleep. Don't listen to Zack and Bethany. They're just mad because I'm not spending every waking second with them. They'll get over it," I mumbled.

She sat there for a while longer; then I felt her get up, and I opened my eyes. She shrugged. "If you say so." She grabbed her granola bar off my dresser and said, "You don't look good. You got dark circles under your eyes. I'm outta here. I don't want it."

And with that, she was gone, pulling the door shut behind her.

"Thanks, though," I called to her back, but she didn't hear me. I closed my eyes again, wondering how much longer I'd be able to keep this a secret. People were talking. I'd have to make a decision soon—either leave Cole or find a way to stop setting him off.

Lying there with my eyes closed felt so good, I kept them that way. And after a while I really did fall asleep, dreaming about lying curled up on Cole's floor, my face all fat and puffy, while soup bubbled away in the kitchen, Brenda making kitten noises and dancing to lullabies, and Mom on the roof with her blazing-fire hair, cackling and dropping things off the edge to the ground below.

At some point Dad's hand, rough and cool, pressed against my forehead, waking me up.

"Huh," he said. "No fever."

I stretched, catching myself at the last minute from turning onto my back, even though my neck was getting stiff from lying in one position.

"I'll call you in for tomorrow, too," he said. "Just in case. Here, this was on your car." He held out a rose, wrapped in green tissue paper, a tiny sprig of baby's breath cradling it.

Dad left the room and I sat up, pulling the note out of the flower and reading it:

Emily Dickinson, you are the love of my life. I'm sorry. Love, Cole

I buried my nose in the flower and took a deep breath.

I had to figure out how to stop making Cole so angry.

TWENTY-NINE

The next day, Cole left another flower on my windshield, so I called him. We talked for hours. He apologized. He promised to do better. To accept my friendship with Bethany and Zack. To stop letting basketball and his parents make him so uptight. To go back to the way things were before.

He convinced me that this was just a rough patch and if we were dedicated to our relationship the way we claimed to be, we would get through it with no trouble. We would be stronger, and the time he punched me in the face would be something ugly that we were too embarrassed to ever talk about again, even to each other.

Even though deep down I didn't believe him, I convinced myself that I did. I had to believe him. I'd already given up so much to be with him. To lose him now would make me feel as if I'd given up so much for nothing.

After two days with a "stomach flu," I finally went back

to school. It was a Friday, and I was so swamped with work and with repeatedly checking and repowdering my face, I barely had time to see Cole, much less Zack and Bethany.

But at the end of the day, when I turned the corner into the tutor lab, there was Zack sitting at the old desk he used to sit at when I tutored him before.

"Hey," I said, my fingers automatically drifting up to my cheekbone. Then, when I remembered that I didn't want to accidentally rub off the makeup, they fell to my necklace instead. "What're you doing here?"

"Hey back!" he said, rolling a toothpick from one side of his mouth to the other while I dumped my backpack on the table and pulled out my notebook. "Ah, she's so busy her best friends need a reason to see her now." He mimed holding a microphone to his mouth. "Tell me, Miss Bradford, what is it like evading the paparazzi? I saw the shower photo in *Questioning Magazine*, by the way. Your, uh... shower cap looked amazing. I stared at it for hours." He mimed sticking the microphone in my face. I laughed.

"No, it's good to see you, Zack," I said. "It's just that... aren't you supposed to be with Amanda right now?"

"Well," he said, "it turns out Amanda's not doing so hot in her own English class. Big stink. So Moody switched us all around. Amanda gets study hall, you get me, and the Big C goes to Jackie Rentz."

"Don't call him that," I murmured, opening my notebook and sitting down.

"Something wrong with your eye?" he asked, changing the subject. "It looks puffy. You must've been pretty sick. Celia said you barely left your room."

I rested my forehead on my hand, looking down and doing my best to shade my eyes and cheek from Zack. "Celia's worse than the paparazzi," I said. "So what do you have to work on?"

He stuffed the imaginary microphone back into my face. "Can I quote you on that?" he said in his TV announcer voice. But when I didn't respond, he tugged at his collar. "Sheesh, tough crowd. I remember this one girl. Name was Alex Bradford. Used to actually laugh every now and then," he said, then leaned over and pulled a crumpled sheet of paper out of his backpack. "Vocab," he said. "Big test Monday." I hated the way his voice sounded so serious, so un-Zack-like. But, really, he left me no choice. I couldn't continue to play the flirt game with Zack. Even though I knew it meant nothing, I couldn't keep inviting fights between me and Cole like that. I had to try my best to keep things from spiraling out of control. In a lot of ways, Cole's mood was difficult to predict and didn't make sense. But in a lot of ways I couldn't blame him for being jealous of my relationship with Zack. Zack was flirtatious. And I egged him on, probably because it always felt so good to get that attention. But now I didn't want it. I couldn't want it, because wanting it made it look to Cole like I didn't want him.

We worked on vocabulary, and then I helped Zack make some changes to a report he had due, the whole time keeping my face tipped down toward the desk as best I could.

Then, just as we were getting ready to pack up, the door flung open and Cole strutted in.

My stomach automatically seized up, and my heart started racing. Cole plus Zack in any room never equaled anything but trouble. And the last thing I needed, on my first day back and while I was trying to hide a black eye, was trouble.

Zack must have sensed it, too, because he let out a deep breath and started packing up, wordlessly.

But Cole's face was open happiness.

"Hey, you two," he said, coming up behind Zack and slapping him on the shoulder good-naturedly. If I hadn't been seeing it with my own eyes, I would never have believed it. "It's Friday—you're not supposed to be working so hard on a Friday!"

He bounced around Zack to my side, then leaned over and kissed me.

"Big C," Zack boomed. "How the hell are ya? Kill any puppies lately?"

Cole laughed out loud—a forced, hearty laugh—then reached across and punched Zack lightly on the shoulder. "No, but the day's still young," he said. Then to me, "You're right, Alex, the guy's got a sense of humor." I responded with a thin smile.

Zack pulled the toothpick out of his mouth and held it in his hand while he shimmied into his backpack. I could tell by looking at him that he was so not finding this funny, but that, like me, he didn't know what exactly to find it, either.

"Yep, I'm a real comedian," he said. "Listen, Alex, you gonna be around this weekend?"

I nodded, unsure what was playing out between them, but getting very nervous. *Please, Zack*, I pleaded on the inside. *I know you don't know what you're messing with here, but I could get hurt if you turn this into a game.* And then my heart sank when I thought of it like that. I could get hurt. Because of a joke.

"I should be," I said. "Got a lot of homework, though."

"Yeah, of course," he said, leveling his eyes at Cole purposely this time. Then back to me. "Bethany's coming over to help me memorize my part. Thought maybe you'd want to come over, too. Since, you know, we don't do the Saturday thing anymore."

"Maybe," I said, hating the shake in my voice and the way I felt electric standing next to Cole, waiting for his response, which I was sure was going to be violent.

"Hey, baby, that sounds like fun," Cole said, bumping me with his hip. "My dad's got me doing some lame-ass chores this weekend, anyway. This way I won't have to feel bad about leaving her alone all weekend, you know, man?" Again with that friendly shoulder punch. I flinched, but Zack stood so steady he almost looked like he was made of concrete.

"Cool," Zack finally said, poking the toothpick back into his mouth. "I'll call you."

He started toward the door, holding his rolled-up script of *The Moon for Me and You* in a tight fist.

"See ya, man! Have a good weekend," Cole called after him.

"Hey, same to you, Big C, you cool, cool guy," Zack called back without turning around.

After he was gone, I finally turned to Cole. "What was that?"

He shrugged, his face still lit up and smiling. "What was what?"

I gestured toward the door. "That. All that 'Have a good weekend' stuff."

He reached for me so suddenly I flinched, but he simply wrapped both arms around my waist and pulled me in against him. "I'm trying. For you. You said you wanted me to try, so I'm trying."

I grinned. "Really?"

"Yeah. I figure if you like him, he can't be all that bad. And if I'm going to be with you forever—and I am—then I better get used to hanging with him. And Bethany, too. Your friends are my friends, baby." He leaned down and gently, gently kissed my cheekbone.

I let out a deep sigh and wrapped my arms around his waist, leaning my head against his chest. It felt so good to touch him again. To feel like this—whatever it was—was over and we were back to who we were before. "Thank you," I breathed. "I love you so much."

He rested his chin on top of my head. "Anything for you. I told you I'd make it up to you, and I meant it. Nothing but good from here on out. Here. I have something for you. Early Christmas present."

He reached into his jacket pocket and pulled out something silvery and shining. He lifted his hand and let it unravel, a silver chain with a delicate silver dream catcher dangling from it. It was tiny, with little red stones dotting a silver-colored web. The feathers hanging from the bottom were made of silver, too, the whole thing gleaming under the fluorescent classroom lights.

I gasped and held my hand to my mouth, looking from the dream catcher, swiveling in the air, to Cole's face, which was shiny and happy.

"Oh my God," I breathed. "Cole, you shouldn't..."

"I had to," he said. "Because I love you. And I hurt you. I hurt the person I love most in this world, and I'll never forgive myself."

I took the necklace from him and studied it in my outstretched palm. "I love you, too," I said. "And it's beautiful. Thank you."

I unclasped the necklace and held it out to him, then turned around, holding my hair up in the back so he could put it on me. When he was finished, the dream catcher lay cold against my chest, about two inches higher than my mom's, which stayed safe under my shirt.

Looking down at it, I dropped my hair and laid my palm over the new necklace and turned back to him.

"I love it," I said. "It's perfect."

He moved my hand and inspected the necklace, then bent and kissed my palm. "I thought you could use a new one. Now you don't have to wear that old one all the time anymore."

I might have argued. Might have reminded him that I hadn't taken off the old one since I was eight years old and I wasn't about to start now. Might have let him know that I had every intention of wearing both of them every day. That I even thought it was cool to wear them together—one to protect me from old nightmares, the other to protect me from new ones.

But at the moment all I could think was, *Thank God*. Thank God I never told anyone what had happened. Thank God I hadn't lost my faith in him. Thank God he came back, the old Cole. And thank God I was right about him in the first place.

Instead, I wrapped my arms around his waist and leaned into him. He hung his arms over my shoulders and rested his chin on top of my head.

We stayed like that for a long time—wrapped up around each other, swaying, our heads stacked, like we were one person split in two and trying to get back together again. Then, finally, he pulled away.

"Hey," he said. "Let's ditch tutoring today. Let's go back to my house. I'll play that song I've been writing for you. Brenda's with her book club, and Dad's working. We'll have the whole place to ourselves."

"Yes," I breathed. "I have had enough of school for one

day." I touched my cheek. "I'm not on the schedule at The Bread Bowl tonight, either." Thank God. That would give my cheek one more day to heal before Georgia's searching eyes would most definitely seek it out.

I zipped my backpack and tossed it over my shoulders. "Ready," I said. Cole turned, beaming at me.

"Let's go out tonight, then," he said. "Your choice."

"Okay," I said, thinking how great it would feel to get out of the house and be just a face in a crowd, where nobody would ask me what was wrong with my eye. "Sounds great!"

He reached over and pulled me in again, kissing me on top of the head. "A whole day and night with the girl I love most in this world," he said, picking up his bag and leading me to the door, our hips bumping as we walked. Just like before there was anything dark and private between us.

Or maybe not quite like before. I'd never seen him look this happy before. This was new. An all-new Cole. An all-new relationship.

He really was trying. He was trying for me. And that's all that mattered, right? Not that a person makes a mistake, but that he learns from it and tries to be better.

I didn't even notice my cheek for the rest of the night.

THIRTY

"Alex! Door!" Celia yelled from downstairs. I'd just gotten home from work and was changing out of my uniform.

I figured it was Zack, wanting to practice his part. I'd heard Celia complaining to Dad about how she'd been helping Zack all week and there was a cemetery scene he was just never going to get memorized. Opening night was just a month away, and he was really stressing about it. She'd probably finally told him to bug me about it for a change.

I sighed, wiggling into a T-shirt. "Minute!" I yelled back. I pulled a pair of jeans on, wishing Zack had at least given me time to text Cole that I was home.

I hadn't seen Cole all day, even though he should've been done with practice by now. I hadn't heard from him, and that worried me because I knew he was stressing out about the upcoming Friday night's tournament. His dad was talking of little else, just like he'd been doing pretty much since games started.

But usually Cole would come over to The Bread Bowl after Saturday practice and hang out, waiting for me to get off. But he hadn't shown up today, and with Dave hanging around all the time, Georgia had adopted a strict no-cell-phone policy, so I had no way of finding out what was going on with him.

Who knew where he was? Probably doing something at home. Usually when he went missing, it had something to do with home. He never gave details about what was going on at his house, but once he told me his mom had slit her wrists more times than he could count. *She never does it seriously, though,* he'd said. *She just wants the attention.* And then he ended, as he always did when he was talking about his family, with *Fucking Brenda.*

I'd just have to get rid of Zack quickly. Tell him I was too tired to practice. Tomorrow. I'd promise to help him tomorrow.

I glanced in the mirror, pulling out my ponytail holder and raking my hand through my hair, then bounded down the steps.

"You still don't have that cemetery scene memorized?" I said, but stopped as I rounded the corner.

It wasn't Zack sitting on the edge of Dad's recliner. It was Cole, looking dark and sparkle-eyed. Energized.

He got up when he saw me. "Hey, baby," he said.

"You didn't tell me it was Cole," I said, but Celia was ignoring us, watching TV, her thumb working her cell phone keypad.

But before I could say any more, he was wrapped around me, hugging me around the waist and picking me up, my toes dangling above the carpet.

"I missed you today," he said.

"Where were you? Practice ended hours ago, didn't it?"

He put me down, kissed me again, and waved the question away. "Missed practice," he said. "Family stuff. Had to meet with my dad's lawyer in Pine Gate. Some old stupid lawsuit. Not important. Just really boring. I saw you leaving The Bread Bowl and followed you home."

Again, he hugged me. It felt so good after a long day of work to be wrapped up in his arms.

Things had been so good between us lately. Christmas break had been great for Cole. Without school and practice, he seemed to really relax, and except for the occasional blowup, we were like we'd been before he punched me. Last week we celebrated our four-month anniversary. It had finally snowed for the first time this year, which was kind of unusual for February, and we cuddled up on the couch together, watching the snow fall and drinking hot chocolate. Romantic bliss, like something you'd see in the movies.

I wanted this to be how life would feel every day, coming home from work and feeling Cole surrounding me. Looking forward to a whole night with him. Just the two of us, everything good.

We kissed, and I heard Celia click her tongue from over on the couch.

"Get a room," she murmured.

"Got one. This one," I said, giggling and kissing Cole again, this time harder and louder just to annoy her.

After we kissed, Cole pulled back. "Get your shoes on," he said.

"Thank God," Celia mumbled. "I'm about to throw up."

"Okay," I said, ignoring her completely. "Where are we going?"

He grinned. "It's a surprise."

I raced upstairs and pulled on a pair of sneakers, then touched up my makeup and ran a brush through my hair. When I came back downstairs, Cole was standing at the front door, his hand already on the doorknob.

"Come on, slowpoke," he said, and we headed out.

In the car, Cole turned up the music and drove fast, pounding his palms on the steering wheel to the beat. Every so often he'd look over at me and smile, then reach across the seat and stroke the back of my neck with his hand.

We got on the highway, and he turned down the radio.

"You coming to the tournament Friday?" he asked.

"Of course. You're playing, aren't you?" I said sarcastically, giving him a big smile and fluttering my eyelashes dramatically.

He grinned, turned up the music again, and leaned his head against the headrest. "That's my girl," he said, then turned the music up another notch.

The car was practically vibrating. Cole was practically vibrating. Definitely intense. But intense in a good way. I felt it radiating off him, but this time I didn't feel dread.

We turned into the mall parking lot, and Cole parked. When he turned off the car, the sudden silence made my ears ring. I looked at him quizzically. We'd been to the mall dozens of times together. Why was this time special?

"Come on," he said. "I have something I want to buy you."

We got out and met at the back of the car, where he intertwined his fingers with mine. We walked into the mall that way—happily holding hands.

When we got into the mall, he started to walk faster, pulling me along behind him. He took me straight past the food court and to the other side, where he finally stopped in front of Book 'Em, Danno.

He held up his arms like one of those game show models.

"The bookstore?" I asked, staring up at the sign. "You want to buy me a book?"

He dropped his arms, rolled his eyes, and came around behind me, ushering me into the store. "Not just any book," he said.

Once we were inside, he grabbed my hand again and started pulling. He pulled me past the fiction and past the cookbooks and past the self-help, all the way to the back of the store, where he finally stopped.

"Travel," he said. He ran his finger along the shelves.

"Kansas, Nebraska, aha! Here." He pulled a book off the shelf and held it out to me.

I read the title out loud. *"Frommer's Colorado,"* I said.

He nodded. "And I found this one, too." He pulled out another book and held it up: *Soul of the Rockies.*

This time I didn't read the title aloud. I couldn't. I was too touched to say anything. Instead, I took it out of his hands and opened it, leafed through it.

The images nearly knocked the wind out of me. The mountains looked so beautiful, so magical. I could almost feel Mom in the grain of the paper beneath my fingers. I sat down on the floor in front of the bookshelf, unable to take my eyes off of the photos.

I'd seen photos of Colorado before. But it was different looking at little thumbnails on Bethany's laptop. These photos were so vivid and crisp, so colorful, that I almost felt as if I was there already. I could understand why someone would want to go there just to see the mountains. Why maybe the beauty would be reason enough.

Cole sat down next to me. "When I found it, I hid it so nobody would buy it before I could get you up here. I knew as soon as I saw those pictures that you would fall in love with it." He brushed his finger across a photo of an ice-capped mountain, the sky behind it so blue that it made me want to breathe more deeply. "You're going to find your answers out there, baby. I can feel it."

"Cole," I said, but I didn't know how to finish. He'd always told me he understood, but so had Bethany and

Zack. And I never quite knew, with all their talk of ski bunnies and hot boy bands and new clothes, if Bethany and Zack actually did understand what the mountains meant to me—that it wasn't just some silly obsession and it wasn't only about taking a vacation.

But now I knew. I knew that at least one person out there got it. Cole understood. He understood everything.

"Oh, and I want to get you these, too," he said. He stood up and walked around to the other side of the bookshelf while I paged through the photographs some more, backing up and looking again at the ones I'd already seen. He came back and dropped two maps in my lap: Colorado and Kansas. "I don't think you guys'll get lost, but just in case. These are the good ones, the waterproof kind."

I held the maps in one hand and closed the book with the other, then scooped the *Frommer's* book into my lap.

"I love it," I said.

"Oh, and one more." He reached behind some Walt Disney World guides and pulled out a paperback: Emily Dickinson. "In case, you know, the mountains inspire you to write some more poetry," he said.

I took the book and held it against my chest, unsure of what to say.

We headed up to the cash register. As Cole pulled out his wallet and handed the cashier a handful of twenties, I knew this was why I'd stayed with him when things were bad. This was why a couple of bruises didn't matter. Because he understood me as nobody ever had before. Because we were perfect together.

I stood behind him while the cashier handed him his change and bagged up the books. I leaned my forehead against his back, feeling so lucky.

"I love you," I whispered into the fabric of his shirt.

THIRTY-ONE

The Bearcats had been having a horrible season, and it was sort of amazing that we made it into the tournament at all. You could feel tension in the stands, radiating off the parents, who were hoping for that big win for their players. The students in the crowd were just there to show off for each other. Get a little freedom. Screw around at school. Make out a little. Fight a little. Wear a little face paint.

I was there by myself. I hadn't seen Bethany for two weeks, ever since the weekend that I'd gone over to Zack's house to help him work on his lines and had felt like a third wheel the entire time. Cole had eased up on Bethany, and Bethany had responded by shutting me out entirely. She'd barely even talked to me all night—not like she was mad at me, but like she didn't know what to say. This was the first time I'd ever felt like an intrusion when it came to Bethany and Zack. We'd always been the Terrible Three, the Three-Headed Monster. Now it was the two of them...and me.

I suspected she was with Zack, working on his lines again instead of at the game. Or maybe they were at a movie. All I knew was I was definitely not in the Zack/Bethany gossip loop anymore.

Even when Zack came in for his tutoring sessions, we mostly just worked. There was hardly anything personal between us anymore. He stopped joking and sat there, answering my questions diligently.

If I were to write a poem about our friendship, I would have to use the word *awkward*. And *stilted*. And *changed*.

So, yeah, I was a little mad at them at the moment for shutting me out when I'd finally worked Cole into saying it was okay for them to be in. And it meant if I wanted to see Cole play, I would have to go to the game alone. Seemed as though I was doing a lot of things alone these days.

And it was a bad game. At halftime the score was 43–12. In the beginning of the second half, the Bearcats managed to put up a couple of shots, but the final score ended up being 62–23, an embarrassment for the Bearcats once again.

People actually booed as the team filed off the court after the game. You could see the disappointment in the shoulders of all of them. Well, all except for one. Number 12. Cole, whose shoulders were taut and stiff beneath his jersey. He'd had such a bad game the coach had benched him for the last eight minutes.

I knew he'd want to be alone for a little while to shake it off, especially since we had plans to go to an after-game party at Trent's house. He'd want to cool down, get in a party mood. And things had been really good between us. I'd learned when to leave him alone. This was definitely one of those leave-him-alone times.

So I sat on the bleachers, thinking about what I would say to Cole to lighten him up when he got out of the locker room.

Next thing I knew my entire row was empty, and when I glanced around, I realized that most of the crowd had gone.

I stood up, and that's when I saw them: Zack and Bethany, at the game, sitting just half a dozen rows behind me, their heads bent together sharing a set of earbuds. Had they been sitting there the whole time? How come they didn't say anything to me?

"Hey!" I shouted, and both of their heads snapped up to look at me.

"Alex!" Zack shouted back. "I didn't see you there!" But I noticed Bethany turn her head slightly to the side to hide a smirk when he said it. Lie. They totally knew I was there and were ignoring me. On purpose.

"I'm sure you didn't," I said sarcastically. "Otherwise you'd have said hi, right?"

Bethany looked up sharply, but before she could say anything, some girl I recognized from hanging around Bethany's locker, but didn't know by name, tapped Bethany on the shoulder. Bethany turned, and her scowling face turned to smiles, just like that. She stood up and hugged the girl, and the two of them chatted happily.

When did that happen? When did my best friend not want to talk to me, and when did she get so close to this other girl that she chatted with her just as she'd always done with me?

Zack stepped over the bleachers, hopping down one row after another until he was right in front of me.

"Hey," he said. "Listen. I'm pretty sure Bethany's gonna ask you if you mind if Tina goes on our trip."

"Who's Tina?" I asked, but then it dawned on me that he was talking about Bethany's new friend. "Her?" I asked, pointing.

Zack nodded. "You'll like her."

"No," I said, furiously jamming my arms into my coat sleeves. "No way."

"They're tight," he said, motioning with his head to Bethany. "She's really funny."

"I don't care, Zack," I said, realizing too late that my voice was way loud. "This trip isn't about having a laugh a minute, or maybe you guys with your RVs and your road trip tattoos and your extra shopping money for real Native American souvenirs don't remember what it *is* about."

He held out his hands as if he wanted to capture the sound waves as they came out of my mouth and hold them right in front of us, keep Bethany from hearing me. But it was too late. She and Tina were already staring at us, matching appalled looks on their faces.

"Whoa," Zack said. "Don't get riled. We haven't forgotten what this is about."

"Well, you could've fooled me," I snarled, stepping over the bleacher in front of me to get around him. "Like I want to share the moment I've been looking forward to my whole stupid life with Funny Tina!" I gave him a sarcastic thumbs-up. "Great plan, guys. Really!"

I hurried toward the steps.

"C'mon, Alex, don't be that way," Zack called to my back.

I started to turn around—Zack didn't do the vulnerable thing very often, and I started to feel bad—but I heard Bethany say, "Whatever. Let her go," in a very annoyed voice, so I straightened up and walked even faster.

But instead of turning right toward the hallway and waiting outside the men's locker room for Cole as I always did, I turned left and pushed through the doors into the parking lot. I couldn't handle the fluorescent school lights right now or the humid, smelly gym. And I couldn't handle running into Bethany and Zack...and Tina...again. Instead, I found Cole's car and paced in half-circles around it.

Despite the horrible game, there was lots of partying going on. People lingering, pulling drinks out of coolers in their backseats. Girls getting piggyback rides. Guys cheering as their friends came out of the locker room, shouting things like, "Hey, man, that was a tough team, but you looked good. You did."

All the parents had left the parking lot, holding sleeping

toddlers on their shoulders and dragging candy-hyped elementary kids behind them. Their taillights were disappearing down the main drag toward town, and the parking lot once again belonged to the teenagers.

But Cole took so long to get out of the locker room that even the teenagers had moved on, leaving skid marks on the blacktop and hanging out windows, yelling for no reason into the night sky. The only cars left in the lot belonged to Cole and Coach Dample, who always stayed for a long time after games, not leaving until after everyone else had gone.

From the sound of things, pretty much everybody was heading to Trent's house. I wondered if Bethany and Zack were going there, too. Great. They'd probably bring Funny Tina.

The thought brought on new waves of anger and despair. Why? Why couldn't anything ever be easy?

I paced some more, thinking. Maybe we could talk this out. Maybe I could make them understand that this trip was too personal to bring along people I didn't know, even though I'm sure she was a perfectly nice girl.

Maybe I could explain to them that now that I was with Cole, I needed to do this more than ever. I needed to understand what was so important out there in the mountains. I needed to prove to myself that no matter what the draw was for Mom out there, I should've been more important, dammit. I needed to put it to rest once and for all — to stop being Alex, the kid her mom left behind, and start being Alex, the whole girl who wasn't so stupidly needy and volatile. I needed them to know that. I needed them to understand how unimportant I'd been feeling lately and how I felt as though I could trace that unimportance back to the day the police were washing Mom's brains off the road. And how I could trace that unimportance all the way from that day to the day I left Cole's house with a bruised cheek. I wished like crazy that I could tell them about Cole hitting me. Then maybe they'd understand why I needed proof that I wasn't unimportant.

But in order to tell them that, I'd have to let them in on my secret. And now that Cole and I had fixed things, I wasn't going to do that. I wasn't going to be the girl who got beaten by her boyfriend. And I wasn't going to out Cole as the boy who beat his girlfriend because he was frustrated and jealous. He wasn't always that guy, but nobody would ever understand that.

I was tired of pacing by the time I saw Cole emerge from the side door of the school. I'd cooled off, so much so that I'd gotten cold. I'd zipped my coat to my chin and then pulled my arms up inside it, wrapping them around my waist to keep warm like I used to do when I was a little kid. I knew I looked ridiculous, hopping around, mummylike, inside my coat, but it helped warm me up.

"I thought you'd be inside," Cole said, coming through the lot in quick, wide strides. The shadows were dense and I couldn't see his face, but I could see that his fists were clenched at his sides. He hadn't gotten over the game yet.

"Sorry," I said. "I wanted the air."

"I'll bet," he said, and he pushed the button to unlock the car.

"Hey, sorry about the game," I said, shivering harder. "You guys totally should've won."

He'd been reaching for the door handle but stopped short. "Should we have?"

Something about his face warned me. This was one of those nights when I would need to watch what I said, for sure. He looked dangerous, and I knew from the past what dangerous could equal for me.

"I didn't mean..." I said, then stopped and chewed my lip. My mind raced. What would I say? What could disarm him? "Aren't we going to Trent's?"

"No," he said, reaching out and grabbing my shoulder. He wasn't clutching it hard, but I couldn't help feeling that cold feeling slide over me again. All I could think of were those two punches and my cheek throbbing. All I could think about was my neck stiff from lying on one cheek for two days, feigning illness so I wouldn't have to show people my bruised, puffy face. I couldn't go through that again.

"No, we're going to stay here, and you're going to tell me your theories on how we should have won that game. Since you know so much about basketball." With that, he shoved me, lightly, knocking me barely to the side. He did it again three or four more times, reminding me of a bear playing with its prey before eating it. "Huh?" he kept saying. "Tell me. How is it we should have won?"

I didn't say anything. In fact, I tried to react as little as possible, hoping he would lose interest and just get in the car and go to Trent's and have a drink and be fine again.

But he didn't lose interest. "Hey, everyone!" he shouted to the empty parking lot. I glanced around but didn't see anyone in the lot. "Listen up! Turns out my slut girlfriend isn't just a shitty poet but a sports expert as well. She's going to tell us all about how to win a basketball game!"

"Cole," I hissed. "I wasn't trying to tell you how to win the game. I was just—"

"What? What were you 'just'? Huh? Go ahead. We're all waiting."

He shoved me again, a little harder this time, forcing me to take a step backward. I glanced around nervously. There was no "we" waiting to hear anything. The realization chilled me—there really was nobody out here anymore. He could basically do what he wanted.

"Please, Cole," I said, my voice wobbly around my words. I hated my voice for sounding like that—like I was pleading for my life—but, in a way, I kind of was. "Can't we just go to Trent's now?"

"Can't we just go to Trent's now?" he mimicked in a high, sneery voice. *Shove.* "Can't we just go to Trent's now? Please, Cole?" *Shove.*

I stepped back with each shove, making no move to step toward him again. He was coming to me instead. *Shove.* Step. *Shove.* Step. We were several feet from the car now, and getting closer to the shadows of the tree line that bordered the parking lot.

I was pleading with him to stop, wrapping my arms tighter around my middle. I wanted to slip my arms back into their sleeves but was afraid to appear as if I was resisting or, God forbid, going to shove him back. I'd never tried to fight back with Cole before, and I wasn't going to start now. I was afraid of how hard he would hit me if I did. "Come on, Cole. Let's just go," I said, trying to keep my voice low and even, so he couldn't mock it. So it wouldn't irritate him. But nothing was working. He was already irritated.

Shove. Step. "You know something, Alex? You're so incredibly stupid." *Shove. Step.* "You think you know everything, too; that's what kills me. You think you have all the answers. You write one stupid amateur little poem and you think you're the shit." *Shove. Step.* "Nothing worse than a stupid slut girlfriend trying... to tell..." *Shove. Step. Stumble.* "...you what to do!"

On the word "do," he gave the hardest shove yet. I tried to keep my balance, but my arms were still inside my coat and it was no use. I was going down.

I didn't make any noise this time. I was too panicked and it happened too quickly. But at the last minute, I twisted my body toward the fall, trying, and failing, to get my hands out of the coat to catch myself. Instead, I went down on the concrete curb that edged the parking lot, my shoulder absorbing most of the blow, but my face hitting hard against the concrete.

And he laughed.

Out loud, laughed. Big, hearty ho-ho-hos.

I finally wriggled my arms into their sleeves and reached up to my face. My hand came away wet, and in the dark, my fingers looked black. Blood. My shoulder ached, but it seemed okay. I could move it. It wasn't broken or anything. But my chin stung, and my lip, too. I felt something hard rattling around inside my mouth and spit it into my palm. A piece of a tooth. Using my tongue, I felt the jagged edge where my front tooth had broken. A big chip.

I pulled myself to my feet, too pissed to cry, too scared to say anything to him, and once again numb. Just incredibly numb, as if someone had found an "off" switch and had shut me down. Thrown a veil over me. It occurred to me that numb was a bad sign—that there were all kinds of things other than numb that I should be feeling, and it worried me that I wasn't feeling them.

Cole was still laughing, clutching his stomach as if this was the funniest thing he'd seen, ever. I walked around him, holding my hand to my face, opened the car door, and then sat down.

I'd always thought if I just stayed away from Zack and Bethany, Cole would be happy. If I just made Zack stop tickling me. If I stopped hugging my friends. If I didn't talk about them or act like they were a part of my life, then I could keep Cole from exploding. But that didn't work.

And I thought if I supported him. Agreed with him when he complained about Brenda. Kept positive about basketball. Showed him that I was always on his side, then maybe he wouldn't blow up anymore. But that didn't work, either.

For the first time, it really hit me. There was nothing I could do to keep Cole from exploding. There was nothing I could cut out or do better or stay away from or say. I had no power over what was happening between us. Cole had it all. The turns our relationship took were the turns that Cole created. He was the one in charge. He was the one with all the say-so. I was just his little puppet, moving the way he wanted me to.

Eventually he came around to the driver's side and got in, too. The bleeding had mostly stopped, but my arm and chin, and now tooth, had started aching big-time. I willed myself not to cry. Willed myself not to think about how bad the tooth must look. Willed myself not to think about what Dad would say when I showed it to him.

"I need to go home," I said as he started the car.

He shook his head. "Going to Trent's. Remember? You really, really wanted to go just a minute ago. Now I'm giving you what you want."

I stared at him incredulously. Did he really expect me to go to a party like this? I looked gruesome.

"My tooth broke," I said.

The air in the car got serious, and he turned to me. "Really? Let me see."

I bared my teeth at him, hating every inch of him but feeling too distant to do anything about it, and he peered at my mouth. "Oh, man, Alex. You really shouldn't go walking around with your hands all caught up in your coat like that." And he had the nerve to sound serious when he said it, as if he was really concerned.

"What do you mean?" I said angrily, unable to hold it in any longer. "I wasn't walking around. You pushed me."

"That?" he asked, thumbing over his shoulder at where we'd just been standing in the parking lot a moment before. Again with that stupid laugh. "I was just teasing you. Just playing. You tripped."

So this was how it was going to work now. He wasn't going to stop hurting me; he was just going to start denying it. Well, that'd be the day. I didn't care if he bought me a million books, if he knew me inside and out. I could not do this anymore. I could not let him hurt me and pretend it was all my fault. I loved Cole, but at this moment, with my tooth poking a sore spot on the tip of my tongue and my chin seeping blood, I hated him far more than I loved him.

For the first time since all this craziness had started, I realized he would never stop doing this. There was nothing I could do to keep from setting him off. There was nothing I could do to make him stop.

As if to confirm my thought, he jabbed a knuckle into my rib.

"If I was going to hurt you, I wouldn't do it in a place where people could see it," he said. "You really are stupid, aren't you, Alex?"

We locked eyes for a long moment, me refusing to wiggle under the pressure of his knuckle, which was growing worse with each second as he pressed it into my ribs.

"Let's go to Trent's," I said, but in my head all I could think about was my new realization, which racked me with fear and grief.

Cole was an abuser. I was abused.

And it was never going to get better between us.

CHAPTER THIRTY-TWO

Trent's house was packed. Of course. Had I looked amazing that night, there would have been nobody there. But I walk in looking like I've just been through a wood chipper, and there's a crowd of about a million; and of course Renee Littleton would be the one standing closest to the front door, because she's got the screechiest voice ever, and if you're within a hundred miles of Renee Littleton, you can hear absolutely every single word the girl says.

"Oh my God!" she screeched as soon as Cole and I stepped through the door. "Alex! What happened to your face?" And every person in the entire house, I swear, looked at me. Even the music seemed to hit a dull note.

I glanced up at Cole, who still had that wait-till-you-hear-this-hilarious-story look on his face. "I fell in the parking lot," I mumbled.

"The doofus had her hands inside her coat," Cole said, spreading his hands wide.

I felt my face get hot, partly from the way Cole was playing this off like it was my fault, and partly from the eyes boring into it. Renee got so close I could smell the alcohol on her breath.

"Ew," she screeched. "You're really messed up."

"I know," I said, thinking, *More than you'll ever know, Renee. More than you'll ever know.* "Where's the bathroom?"

Her hands flew up to cover her mouth, and her eyes grew wide. "Oh my God! Alex! Your tooth!"

Cole nodded elaborately. "That's what I'm saying. Who knocks out a tooth in the freaking parking lot? Dude!" he called to Ben Stoley, who was manning a cooler in the dining room. "Over here." He held his hands receiver-style, and a can blurred through the air, landing with a *thunk* in the center of his chest. Several kids cheered and, thankfully, forgot about me. Including Renee Littleton, who was busy screeching to the boy next to her about her recent trip to Padre Island.

Quickly, I ducked away, keeping my face pointed to the floor as much as possible, and trying to avoid eye contact.

I slipped down a hallway on just the other side of the kitchen. Surely there'd be a bathroom there. The first three doors that I checked were bedrooms—two of which were occupied (one by a crowd of about ten, playing Twister and laughing their asses off, and the other by a couple who were quickly moving past the just-making-out stage). The third bedroom looked like a master bedroom, so I ventured in, and sure enough there was a bathroom.

I closed the door behind me and flicked on the light. I turned and looked in the mirror.

My hands went to my face of their own accord, and I let out such a huge gasp it was almost a cry. I'd been too afraid to look in the mirror in Cole's car—too afraid that I'd see how bad it looked and would cry, and I didn't want to give him the satisfaction of seeing me cry. But, oh my God, it looked so much worse than I'd thought it would.

Apparently my nose had been bleeding, too, though I didn't even feel it hit the ground. But there was crusty blood all around my nose and mouth, standing out against my pale skin, making me look like I'd kissed a clown. My chin had a scrap of skin hanging from the bottom of it, and my top lip was fat.

I opened my mouth, then snapped it closed again. As I suspected, my tooth wasn't just a little bit chipped. It was chipped almost in half, at an angle, pointing down sharply at my tongue. I bared my teeth and stuck my tongue through the gap, then immediately pulled it back from the sharp pain in my tooth. I wouldn't even be able to eat with my tooth like this.

Trying to stay calm, I turned on the warm water and began splashing it over my face. Surely once I got myself cleaned up it wouldn't look so miserable. Surely it would just look like a little scrape, a fat lip. Maybe not so obvious.

But my tooth... that was obvious.

The numbness wore off then, and I started to cry, staring at myself in the mirror as I scrubbed, gently, at the blood on my face, only to find that not much of it came off. I was one giant scrape. No wonder my face burned so badly. It was all raw skin.

But it was a soft cry. A giving-up cry. I honestly didn't know what to do at that point. I wanted to leave him, but I was afraid to do it. I wanted to love him, but I didn't want to be the person who loved someone who did this to them.

There was a soft knock on the door then, and it opened, just a little at first, revealing Bethany's glasses on the other side.

"Renee said you got hurt," she said. "Can I come in?"

I bristled but nodded, and she stepped into the bathroom with me.

"Wow," she breathed, grabbing a washcloth off the towel rack next to her and soaking it under the running water. "What happened?"

The sadness felt so heavy I couldn't speak. I didn't know how to say it. I didn't know if it was still safe to say anything to Bethany. I opened my mouth, but everything was stuck, somewhere down deep in me, just as it had been that night on the patio with Georgia, and I knew it was not going to come out here, in Trent's parents' bathroom, tonight.

"I fell," I finally said. "In the parking lot."

She stopped dabbing my chin and looked at me skeptically. "You fell," she said, only it wasn't a question, but a statement. A statement of incredulity. Cole may be right about me—I may be stupid as hell—but he could never accuse Bethany of being stupid.

"On the curb by the car," I said. "I was..." I grasped for the first thing to come to mind. "I was running."

She blinked, used the back of her wrist to push her glasses up on her nose, and then went back to dabbing. "Were you running away from someone?" she asked in a dull voice.

"What's that supposed to mean?" I winced when she touched a particularly sore spot.

She sighed, dropped the washcloth into the sink, and looked me in the eye. "Listen, Alex, don't take this the wrong way, but...Zack and I've been talking about you and..."

I straightened up. "Great. You're talking about me behind my back now, too? Is Tina in on the big conversation?"

She reached out and smoothed my shoulders softly. It was such a departure from the cold grip Cole had used just a few minutes earlier that I couldn't help pulling away. "Don't, don't," she said. "It's not like that. We're worried."

I reached down and picked up the washcloth, squeezed it out, and blotted the space between my nose and upper lip. "Well, don't be," I said. "I fell. It's not a big deal."

"It looks like a big deal from here," she said. Then, softening again, she took the washcloth from me and began blotting where I'd left off. "Alex, we're your best friends. More like sister and brother, really. If that asshole's hurting you..."

I backed away suddenly, shaking my head. Bethany watched me in the mirror, her hand still holding the washcloth in the air where my face had been a second before.

In my mind, I was thinking this was it. This was my chance to finally come clean. This was my chance to let Bethany in on what had been happening to me. This was my chance to have someone on my side.

But then I remembered what had happened at the game. *Whatever. Let her go*, she'd said. *Whatever. Let her go*, while she hugged and chatted with Tina, and made plans for Tina to go to Colorado with us. I loved Bethany, but I no longer was positive that I could trust her. I had been so totally devoted to Cole for months now, and I didn't know who else I could turn to anymore.

Besides, this was something that had been between just Cole and me for months. Our secret. If I told her about him pushing me and breaking my tooth, I'd have to tell her about the punches in his bedroom. And about the wrist in the tutor lab. So many secrets. So many of them. She would be mad that I'd kept these things from her. She would tell. I would have to repeat the stories over and over again, everyone angry and disappointed with me. It would be so humiliating.

I started to feel dizzy.

"Alex," Bethany said, her hand looking comical, still in the air like that. "You can tell me anything."

But I kept backing away, holding my hands up against my temples thinking, *This is it. This must be the part where*

I go goosehouse-shit crazy. I backed into the bed but scrambled up quickly.

"Please," I said. "Please don't say anything to anyone."

She stood up. "So he is? You have to tell."

I felt tears well in my eyes. "No," I said, pointing at her with one hand, the other still on my temple. "He's not.... Please don't say anything to anyone, Bethany. Please. I have it under control."

She started toward me, but I bolted for the door.

"Alex," she pleaded, and I noticed that she, too, was crying. I wondered what on earth was making her cry. It's not like she'd lost everyone she ever loved. Not like she'd lost her mom in a car accident before she was old enough to even remember her. Not like her dad had ever crawled into a mental hole and never come out again. Not like the boy she loved had punched her in the face. Not like her best friends had moved on without her. What the hell did she have to cry about? She still had everything, and I still had nothing. Just as it'd been our whole lives. "We'll help you," she said, her voice thick with tears.

"There's nothing to help," I said, or maybe yelled, because now that the door was open, the music was beating into my temples on top of everything else, and I seriously couldn't pay attention to anything but the noise in my head.

I left her there. Standing halfway between the bathroom and bedroom, clutching a dripping, bloody washcloth on Trent's parents' off-white carpet, tears streaming down her face, the water faucet gushing behind her. Promising to help a friend who no longer trusted her. Promising to be there for someone who insisted that there was no "there" to be.

I found Cole in the basement, playing pool with Trent and a couple other guys from the basketball team. It was just the four of them down there, no music, no Renee Littleton, no Bethany. I could think down there.

"Hey, there she is!" Cole said when he saw me. He took a long drink out of his beer can.

I ignored him and slouched back on the couch and turned on the TV. Some old black-and-white movie was on, and I vegged out in front of it, not paying attention at all to what it was, figuring the lamer I could make it down here, the better chance I had of nobody else wanting to come down and hang out.

Eventually I fell asleep, only to snap awake again when someone flopped down beside me, slinging an arm over my sore shoulder. I opened my eyes. It was Trent, and he was way drunk. I crinkled my nose at the smell of his breath, and was immediately reminded of my skinned-up face from the movement, which made my face feel as if it was being shredded up by razors.

"Heeey, Alex," he slurred. "You look like shit."

I glanced over the back of the couch. The pool game was over, and all the other guys were gone.

"Where's Cole?" I said, clearing the sleep out of my throat and sitting up.

Trent laughed in my face, pelting me with drunk-breath,

and leaned into me. "You fall down go boom?" And then he laughed some more.

I edged my way out from under him, leaving him to melt into the couch, still giggling over his joke. Hopefully he would pass out. Sleep it off. Hopefully the rest of the party wouldn't destroy his house while he was down here face-first in the couch.

I went upstairs and plunged back into the party, which seemed to have thinned out a little. According to the clock, I'd already missed curfew. Which meant I needed to get home before Celia realized it and woke Dad.

Problem was, I couldn't find Cole anywhere. I checked every room. I checked outside. His car was gone, too.

Great. Abandoned. Very nice.

This was shaping up to be a really shitty night.

I sat on the porch to try to figure out what to do. People stumbled past me, got into their cars, and rumbled away. Soon I imagined everyone would be gone. Just me and Trent, snoring away on the basement couch, my broken tooth rotting and me getting grounded for pretty much ever for not coming home.

I found Bethany and Zack playing PlayStation on a big screen in the den. It was some sort of racing game, from the sounds of roaring engines filling the room, and Bethany won, standing up and giving a victory dance.

Her eyes landed on me and her smile faded, stopping her in mid-dance.

"You're still here?" she said.

Zack turned, still holding the controller in his hand. "Oh, hey, Alex. I thought you'd left."

"I fell asleep downstairs," I said. "Cole left."

They exchanged a look that I couldn't quite decipher; then Zack leaned forward and turned off the PlayStation. "I'm ready to go, anyway. Kicking Beth's ass was getting old."

She slapped him on the shoulder but set down her controller and left the room, saying something about finding her purse.

I sat in the backseat by myself and pretended not to hear them joking with each other up front. Pretended not to notice that neither one of them said a single word to me all the way home. Pretended not to be so relieved when we finally pulled into Zack's driveway, where I could bolt across the yards and into the darkness of my house, alone.

CHAPTER
THIRTY-THREE

Half an hour later, I was showered, bandaged, and lying in bed, staring at the lights coming in through my window onto my ceiling.

My chin still burned, even more so now that I'd clipped off the hanging piece of skin. My nose felt sore, too, and my tooth, while it didn't exactly ache, irritated me by poking into my tongue.

I couldn't leave it alone. As I lay there, thinking, I pushed my tongue under the sharp edge of the tooth over and over again. *Jab. Jab. Jab.* Something about the pain felt familiar and—as weird as it sounds—good.

Because at least the pain in my tooth was something I could count on. Something I could expect. *Jab.* Pain. Sharp edge. *Poke.* Ouch. Good. I knew that was coming. I could predict and understand my broken tooth.

The rest of my life... not so much.

How did everything get so out of control? Where did I go from here? I was afraid to face everyone.

It must have gotten very late, because I lay there so long I actually began to contemplate just running off to Colorado myself right then and staying there. Not telling anyone where I'd gone. Just going and being a memory. I had enough money saved up to get out there. I had a car. All I needed to do was get a job once I got there. All I had to do was get away and leave the pain behind me.

Just as I finally started to drift off, yelling outside pulled me awake again.

I sat up and looked out the window. I couldn't see anything, so I got out of bed and pulled the blinds all the way open.

Cole's car was at the curb, idling, the driver's side door open. He was standing in the side yard, yelling something to someone who was standing in the shadows of Zack's front porch.

It was hard to understand what he was saying. His words were slurred, and there was a yard and a pane of glass between us, but it didn't take a genius to make out what was being said.

"Because I want to shee her and iz nona your business!...She's not your girlfriend, dude, get a grip..."

I gasped, bringing my hand up to my mouth, unsure what to do. A light had gone on in the house across the street, and I saw the neighbors lift up their shade to peer out. God, if Cole kept this up, Dad would wake up, and the last thing

I needed was to try to explain why my boyfriend was screaming in my yard, so drunk he could hardly stand up, at three o'clock in the morning. *Oh, and by the way, can you schedule me a dentist appointment for, like, immediately?*

I started to unlock the window so I could pull it open and, hopefully, shush Cole. But before my fingers could work the lock, he yelled again.

"Shit, I'd liketa shee you try," he said, and there was a streak of blue jeans and suddenly Cole was on the ground, rolling around angrily with Zack, both of them punching wildly.

Lights went on in another house across the street, and someone stepped out on their front porch and shouted, "Hey!"

My fingers worked double-time then, and I yanked open the window. Cold air rolled in at me, and the grunts and thwacks were loud and crisp. But I realized I didn't know what to say.

Really, Cole was no match for Zack, who was at least as big as Cole, and not drunk. He hit Cole five times to every one of Cole's strikes, and eventually Cole stopped hitting back and went to simply covering his head. Zack rolled Cole onto his back and grabbed his shirt, pulling him up off the ground, then letting him drop. Zack's hands went slack at his sides.

"You touch her again," Zack shouted in Cole's face, "I'll break your whole fuckin' body."

He got up and walked back to his house, flicking a glance at my window, where I stood, my hands pressed against the screen, my mouth hanging open. His lip was bleeding and he was out of breath, but otherwise he didn't look so bad.

Cole looked much worse. Bloodied nose. Bloody lip. Blood gushing down his chin.

He kind of looked like me.

After Zack's door slammed shut, Cole rolled on the ground a little, then stood up, spitting onto the ground.

Several neighbors were outside now, one of them holding a phone to her ear.

Cole stumbled, cussing, back to his car, stopping to spit every few steps. Then he got in and left, just before the police rolled down the street. They paused at Zack's house but must have decided that whatever had gone on was over now, and rolled away silently.

I crawled into bed and went back to feeling my jagged tooth with my tongue, replaying over and over again in my head the look on Zack's face when he glanced up at the window.

There was no way I'd ever figure out this night, which began with the boy I loved, who was supposed to be my ultimate best friend, hurting me, and the best friends I hurt at the basketball game standing up for me.

Zack had looked up at my window as if he'd expected me to be there. As if he knew I'd been watching him beat up Cole. As if he'd not only been warning Cole but warning me as well that he wasn't afraid to take on Cole if he had to, whether I liked it or not.

There was another look in his eye, too. A look that said he wasn't going to just let me be devoured by Cole. A look that said he'd always had my back and wasn't about to stop now.

Maybe I wasn't as alone as I'd thought I was. Maybe it was finally time to tell.

THIRTY-FOUR

"Let me see," Bethany said when I slid into the seat next to her. It was opening night of *The Moon for Me and You*, and I'd had a late dentist appointment, so I'd had to meet her there. The community center was packed. I was nervous for Zack, even though I knew he was backstage goofing around, not a nerve to be had.

I smiled wide, showing off my newly crowned tooth.

"Very nice," she said. "Did it hurt?"

"Only on the drive over," I said, closing my lips and running my tongue over my top teeth to remove any lipstick stains. I dug through my purse for a mirror so I could check them.

"Big lecture, huh?"

I nodded. "Oh, yeah." I located the mirror and held it up in the light, looking myself over. My scraped nose, lips, and chin had long since crusted over, the scabs fallen off.

All that remained were faint scars that I was mostly able to cover with makeup. " 'I can't afford to fix your teeth every time you decide to jack around in a parking lot,' " I said, adopting a gruff voice meant to mimic my dad's. "Seriously, I was so close to just saying forget it, I'll live with the temporary tooth. I'd kind of started to get used to it, anyway. This tooth feels so big in my mouth now."

In my head, I replayed the conversation between Dad and me on the drive to the dentist's office. There'd been more than just a lecture.

"That boy's been leaving roses on your car again," he'd said, the question lying, unasked, between us.

"Yeah," I'd answered, not sure what to say.

"Is it serious?" he'd asked.

I shrugged. I had no way to answer that question. I wasn't sure what "it" was between Cole and me anymore. He had come in to school that Monday, beat up but acting as if nothing had ever happened between us. He had started leaving the roses on my car again, with sweet notes, calling me Emily Dickinson and saying he was sorry and begging for my forgiveness. Just like always.

Only now...my skin crawled every time he touched me. He irritated the hell out of me every time he spoke. He scared me. But I hadn't left him. At this point, I didn't know how.

"I don't know," I said to Dad, staring out at the trees whipping past us. We passed the spillway, and my stomach turned in knots. *If only we could get that magical time back*, I thought. *If only I could get a lot of things back.* And before I even knew what I was doing, I blurted out, "Dad, why did Mom leave?"

At first he didn't say anything. Just stared straight ahead, his hands resting at the bottom of the steering wheel. Silence, like always. No answers, just…silence. I rubbed my forehead with my palm, waiting for what I was guessing would be only more silence.

But, surprisingly, just as the dentist's office came into view, Dad said, "She got mixed up with some guy who claimed to be a spiritual healer." He shook his head, gave a sardonic laugh. "He was an unemployed blackjack dealer. But she believed him."

I sat up straighter. "She had an affair?" My fingers felt cold, and I couldn't make sense of it.

But Dad shook his head, pulling into the parking lot and swinging the car into a space. "No," he said. "It wasn't an affair." He held the keys in his lap, tossing them lightly between his fingers. "Alex," he said with a sigh, "you were always the one who missed her the most. But you need to understand. She was sick. Mentally. And she was drunk that night she left. It was all just a big, sad accident."

He opened his door and got out, but I stayed rooted in my seat. It didn't make sense. Why would Mom need a spiritual healer? What was their relationship if it wasn't an affair? And why would Mom risk everything to be with him? I wanted to ask Dad so many more questions, but he was standing at the back of the car, stuffing his keys into his pocket, and I knew he was done talking about it.

I wanted to tell Bethany and Zack. See if they had any more answers than I did. See if it made sense to them. But I was still learning how to talk to my best friends again after all that had happened. I wasn't sure anymore what they were interested in. I wasn't even sure they were still interested in our trip. At least, with me there.

"Well, I think it looks good," Bethany said, snapping me out of my memory. "Hopefully this one won't get knocked out. Imagine what your dad will say if he's got to pay for it a second time."

I dropped the mirror back into my purse and zipped it shut vigorously. "Bethany, please. Don't start. I know what you think, but I really was wrapped up in my coat, and if I hadn't been, I would've been able to brace my fall. It was my fault. Really."

She raised her eyebrows. "I know. I was just saying I hope you don't fall down on your face again is all. A lot of people die from falls every year. I just don't want you to be a statistic." She didn't have to spell it out for me to know what she meant. She believed it was "just a fall" about as much as she believed I could fly.

We stood as a couple shimmied in front of us down the row to their seats.

"I'll be all right," I said, when we settled back again. "Can't you guys just let it rest?"

She held up her hands. "Okay," she said. "But if you need help cutting it off…"

As the house lights dimmed I wondered if maybe it

was just a matter of getting help cutting it off. Maybe I wasn't just afraid of what he would do to me or to Bethany and Zack if I broke up with him; maybe I was afraid of being without Cole. Maybe being with an abuser was better than being totally alone again.

And before I could even stop myself, the words tumbled out of my mouth: "I think...I don't know, like, I deserve it sometimes."

She reached over and put her hand on my wrist on the armrest. "Alex," she whispered, but the house lights went totally down and the orchestra's opening music crashed to life, breaking whatever spell I was under. "Alex," she whispered again, but then faltered when the man in front of her shot her an angry look.

I shook my head and pointed to the stage, where Zack had emerged in a 1950s-era suit, singing something about payday.

The lights came up again for intermission. We both clapped and cheered Zack's successful first half, which was way better than any first half Mickey Hankins had ever had, but somehow the excitement never quite reached our eyes.

We might have talked more about it. I might have told her about the night Cole punched me. I might have taken her into the ladies' room and told her about Brenda's suicide attempts and Cole's dad, who I was pretty sure beat Brenda, too. I might have told her about the wrist and about Cole calling me a slut whenever he was mad at me. I might have been swept away just enough by Zack's singing and Bethany's soft hand on my wrist to have told her everything.

But the lights were up again, and it was bright and I felt exposed. The family next to me began pushing their way down the row, and the audience, including Bethany and me, made a mass exodus toward the restrooms, and the moment was gone.

Bethany made a beeline for the restroom, but all I really wanted was something to drink, so I turned toward the booth set up by the culinary students and got a soda. I paid for it, then turned, taking a sip, and almost bumped right into Cole's chest.

"There's my beautiful lady," he gushed, kissing me on the ear. Immediately I felt the familiar tension rise in my shoulders. Lately, I'd had that tense feeling in my shoulders every time he touched me. I smiled thinly. "You are gorgeous tonight. I didn't realize people got so beautified to go to school plays."

My heart was so busy racing, I could hardly take in what he was saying, much less answer him. Was he going to insinuate that I was trying to look good for Zack? That was a path that was too familiar and too ugly to want to go down. I sipped my soda casually.

"So I was trying to surprise you," he continued, stretching one arm around my waist and pulling me toward a corner where nobody was standing. "But I got here right as the show was starting and I couldn't find you in time. Sure looked like you and Bethany were having a serious conversation down there."

He paused pointedly, and I had no choice but to swallow the soda I was holding in my mouth and speak up. I braced myself for a poke or a jab or a pinch that would mean *I know what you were telling her.* I shook my head. "We were just talking about my new tooth. See?"

I bared my teeth, and Cole's face lit up. "There's the mouth I know and love." He leaned over and kissed me, then smacked his lips together elaborately. "Mmm…sweet!" He leaned in and whispered into my ear, "The soda's not half-bad, either." Our old joke.

Slowly, I started to relax. He was the old Cole, sweet Cole. Cole who was trying to make the best of it with Zack and Bethany. Cole who whispered that I was beautiful and left roses on my car and assured me we'd have a great, calm life together with lots of beautiful children. Why couldn't he stay *that* Cole?

The lights flickered, and the crowd started to move back into the auditorium.

"Oh, hey," Cole said, pulling two ticket stubs out of his back pocket. He held them up. "I've got two seats."

I glanced over at Bethany, who was flicking worried looks over her shoulder at me as she filed back into the auditorium with the rest of the crowd. After what I'd told her, she'd never in a million years understand why I'd even be standing next to the guy, much less why I would sit with him over her for the entire second half of a musical.

She might even try to get me to move back to my original seat. Cause a scene. Make people stare. Force me to deny having ever said anything. Force me to make her look like a fool in order to save myself.

But as much as I worried that Bethany wouldn't understand why I wasn't sitting with her, I knew that Cole would be pissed if I chose her over him. And of the two of them, Cole was the one I was far more afraid of.

"Okay," I said, taking his arm. "Let's go."

Turned out, our seats were only a few rows behind Bethany, who scanned the auditorium almost obsessively until the lights started to go down.

And when they did start to fade, she finally found me.

I didn't need light to see the disappointment and sadness in her eyes.

THIRTY-FIVE

As soon as Cole took the corner toward the lake, I knew where we were going. This was the first time we'd really gone anywhere alone since the musical. Not that Cole hadn't been trying. I'd been avoiding it.

I was afraid to be alone with him. Afraid that he'd hurt me again. Afraid that I'd be forced to break up with him and then he'd do something crazy. Afraid that there was a lot more of me to be broken than just a tooth. Unbroken parts of me on the inside, where scars don't show. And afraid that he would find those unbroken parts of me and smash them to bits.

But no matter how I tried, and no matter how many times Bethany tried to talk me into it, I couldn't break up with him. There was something familiar about Cole. I loved him. I understood him. We understood each other. And you don't come by that every day. If you give up on your soul mate...if you let him slip through your fingers...will you ever be loved again? I didn't know, and I was afraid to find out.

We didn't talk much as we drove along through the woods. Cole's hand was in my lap, his fingers entwined with mine. He sang along to the radio; I gazed out the window at the bare tree branches silhouetted against the crisp early-spring sky. Things felt comfortable between us.

Finally, Cole pulled off on a gated road and parked in a patch of dry weeds. We both got out and tromped through the familiar foliage, coming out on the other side at the top of the spillway.

Cole marched right across, just like always, but as I raised my foot to join him, I felt the familiar pang of fear reverberate in my chest. It had been a while since we were last here. It was so high. So dangerous. And a lot had happened between our last visit and now. Cole himself had gotten so much more dangerous since then.

"Come on, Emily Dickinson," Cole said, stretching his arm out toward me. "I won't throw you off." He laughed as though he'd just made a particularly funny joke, but my knees shook when I realized that this was exactly what I was afraid of.

"I can't," I said, and choked out a laugh. My teeth chattered. "It's been too long."

Cole rolled his eyes and came across to me. "Chicken," he teased. Then, just as he'd done on our first date, he grabbed my elbows and, walking backward, led me to the middle of the spillway ledge.

"See? You made it, chicken," he said. He sat, dangling his legs over the edge of the concrete, and scooted back, patting the ground in between his legs, just like before. "Come on. Sit down." When I just stood there, my arms crossed against the constant cold breeze, my whole body shaking, he rolled his eyes again. "Alex. I'm not going to let anything happen to you. Sit down. I want to tell you something."

Slowly, slowly, I lowered myself into his lap, my legs dangling over the edge now, loosing rocks into the water below. I leaned into Cole, taking in his familiar scent, feeling the shape of his chest that I'd memorized over the past several months, and closing my eyes, the memories flooding back so hard it almost hurt.

He pressed his cheek against my ear.

"I told my parents yesterday that I'm done with sports for good," he said.

"Really?" I asked, turning so my forehead was leaning against his chin.

He nodded. "I was afraid I was going to lose you." He reached up and grabbed my chin, gently lifting it up so I was looking into his eyes. "I can't lose you. I love you too much." He bent and lightly kissed me. "All that stuff that happened, Alex. It's over. It won't ever happen again."

I ducked my head, my chin pushing against his hand. "You've said that before," I mumbled.

I felt his belly move outward and back in again as he took a deep breath and released it. "I know," he said. "But this time it's different. I went to an anger counselor yesterday. I'm changing. For you, Alex. I'm changing because I love you."

Relief flooded my body. Cole had talked about changing before, but this time felt different. He'd never talked about counseling before. Despite myself, I started to let myself believe that maybe this time he really meant it. I turned the whole top half of my body so that I could look into his face. I didn't know what to say. Everything could be different now. Everything could be like it had been in the beginning. I could be getting my old Cole back for good. I wanted to cry, I was so happy.

Cole picked my hand up off his thigh and held it in both of his, gently stroking my fingers. "I want to marry you, Alex," he said. "I want us to be together forever."

And suddenly, I found my voice. "I want that, too," I said, and was surprised at how true that was. Despite all that we'd been through, I wanted this future with him. And I believed in it.

Cole scooted backward, away from the edge of the spillway, pulling me along with him. When it was safe, I turned to face him, wrapping my legs around his waist, and we kissed, forgetting about fear. Forgetting about how high we were and how the tiniest slip could take us a long way down.

CHAPTER
THIRTY-SIX

Things were good. Cole was going to counseling and seemed to be making a renewed effort to make it work between us. He was back to calling me Emily Dickinson and buying me things and making everyone pretty much think we were the perfect couple. It felt as though we'd made it through a dark winter and were blooming again, right along with the early-spring flowers.

He was working so hard at making things better, I even began to let my heart believe in us just a little again. And then a little more. And after a month with no violent outbursts, it started to seem as if all that other stuff that had happened was in the past now, and he and I would make it.

One night, lying on his bedroom floor listening to TV noise drifting through the hallways of his house, we decided it only made sense for Cole to go to Colorado, too. He was sorry about throwing the papers out the window before, he said. He'd never stopped wanting to go, he said. He said he knew as much about me as Zack and Bethany knew—maybe even more than they knew—and it seemed like the best place for the two of us to grow a stronger bond.

I knew Zack and Bethany would hate the idea. But it was worth it to fight them whenever I thought about hanging out in front of a roaring fire, letting go of my past, snuggled in Cole's arms, then making love in a down-filled cabin bed. It sounded like the romance we really needed.

Plus, Cole had been talking more and more about spending the rest of our lives together. Maybe he would officially propose and we would go ahead and get married there. We'd be eighteen. A mountaintop wedding. Beautiful.

I decided I would bring up the idea to Bethany and Zack the next time I saw them. After all, they'd asked to bring Tina along. My asking to bring Cole made so much more sense.

I waited until I saw them together at Zack's house. Every day I watched and waited, and as soon as I saw Bethany's car pull up in Zack's driveway, I threw on my jacket and rushed over there.

"Hey," I said when Zack's mom opened the door. "Are they here?"

"Alex!" she declared, much too loudly. I almost thought I detected a hint of something in her voice that I couldn't quite pinpoint. How much had Zack told her about Cole? Did she know about the fistfight in the front yard? "Well, honey, it's been so—come on in—Zack's just right down— Zack, Alex is—I just made a snack—you need anything?"

I shook my head and said, "I'll just go down," and before she could argue, I was through the living room and halfway down the stairs to the rec room.

As I expected, Zack and Bethany were sitting cross-legged on the floor in front of the TV, playing the same racing game they'd been playing at Trent's party. Bethany paused the game when I came into the room.

I hoisted myself up on the washing machine, which sat just a few feet from the TV stand, and crossed my legs at the ankles, casually kicking the machine softly with my heels—*bong, bong, bong*—just as I'd done a billion times over the past seventeen years.

"Who's winning?" I asked.

"We just got started," Bethany said. "You want in?" She held her controller up for me.

"Nah," I said. "I just wanted to talk. About Colorado."

They exchanged glances…again…as they'd done so much lately—as if anything they might have to say about me has already been said and they didn't need to waste anyone's time saying it again. "Yeah?" Bethany said, pressing the button to un-pause the game. The basement was awash with the sound of cars zipping around a racetrack.

"Yeah," I said, and took a deep breath. There would be no easy way to say this. I had to just come out with it. "I was sort of wondering if Cole could come with us."

Zack let out a bark of laughter—just one "ha"—but kept playing the game. Bethany, however, set her controller in her lap and took off her glasses.

"You're kidding, right?" she said. She didn't look at me. Zack kept playing, the "ha" his only contribution to the conversation.

"No," I said. "Listen. I know you guys don't like him, but he promises he's going to try to get along and...I think he might propose to me."

"Oh. My. God," Bethany said, picking her controller up out of her lap and tossing it to the side. Zack pressed the pause button this time and stared at me as Bethany stood up and paced to the rusted refrigerator at the far end of the basement. "You can't be serious."

I hopped off the washer. "Yeah, actually, I am. We'll be eighteen. Why couldn't we get married out there?"

She opened the fridge and pulled out an orange soda, popped the top, and took a sip. "Well, for starters, he abuses you, Alex." I flinched, blinking. It was the first time she'd ever said so plainly what I'd been denying even to myself.

"He hasn't done anything in a long time," I said, which was true. "And it'll be different if we're married, because then he won't have to deal with the pressure of his parents and school and everything. He's going to counseling because he wants to make it better. For us. For our future."

Zack laughed again—this time like "ha-ha"—but there was no laughter in his face whatsoever. "You're an idiot," he said.

"Excuse me?"

"He's right," Bethany said. "I'd kind of given up on the trip anyway, since you stopped showing any interest. But if

312

you're bringing Cole along, I'm out. I won't have anything to do with that guy."

"Ditto," Zack said.

I could feel fury filling me from the toes up. "You'd love that, wouldn't you?" I shouted. "You'd love to shove me right out of your little friendship, just like you've been trying to do ever since I met Cole. Maybe you should go together, just the two of you. Better yet, maybe you should take Funny Tina with you. I hear she's a freaking riot!"

"You'd think you'd be more appreciative," Bethany said, waving her soda can in my direction.

"I should be more appreciative?" This time I was the one who laughed, a hoarse chuckle.

"Yeah," she said. "Zack almost got arrested trying to protect you from that asshole. He almost got suspended for defending you in the locker room. And he got his mouth smashed up. All for you, Alex."

"Ah," I said. "So you're jealous. Because he didn't do it for you."

She walked back to where she'd been sitting and set her soda down. "No. Actually, I've been too busy being hurt that my best friend's been treating me like shit to even care about much of anything else."

"Oh, well, I'm sorry if I haven't properly revered you, Your Highness. I'm so sorry that I have a boyfriend and you don't because you've never had the guts to even talk to the guy you like, much less try to get with him. Or maybe you won't talk to Randy Weston because you're really in love with Zack. God, Zack, why don't you just go ahead and do her already, so she can lighten up a little bit?"

Both of them shot angry, shocked looks at me. Zack's face had gone as gray as the concrete floor. Bethany's whole body was red. I'd even shocked myself. I stood there, panting, unsure of what to do next.

I had just sounded...like Cole.

Oh my God. I was turning into him.

"Go home, Alex," Zack said. He pressed the pause button, and the racing noises started up again.

Bethany wiped her glasses with her shirttail and put them back on, then picked up her controller and started playing, too.

Suddenly it was as if my legs couldn't move. As if I'd forgotten how to put one foot in front of the other and make myself go forward. I stood there, my hands on my hips, trying to catch my breath, trying to figure out what just had happened.

"I said bye-bye," Zack said again. No yelling. No cussing. No emotion whatsoever. It was as if he were talking to a stranger. Or a dog.

"Fine," I said, trying to sound tough. Trying to save as much face as I could. Trying not to sound like I instantly regretted what I'd just said. I stomped to the stairs. "But if you guys don't accept Cole, you don't accept me. You're out of my life."

"Your choice," Bethany said. Then she muttered something I couldn't make out under her breath, and Zack mumbled a response.

I crept up the stairs, only to find Zack's mom standing in the entryway waiting for me. She looked grim. Sort of like a fairy godmother who'd screwed up and sent someone to a gas chamber instead of to the prince's ball.

"Oh, honey," she said, reaching to stroke my hair. "Oh, honey, I'm sure they—did you fight?—things will smooth—Zack and that boy just don't—oh, sweetie, I wish there was something I could do to help."

And suddenly there was something so motherly about her that I wanted nothing more to do with her. *This is all your fault*, I raged inside. *If you hadn't made it look so good all these years, maybe I wouldn't have ever missed her.* Maybe I'd be hard like Celia and Shannin, and I'd never have gotten into this mess. I ducked from her touch.

"There isn't," I said, and escaped through the twilight-dim cold air, through the yards, back home to my room, where I could pretend everything made sense.

THIRTY-SEVEN

When I was a little kid, I leafed through the photos of Mom and Dad constantly. After I'd rescued them from the garbage, I'd hidden them in a shoe box under my bed, and every time I felt sad or lonely I'd get them out and stare at them until I had every grainy little millimeter of them memorized.

I would tell stories about them. Talk to Mom in them. Tell her she looked beautiful. Imagine what the next frame would look like if the photographer had snapped another and then another and then another photo of them, making them come alive, like in the movies.

I had my favorites—the one of their silhouettes sitting cross-legged under a tree, their knees touching; the one of Mom's arms being pulled in opposite directions by her friends, her smile so bright; the ones where you could see it in Dad's face. His love for her. It was all-consuming.

I used to kneel next to my bed and line them up in what

I imagined their order to be. The one of them on the concrete steps, Dad in a cheesy Hawaiian shirt. All the way to the one of the amusement park ride, Mom looking so miserable, like she was going to throw up.

Trying to find the perfect order. Holding the one wedding photo (why just one?) in my hand and trying to find exactly the spot where it belonged. Like if maybe I could get the order right, more photos would suddenly appear in the box: photos of things that never got to happen because she was gone. Things that would forever happen without her. Christmases and birthdays and marriages and births. Or maybe, God, I don't know...just something. Something that would say this life was important, too. Not just whatever life lived for Mom in Colorado, but this one. The one she had right here.

With me.

My life.

What I wouldn't have given for one photo of Mom holding me or standing with me or playing with me and looking happy about it.

After the fight with Bethany and Zack, I locked my bedroom door and knelt beside my bed. I rummaged behind books and old pencil boxes from elementary school until my hands landed on the familiar cardboard of the shoe box. I pulled it out and sat on the bed with it in my lap.

It'd been so long. Would their faces look the same to me now as they did then? Or would I open the box only to discover that Mom never looked happy? That she only ever looked like she was trapped on a ride and wanted, more than anything, to just get off.

Slowly, I pulled the lid off the box. My breath caught. There they were. Just as I remembered them. Look. Mom's smiling. Look. They were holding hands. Look. They had a happy life, and it wasn't until Shannin, Celia, and I started showing up in the frames that she got that distant look in her eyes. It wasn't until we landed in the photos that she started dreaming of Colorado.

I pulled out a photo with shaking hands. I remembered this one, of course. Mom was standing on the side of a road, a fanny pack strapped around her waist. She was grinning goofily and holding a flower so that it looked like it was growing out of the top of her head. I recalled all of those details about this photo. But what I'd never noticed before was what was in the background. Blue-black, hazy, monstrous. A mountain.

I leaned over the picture, my eyes straining to find some sort of clue. Where was this taken? Where, Mom? Where were you headed? You and your spiritual healer friend?

I would never know. Now, thanks to Bethany and Zack or thanks to Cole or, hell, I don't know, thanks to me, probably, I would never find out.

I dug around in the box, pulling out photos at random and staring at them and then dropping them back in, only to dive in for the next.

I didn't even realize I was crying until Celia barged into my room.

I jumped, scurrying to hide the box from her. Even after all these years, I still wanted this life inside the photo box to be all mine. Celia and Shannin didn't deserve it. I pushed the box next to my hip, and it slipped down the crack between the bed and the wall. I could hear the scraping of the cardboard against the wall as it fell, and the papery swishing sounds of the photos falling out and landing on the floor.

"What do you want?" I said, wiping my face with my shirt.

"Zack told me what happened at his house," she said.

"Goody for you. Get out," I said, thinking, *He certainly wasted no time getting the news out. Maybe he should take out a billboard.*

"You're not going to Colorado now," she said. "At least not with them."

"Nope," I said, pulling a magazine off my nightstand and opening it, trying to look nonchalant about it. A folded-up piece of paper fell to the floor. I bent over and picked it up, holding it in my palm. "You can leave now."

"Um, forget something?" she said, standing on the throw rug in the middle of my room with her hands on her hips.

"Nope," I said again. "Bye."

"Yep," she countered, bobbing her head. "The cake. You forgot Dad's cake."

I brought my hand to my forehead. The cake. Of course. The party was tomorrow, and I'd totally forgotten the cake.

"The grandmas went to pick it up," she continued, her voice dripping with snottiness. "And it turns out you hadn't even bothered to order it."

"Oh, man." I sighed. "I forgot. I'm so sorry." I felt guilt rise. Now if Dad's birthday party was screwed up, that would be all my fault, too. It was like I couldn't do anything right. I'd let down my sisters, my friends, my dad, everyone.

But Celia had seen her one-up opportunity, and she wasn't about to let it go. "How? How is it even possible that you forgot? You've had months to do it, and I reminded you, like, a billion times. God, Alex, I can't even believe you."

"I said I'm sorry," I said. "I'll order it today. I'll have them put a rush on it or something. It's not the end of the world, Celia."

"The grandmas already ordered it. Shannin's superpissed, just so you know."

I rolled my eyes, shutting the magazine with a slap. "Of course she is. Because everyone in the world is mad at me right now. I don't care, okay? I've got my own problems. Why don't you go get Shannin and Zack and Bethany and everyone else in the world and have an 'I Hate Alex' party, okay? Just...leave."

I hopped off the bed and picked up my Bread Bowl uniform pants off the floor. I headed to the dresser to get a shirt, fuming.

Celia was quiet while I dug for a shirt and clean underwear. Then, just as I turned to go into the bathroom to get ready for work, she said, "Are you really going to marry him, Alex?"

I turned. "Zack told you?"

She nodded. She was still standing in her pissed-off pose, but her eyes were big and moist. Even though she was in high school now, she suddenly looked like a little kid. "He told me some other stuff about Cole, too. Is it true? He hurts you?"

A million images and thoughts and memories crossed through my head all at once, nearly knocking me down under the weight of them.

Finally, I shrugged. "I don't know what I'm going to do," I answered. Probably the most honest thing I'd said in a long, long time.

"Well, you have to do something," she said softly, then turned and left the room, shutting the door quietly behind her.

I dropped my clothes on the bathroom floor, then unfolded the piece of paper that had fallen off my night-stand when I picked up the magazine.

I cannot swallow your squared eyes
Sightless of my shrinking heart
My caving chest
Shoulders to the polished floor . . .

My poem. How did it get on my nightstand? I didn't remember putting it there. I read it, even though I had it memorized by now, my chest feeling heavy and full, remembering the day that Cole sang it for me that first time on the curb at The Bread Bowl. A sob escaped me. I wanted that moment back so badly.

I lifted my eyes to the top of the paper, sniffling. I'd still never titled it.

I turned and rummaged through the vanity drawer, pulling out an old eyeliner pencil. Leaning over the bathroom counter, I scrawled "Bitter End" across the top. Cole was right—that title was perfect.

Then I wadded up the poem and threw it in the trash.

Straightening up, I caught sight of myself in the mirror. I stared at my eyes long and hard—looking for that lost, empty look I'd seen in Mom's eyes in the photos. Was it there, in my eyes, already?

The one good thing to happen to me all day was that Dave had already been at The Bread Bowl and gone home again. Georgia was in the lightest mood I'd seen her in since he'd started hanging around, and Jerry seemed happy, turning up the kitchen radio and singing along when there weren't any customers in the dining room.

I needed some lightening up myself. Craved it. So I joined in, singing along up front, joking with Georgia, even making some ugly little dolls out of cauliflower and calling them the Granite-Ass family.

Georgia had good news. Lily had been accepted into a progressive program for special-needs kids, and Georgia was convinced it would be the best thing to ever happen to her daughter. We grazed off the chocolate chip cookie tray to celebrate.

It was like one big party, and I was in a partying mood. Bring it on.

Which was why I was so caught off guard when the girl whose order I was ringing up suddenly took a hold of my wrist and pulled my arm toward her, bending down to look at the underside of my bicep, a stricken look on her face.

I jerked my hand away, my face getting warm. She looked familiar, but I couldn't quite place where I knew her from.

"What's...?" I asked, but before I could get the whole sentence out, she spoke.

"You're still with him?"

Honestly, at first I had no idea what she was even talking about. Then it occurred to me. She was looking at the pinch marks on the back of my arm, the lowest two of which barely showed if the short sleeve of my uniform pulled up just a few inches. Cole had pinched me yesterday, hard enough to leave marks, saying he was "just playing" and that I should "lighten up a little. Not everything is an after-school special."

"You're still with Cole?" she repeated, pointing to my arm.

And suddenly I knew where I'd seen her before: the movie theater.

Maria's kind of a psycho, Cole had said. *Nuts.*

"You're that girl from Pine Gate," I said, and she nodded. "Maria, right?" The man standing behind her shifted his weight impatiently and sighed.

"Cole's ex-girlfriend," she said, glancing over her shoulder as if she expected to see him standing right behind her. "You're still dating him."

The guy behind Maria cleared his throat.

"I've got customers," I said. But as I said it I knew, at that moment, I didn't want Maria to leave. I had questions. I wanted answers. Things that didn't make sense back at the movie theater when everything was good between Cole and me—they were now making perfect sense. She'd looked like she wanted to bolt back then. She'd looked...afraid.

Maria's kind of a psycho had been Cole's explanation. *Her parents are friends with my parents. Used to be, I mean.* Why "used to be," Cole? Why in the past? I knew the answer now, I thought.

She started toward the other end of the counter, where Jerry already had her order on a tray.

"I get a break in fifteen minutes," I said. She nodded and headed to a table in the back by the patio entrance.

When the line finally died down, I called to Georgia that I was taking my break and rushed to the dining room. Maria was done eating but was still sitting, sipping her drink and reading a paperback.

"I'm not really supposed to talk about it," she said, without looking up from her book. I pulled out the chair across from her and sat down. She slipped a piece of paper into the book to mark her spot and stuffed it into her coat pocket. "Part of the lawsuit."

"I don't know anything," I said. "He said your parents were friends."

She gave a sardonic chuckle. "Not so much," she said. "More like my parents wanted the money to pay the hospital bills after he broke my arm."

Without thinking, I grabbed my wrist, the one he'd held so tightly in the tutor lab. She looked grim.

"I take it he's still twisting arms?"

I don't know why, but I moved mine to my lap, hidden under the table.

"I'm not the first," I whispered.

"No," she said. "He also used to hit this girl at my school, Jillian, when he was dating her. She dumped him, and he harassed her for a long time. They had to get a restraining order. I didn't know any of this until after, you know." She held up her arm.

"So that's why he moved here?"

She nodded. "None of it was in the papers because we're all minors. But, you know, people talk. And pretty soon everybody knew about it. Some of the guys would say things to him. Threaten him and stuff, you know."

I sat there, stunned. It had never occurred to me that I might not be the only girl Cole had ever tormented. There'd always been that doubt, that part of me that insisted that he only did this because I was so difficult to live with. That he only did it because I pushed him, I asked too much of him, I didn't respect him enough.

"I can't believe it," I said, my voice barely more than a whisper.

"Listen, I don't know you, and if you want to stay with him, that's your business. But I thought I should tell you, since I saw the bruises on the back of your arm, that it's only going to get worse. I thought he really loved me all the way up until I was in the ER. I actually still cried when my parents made me break up with him. He was always so sorry. So romantic about it. Did he put roses on your car?" When I didn't answer, she nodded. "Yeah. But he's going to kill somebody someday, and if I can stop it from happening to you, then maybe I didn't live through the most horrible time of my life for nothing. Hopefully the counseling the judge ordered him to get will work."

I sat, stunned, my mouth open. A judge ordered the anger counseling. Cole wasn't going because he wanted to get better for me. He was going because he had to make up for what he'd done to Maria.

She stood, picked her purse up off the floor, and pulled a set of car keys out of her coat pocket. I picked up her tray.

"Good luck," she said. "If you stay with Cole, you're going to need it."

THIRTY-NINE

It didn't take a rocket scientist to see how much my mood changed while I was on break. I came back dazed and emotional, not wanting anything to do with Jerry's songs or Georgia's celebrations. I threw away the cauliflower Granite-Ass family.

All I could think about was that Maria wasn't the only other one. He'd beaten not just me but other girls. Which meant Cole had a problem. And so did I, if I was going to stay with him.

My God, what was wrong with me that I was even considering staying with him? *Girls.* Plural.

The dinner rush was long and busy, thankfully distracting me, but as soon as it was over, I was left with the thoughts in my head again. Images racing. The times he made me feel small. The times he scared me. The times he hurt me.

And he'd hurt Maria worse.

He's going to kill somebody someday, she'd said, and I almost immediately thought of his fingers digging into my neck so tightly while he punched me with his other hand.

And look at all I'd lost, being with him. Celia hated my guts. I'd let Shannin down. The grandmas knew something was up, for sure.

And then there were Bethany and Zack, the brother and sister who'd always understood me before. Suddenly they were a duo. A clear duo, telling me to stay away, forcing me to choose. And what had I chosen?

He's going to kill somebody someday.

I'd even hurt Georgia, leaving her alone on the patio when she'd tried to reach out to me.

And then it struck me: Georgia. Of course.

I needed to talk to Georgia. The secret was out now. Maria knew. So did Zack and Bethany. Probably Zack's mom. They'd even told Celia. Soon Dad would know, too, and what would I say to defend my decisions? How would I convince them I still needed this boy? How could it possibly not be over for Cole and me now?

I needed to tell Georgia. I needed to cry on her shirt and have her tell me it was okay and it wasn't too late and this still wasn't going to define me.

I moved super-slow on dining room cleanup after closing, to give Jerry plenty of time to get the kitchen cleaned and prepped for tomorrow. I swept carefully. I washed the windows. I filled each salt and pepper shaker painstakingly.

I loaded up the condiment bar with napkins and half and half and little packets of mustard and horseradish sauce.

By the time I was done, Georgia was standing at the front counter, staring out into the dining room, her arms crossed over her chest.

"Wow," she said. "Geoffrey isn't going to have to do a thing in the morning."

I didn't say anything, just shoved stock back into the cabinet under the condiment bar.

"Come on," she said. "Let's close up." And then, when I still didn't respond: "Earth to Alex. Come in, Alex."

I closed the cabinet, and slid down to the floor. Just like that, it was as if an avalanche had fallen onto me. As if I were buried under feet of mud and rocks and I couldn't breathe. I couldn't speak. I couldn't move.

All I could do was cry.

Months of pain and heartache and confusion and secrets, all pressing me down to the floor. That lump I'd worked so hard to keep down in the pit of my stomach finally broke loose.

"Hey," I heard Georgia say, and then heard her footsteps coming nearer. "Hey," she said again, crouching down next to me. "What's going on? Something happen?"

It was one of those cries that felt like it had no end—like the breath had been stolen out of me. And when I finally managed to make my lungs move again, I gasped loudly, a torrent of tears coming out of me in raw, ragged jags.

"Honey," Georgia said, but she trailed off, easing her

bottom down onto the floor next to me and putting her arm around my shoulders.

And I let her. And I leaned into her. God, I needed her. I turned my face into her shoulder and clutched her arms with clawlike hands and melted and melted until there was nothing of me left.

We stayed like that for a long time, and when I felt so spent I was almost dizzy, Georgia began to speak.

"I've been suspecting," she said. "He's been hurting you, hasn't he?"

Again, a long pause. I suppose she was waiting for me to say something, but I couldn't. All I could do was sit in my dark rubble and wait.

"The little son of a bitch," she muttered. "How bad has it been, honey?"

I turned my face to the side, the air cold against my nose, but I still didn't open my eyes.

"Damn him," she said. "I knew I should have done something. Alex. Honey. Talk to me, okay? You can trust me. I'll help you. I'll do whatever you need me to do. But you need to tell me what's going on."

She looked down at me—I could feel the movement—but I couldn't make myself open my eyes. Couldn't make myself admit that, yes, she was right. Couldn't make myself admit that I now knew that I should have stayed on the patio with her that night. Should've let her warn me about him then.

"You'll think I'm stupid," I said.

This time when she moved, she moved her whole body, holding me out with her arms so I was forced to sit back and open my eyes. Her face looked haunted, ashen, as if she were just coming back from the dead.

She shook her head. "That's what he wants you to think. But I know you, Alex. You're not stupid. You're just caught up in something too big to handle on your own. Let me help."

She stretched up, pulled a napkin out of the dispenser above us, handed it to me, then got another and dabbed the corner of her eyes with it. I held the napkin she'd handed me in my lap and blinked.

"I don't know what to do," I said, tears starting anew, but softer and less desperate this time.

"You get away from him now while you still can," she said. "You tell him good-bye."

"What if I can't?"

She reached over and touched my arm. "You love him."

I nodded, wiping my nose with the napkin and folding it into a tiny square.

"Oh, honey," she said, reaching over and pulling me in again. "I know," she whispered. "I know."

We talked for another hour, Georgia heating up hot cocoa just as she'd done before, and pulling two cookies out of the cookie case for us. Only this time instead of sitting on the patio, we stayed on the floor in front of the condiment counter, our backs leaning against the cabinet.

I told her everything that had happened. I told her about

the spillway and his promises. I told her about the time he punched me, and about my tooth and the pinches on my arms. I told her why Bethany and Zack never come around anymore and how I felt as if I'd lost my best friends. And I told her how nice he always was afterward—giving me flowers and apologizing and telling me he loved me, and how a part of me believed him and felt sorry for him. How even when I was in pain, I was still in love with him.

And I told her about the photos. And about Colorado, and how I wanted to go there to find my mother's spirit, and how I couldn't explain it any better than that, and she said she understood. And I told her that I always thought of her as my mother, and she cried a little but laughed, too, and said, *Well, then I order you, young lady, to get away from this boy or you're grounded.*

And by the time we washed our mugs and swept up our cookie crumbs and turned out the lights and locked the door, leaving the place sparkling for the morning shift, I had decided.

It was time to tell Cole good-bye.

FORTY

Georgia had ducked back inside to leave a note for the opening manager about some report Dave needed written up by day's end, and I went on ahead of her, pulling my hoodie around myself.

My nose felt clogged and my eyes scratchy, and my chest hurt. And I was scared. But still I managed to feel better than I had felt in a long time. As if a weight had been lifted off. I was going to do what needed to be done forever ago. I would be honest. I would be unforgiving. Unflinching. I could do this. I was strong. I would do this. Next time I saw Cole I would know exactly what to do.

But I didn't get a chance to prepare.

I rounded the corner and there, leaning against my car, was Cole.

"Have a nice party?" he said, and already I could tell by

the tone of his voice he was pissed. "Took you long enough. Been waiting forever."

"I had to close," I said, edging up to him boldly—more boldly than I ever had before, even though I was so scared I was shaking. Even my voice trembled.

"I saw you talking to Maria," he said. "Earlier."

I shivered harder. How long had he been out here? My mouth moved as I tried to form words, but I didn't know what to say.

"Let me guess what you two were talking about," he said. "The weather?" He laughed bitterly at his joke. I pulled my car key out of my jacket pocket and thumbed the locks open. He grabbed the key out of my hand and pushed the button to lock the doors again.

"Cole," I said, "give me my keys. I'm going home."

Quickly, his arm darted out and grabbed the back of my hair. I made a noise, but he only pulled me in harder, twisting my head back so I'd look directly into his eyes.

"That bitch tell you a bunch of lies about me?" he asked.

I tried to shake my head. "No," I said. "We were just talking. Let go."

Immediately, I hated myself for going right back to that place of just saying anything, doing anything to make Cole happy. As if Georgia and I had never talked at all. As if nothing had changed. For a despairing moment I thought I'd never be able to tell him good-bye. That we'd always come back to this place—Cole with the upper hand, always.

Cole let go of my hair, glaring at me. "Liar," he said. "You're such a fucking liar, Alex."

Inside, I rallied my strength. I had to do this. I had to tell him good-bye. Stand up for myself. Stand up for my future.

"Shut up," I said, my voice barely more than a whisper.

He arched an eyebrow and took in a deep breath. "What? I'm sorry, did my slut girlfriend just tell me to shut up?" he said. "She wouldn't dare, because she knows I'd kick her ass for even thinking it."

He was up off the bumper now, leaning over me, causing me to stumble backward, farther and farther away from my car. "Don't touch me," I said, shivering so hard my teeth were chattering.

I swear the pupils of his eyes glowed, every muscle in his body standing at the ready. His eyes slipped down from mine to my neck, and for a moment I thought he was going to strangle me.

"I thought I told you to stop wearing this piece of trash," he snarled, snatching Mom's dream catcher off my neck and yanking it free. I felt the leather strap pop, and for the first time since I was eight years old, I was alone, naked, the barrier between me and my nightmares gone.

He held the broken necklace in his hand above my face and tossed it across the parking lot. I lost sight of it in the dark. It was gone. Everything important to me was crumbling, breaking. Everything was gone.

Something snapped inside of me. I straightened up, the

shivering dying immediately, and shoved him in the chest with both hands, giving it everything I had. He stumbled backward, his back popping the side mirror of my car out of place. It landed back in place with a *thwump*.

"You broke it!" I screamed, because I didn't know what else to scream. "It's over. Get away from me. Don't ever come near me again."

He laughed. Like what I'd just said was the funniest thing he'd ever heard in his life. Like my shoving him tickled. He threw his head back and laughed, long ragged laughs into the night sky.

And then, when he straightened up, he reared back so suddenly I didn't even see what happened until I opened my eyes again and found that I was on the ground next to the tire of my car.

My face hurt. Not like it hurt before. This time it was different. It hurt and tingled and felt numb and hot. When I reached to my eyebrow, my finger slipped into a gash, and my hand came away wet with blood. I had also bitten my tongue and tasted blood in my mouth. I gagged, spat, trying to make sense of what had just happened.

"You think you're all big now, huh? You talk to that crazy bitch, and you suddenly think you can just push me and tell me it's over? It'll never be over, Alex, do you hear me? Get up! Get the fuck up!"

I rolled to my side, trying to figure out how to get up. I was dizzy and the world didn't make sense to me. I must have taken too long, because I saw Cole's shoes take several long strides into my vision, then saw one leave the ground, and the next thing I knew I was gasping for air, the toe of his shoe buried in my stomach.

I couldn't get my breath, but that didn't matter to Cole, who was still ranting about me being crazy if I thought he was just going to let me and Maria tell lies about him. He reached down and grabbed my arm, twisting it and pulling upward so fast and violently I felt something pop. I cried out, scrambled, and got my feet under me.

"Please," I started whimpering, just as I had that day in his bedroom. "Please, okay. Okay. Stop. Please."

"Hurts, doesn't it?" he asked, rapping me on the back of the head twice with his knuckles.

"Cole," I whimpered. "Please. Just let me go home."

"Home to Zack?" he shouted in my face, wrenching my arm up tighter. I cried out and he shoved me backward so hard, I felt light and floaty when the back of my head hit the pavement.

I don't know how long the beating went on. All I know is I ended up curled into a ball on my side, his feet connecting with every inch of me that they could reach: my ribs, my tailbone, my cheek, my ear.

This is it, I thought. *Maria was right. He's going to kill someone and it's me. I didn't get out fast enough. It's my own fault.* And just when it started to not hurt anymore and my thoughts started to drift to other things, he stopped.

"Hey," a voice shouted. I opened one eye as far as it would go and saw Georgia running toward us, dropping her purse and her deposit bag and her keys on the sidewalk while she ran. "Get off her! Get off her!"

Cole stepped back and held his hands up, as if he'd never been touching me to begin with, and Georgia shoved between the two of us, holding her arms out to shelter me.

I could only open one eye. But even through that one eye I could see that the look in Cole's eyes was like no other I'd ever seen on him before. He looked crazed.

He's going to kill us both, I thought, and I wanted nothing more than to have not brought Georgia into this.

But he didn't. "Okay, okay!" he shouted, breathing hard, as if beating me had given him a good workout. "You'll be back, bitch," he said, but I didn't respond. I was too busy closing my eyes and drifting off to the place where my bones weren't broken and I wasn't draining blood into the cracks of the parking lot feeling like a split sandbag, splayed out on the blacktop, sure I would never move again.

I floated in that black place, hearing Georgia's voice barking The Bread Bowl's address into her cell phone and crooning to me that everything would be okay. I heard her say, "Your daughter's been hurt," too, and I wondered if it was bad enough that someone would have to wash my brains off the pavement. And I heard the sirens and voices talking to me and felt myself being carried, but I never opened my eyes through any of it.

As black as it was behind my eyelids, it didn't seem anywhere near as black as the world would be if I opened them again.

FORTY-ONE

There were visitors. A lot of them. Kids from school. Cousins I hadn't seen in ages. Neighbors. Bethany and Zack, who looked sad and grim and tried to crack jokes, but left too quickly. I wanted them to stay. I missed them more than ever.

And there was Brenda, who came in, sheepishly carrying a pot of flowers, which looked so vibrant against her skin it was almost like those photographs, all in black and white but with one thing in color. She set the pot on the windowsill and then just stared at me, wringing her hands.

"They arrested him," she said, barely a whisper.

I was still not moving much — not even opening my eyes much, they were so swollen — but I nodded. I already knew this. Georgia had been at my bedside as soon as I opened my eyes, and it was the first thing she'd told me.

Brenda scratched her arm where the flowers had just been, and again I was struck with how skinny she was.

"He said you pushed him first," she said. Then she shook her head and gazed out the window, as if she regretted saying it. And then she just walked out. And never came back. I guess she needed to see for herself what her son had done this time. I guess what she saw must have hurt even to look at.

Celia had come in, too. With Shannin and Dad and the grandmas. They brought Dad's birthday cake and we had a small family party in my hospital room, which Celia looked so bitter about it made my heart ache, but later, when Dad and Shannin and the grandmas went down to the cafeteria in search of coffee, she came back, carrying a book in her arms.

She held it out to me. It was a photo album.

I looked up at her, searching her face, then held up my splinted arm. "I can't..." I said.

She looked unsure for a moment, kind of wavering in place. Then she came around to the side of the bed, climbed in next to me, just like we used to do when we were little kids, and opened the album in front of us.

I gasped, pressing my good hand to my mouth. The photos. They were all there.

"Where did you..."

"I slept in your bed last night," she said. "I thought you were going to die. Leave us like Mom did. And I...I just happened to find the box in the space between the bed and the wall. I didn't even know these existed anymore."

She turned the pages—*flip, flip, flip*—and there they were. Mom and Dad, beautiful and happy and together.

"Dad put them in order," Celia said. "Last night. And he added these. He's been keeping them in his closet."

She flipped a couple more pages and opened the book again. Wedding photos. Dozens of them. Page after page after page. Mom and Dad so happy. In love. Perfect.

A few pages later were more additions: baby photos. Shannin's, mine, Celia's. Mom looking tired and in love. Dad looking so proud. Toddler photos, school photos, photos of us in pumpkin patches and sliding down slides and at birthdays. They were all there — proof that our mother loved us.

Proof that I had it right all along.

Later, when the grandmas took Celia out to dinner, Dad sat by the bed and flipped through the album silently. More than ever, he seemed heartbroken.

When he got to the photo of Mom holding the flower on her head on the side of the road, he just chuckled, touching the photo.

"Where was that, Dad?" I asked. "What mountain is that?"

He stroked the mountain in the background. "Cheyenne Mountain," he said. "Colorado Springs. We went there on our honeymoon."

Cheyenne Mountain.

"She always said the last time she felt whole was when we were in the mountains."

"Is that why she wanted to go back? Because she missed your honeymoon?"

God, that couldn't be it, I thought. She couldn't have

killed herself just to get back to the mountains for sentimentality's sake.

He shook his head and closed the book. "Alex," he said, looking deep into my eyes, "your mother was mentally ill. And after you girls were born, she just got sicker. She wasn't thinking right. Said she loved you girls so much, every time you cried she felt like a piece of her was being chipped away. She was convinced that she wasn't a good-enough mother."

"I don't understand," I said. "Why Colorado? Why a spiritual healer? It doesn't make sense."

Dad shook his head. "No, it doesn't. He had her convinced that if she would just get back to the last place she felt whole, she would be all better and could be a better mom to you girls. Sounds crazy, and it was. But she believed it."

My mind reeled. She wasn't leaving us. She was leaving *for* us. She was going to come back to us, all better. She was trying to heal herself so she could love us better.

I couldn't help wondering how different the past year would have been if I'd known this. How different my whole life might have been. Why couldn't Dad have just told me this before? Why couldn't he come out of his own grief to tell me the one thing I needed so desperately to hear—that my mom loved me. That I mattered. That I was important.

That Mom's death was all just a big, sad accident.

After Dad left the room, I curled onto my left side, which hurt less than my right, and cried. Mom was gone, and we'd never bring her back.

But I was still alive. There was still hope for me.

FORTY-TWO

I'd been home from the hospital exactly four hours when he called my cell.

The first calls I ignored. I lay under my blankets and shivered, like I was right back to that night. Ignored the voice mails he left.

But he wouldn't give up. Every few minutes he called, his cell phone number popping up in the ID. He was out of jail already. He was back home.

The thought made my spine go cold.

But I was curious. Even after everything that had gone on, I was curious. And I wondered how awful it had been for him. How awful it would still be. Would he have to go to court? Would my dad show up? Would my dad try to sue his family?

By the end of the day, I had given in. When he called, I answered.

"Alex," he said, his voice muffled as though he was leaning hard into the phone. "My Emily Dickinson."

He didn't say anything more. I didn't say anything. Just sat there, the open-air sound of the phone line stretching between us.

And it occurred to me that curiosity wasn't enough. I just... didn't have anything to say. Not anymore.

"God, I'm so sorry," he said, at last, and I pulled the phone away from my ear, hung up on him, turned the phone off, and put it in my nightstand drawer.

And it stayed there.

EPILOGUE

We waited a year. Part of that time was to let my stitches heal and my bones get strong again and let me make peace with the internal scars that would be my forever companions. Part of that time was to work—get myself back to a place of normal, or at least as normal as you can get when you've been through what I'd been through. Part of that time was to speak out—to travel to all the schools I could get to and tell them my story. The therapists all said it would help. I guess they were right. It felt like the right thing to do, anyway. Even if it sometimes made me feel like a freak and sometimes made me miss Cole and sometimes left me sobbing in the driver's seat of my car, unsure how I would ever get home.

And part of that time was for Bethany and Zack to forgive me.

When I say it that way, it sounds like they were bitter

and hateful and didn't want anything to do with me again, and it wasn't like that at all. They were hurt. And I couldn't blame them. And it took a while for that hurt to go away and for them to come back to a place of feeling as if . . . well, as if I belonged to them again. Cole had stolen me away and they had gotten me back, but it was as if they didn't know what to do with me when the tug-of-war was over.

Plus, life did move on. For those who weren't lying in bed living on painkillers and wincing every time they tried to turn over and trying desperately to forget the good things about the guy who just a week ago was holding her hand, life did move on.

There was prom and finals and graduation. There were summer parties. Movies. Mini golf and dates and college orientations. There was life, moving on, and I missed it. Not because I couldn't go physically but because I couldn't go emotionally. There were whole days when I couldn't leave my bed, not because of the bruises and scars but because getting up and facing the world for another day felt too frightening and too pointless. In some strange way, Cole had given me what I'd so desired all these years. Because of what he'd done to me, I was finally able to understand why my mom had done what she'd done. Because of him I truly understood the meaning of bleakness. Of desperation. Of sadness.

Bethany went to college, just as she always said she would. She was three states away, which, at times, felt like the other end of the world. She made new friends and got serious with a guy named Bryce and joined an environmental activist group and a sorority — "an academic one. You know me," she'd said, but from the lilt in her voice I guessed that it was a very social academic sorority.

And Zack got a job on a cruise ship — "just a waiter for now," he'd said, but he was working hard for a part in one of their shows. He sometimes really was at the other end of the world. And he hardly ever called.

But when they both came home for Christmas break, we went to the mall together, and over smoothies in the food court, I brought up Colorado and, though they gave each other that same hesitant look I'd seen them give each other so many times, they agreed.

"It's our gift to ourselves, remember?" I'd said, though the truth was I just wanted to see things through to the end. My questions about Mom had been answered. Now it was time for me to let it go, and part of me needed this trip so I could say I'd made it just like I'd always said I would. So I could adopt at least some of Bethany's determination.

The drive was like every road trip movie I'd ever seen. The three of us, rattling down the road in the RV Zack's grandpa rented for us, all of us squished in the cab together, laughing, leaning on one another, playing license plate bingo, eating far more potato chips than could possibly be considered healthy, and switching off behind the wheel.

Just past the Colorado state line, we pulled into a gas station parking lot and made sandwiches, then ate them in the loft sleeper, pulling the curtain shut and whispering just as we'd done in our bedroom closets so many times as kids.

"When do you want to go to the mountain?" Bethany asked, pushing a wad of sandwich into her mouth. "Right away? Or...?"

I sipped my soda, digging my bare toes between the mattress and the wall of the RV, and grimaced as the fresh tattoo on my shoulder rubbed up against the RV wall. I smiled. I still couldn't believe we'd let Zack talk us into matching tatts after all. Georgia was going to throw a fit when she found out.

"Doesn't make any difference to me," Zack said, answering Beth's question. "This is Alex's show."

"I don't know," I said. "Now that I'm out here, I kind of...I don't know..."

"Don't want to do it," Zack said. Statement, not question. "You're afraid."

I nodded, tears welling up in my eyes. "What if I don't feel her up there?"

Nobody answered. We just ate our sandwiches, our faces shadowed by the gingham curtains, our legs intertwined, our backs up against the wall of the RV. We'd never, in our lifetime together as a threesome, considered what would happen if the trip was a failure.

Turned out, all it took to make up my mind was seeing the mountain pop up in front of the windshield—one minute not there and the next so big it filled our whole vision— twinkling in the dusk.

We all gasped. And then we got giddy. We practically had to force ourselves to pull in to the hotel parking lot and check in; we just wanted to keep driving, keep rattling up and up and up until the clouds were on our heads. After we checked in, while Bethany ordered pizza for a late dinner, I strode directly to the tiny balcony attached to our room.

I watched. I waited. I breathed in while the breeze whipped my hair around my face. I looked for her. Felt for her.

Nothing.

After a while, the adjoining door between our rooms burst open and Zack plowed through, singing a song from *The Sound of Music* at the top of his lungs. Bethany giggled, joining in—something about the hills being alive—but I couldn't move. I couldn't take my eyes off the mountain. What if I missed something? What if she showed up and I missed it? It was as if I was looking at my whole life, jutting out of the ground in front of me. I couldn't blink. Who could?

The sliding door rumbled open behind me, and Bethany's arm wrapped around mine.

"You okay?" she asked.

I nodded, but didn't realize until Zack stepped up on the other side of me and reached over to wipe a tear from my cheek with his thumb that I'd gone so long without blinking that my eyes were watering. "Yeah. No," I said. "She's not here. We came all this way, but...she's not here."

Bethany sighed and laid her head on my shoulder. Her hair smelled like apples and I had a thought that this was just one more change in all the changes that Bethany had gone through since going away to college. But her hair felt so good when it blew in my face. So comforting.

"She's here," she whispered. "You'll find her."

Zack reached around my waist, pulling me in close.

"Plus we're here. We're always here," he said, his words tight around a toothpick.

"We don't have to go up there," Bethany said. "We can just go home."

My free hand reached up to my collarbone and felt the familiar leather strap of my necklace, which Celia had found in the parking lot of The Bread Bowl the day after Cole had left me there bleeding, and had fixed by clamping a clasp to the broken ends like a regular necklace.

Bethany was wrong. We did. We needed to go up there. And not just me, either. All of us. Because, in a very real way, we had all been victims of my mother's death. We had all suffered. We all needed to go up there and see that the mountain was just a mountain and she was no more there than anywhere else. We needed to see that we couldn't fix her...we couldn't fix me...by climbing a mountain, any more than she could fix herself by doing the same.

I held my fist around the dream catcher, feeling the little feather in my palm. And for the first time ever it occurred to me what I would do.

I would climb, broken, to the top of Cheyenne Mountain.
And I would leave her necklace there. In a tree, maybe.
Or on a rock. Or maybe I would dangle it over a cliff and
just let it go.

And I would climb back down, both of us—all of us—
whole again.

There was a knock at the door—the pizza being
delivered—and Bethany left to pay, leaving Zack and me
out there alone. I gazed at him. We locked eyes. He smiled,
very gently, and pulled me in tighter. Then he reached over,
brushed a strand of hair out of my face, then pulled the
toothpick out of his mouth, leaned in, and kissed the top of
my head lightly.

"Race you to the top," he said.

I grinned. "You're on."

He chuckled. "Those are some big fightin' words. You
sure you're up to it?"

"I'm up for anything," I said. "I only look all patched
up like Frankenstein. On the inside, I'm buff, baby." And I
was almost surprised by how much that was true. There
were still scars, both inside and out, but something about
being here made me feel as though I could finally let them
go. All of them.

He reached down and brushed the hair out of my
eyes again. "You are the strongest person I've ever known," he
said, and something about the way he said it made it the
truth.

"Pizza's here," Bethany said, stepping back out onto the

balcony, but she twined her arm back into mine and rested her head on my shoulder again, just as she had been before.

None of us made a move toward the pizza. Instead, we just stood there on the balcony, arms interlocked, staring at Cheyenne Mountain, until darkness took it away from us.

ACKNOWLEDGMENTS

First and foremost, thank you to my amazing agent, Cori Deyoe, for the endless encouragement, advice, and friendship. You make me believe in myself.

A huge thank-you to my editor, Julie Scheina, for your tireless enthusiasm and hard work and for pushing me to always look deeper. And thank you to everyone at Little, Brown who worked to make this novel the best it could be, including Jennifer Hunt, Diane Miller, and Barbara Bakowski. Also, thank you to Erin McMahon for the cover design.

A special thanks to my friend T. S. Ferguson for the idea, and for the help with the early stages of the manuscript.

And thank you to my personal in-house teen editor, my daughter Paige, for telling me when I use a word that teens don't use or name a character a "gross" name and for always being willing to read the rough drafts. For the record, I totally think Alex and Zack should get together, too.

Thank you to the 2009 Debs for all your help and support and for holding my hand when I'm feeling that I'm made of lame, especially Michelle Zink, Malinda Lo, Saundra Mitchell, and Sydney Salter.

Thanks, as always, to Cheryl O'Donovan, Laurie Fabrizio, Nancy Pistorius, Susan Vollenweider, and Melody O'Grady for never tiring (outwardly) of hearing me drone on and on about the horrors of being a writer.

Finally, thank you to my family, especially to my husband, Scott, and to my kids, Paige, Weston, and Rand, for the patience and the love and for pretending not to see me cry when the revisions came. I love you so much.

AUTHOR'S NOTE

In college, I majored in psychology. I'd always had an intense interest in human thought and behavior. Always wanted answers to why people did what they did, what motivated certain actions or inactions.

During my junior year, I took two courses in psychology of women. The first was a classroom course, but the second was an independent study, and I got to choose my own topic for the semester. I chose domestic violence.

I wanted to learn about the cycle of abuse, about what happens to a woman emotionally and cognitively when she suffers abuse. My goal was to discover the answer to the ever-popular question, Why doesn't she just get out?

I've heard myself say the words "I would never..." plenty of times. "I would never let someone abuse me. Hit me once and I'd be outta there, baby!" In fact, I've heard lots of women say something along those lines. "If a man ever hit me..." we like to say, and then we have all kinds of strong and powerful things to follow up that phrase. I wonder how many women stuck in an abusive relationship with no idea where to go or what to do had once said, "I would never..." or "If a man ever hit me..."

So I spent the semester learning about the cycle, or pattern, of abuse. I learned about the tension-building stage and the abuse stage and the honeymoon period of an abusive relationship. I learned all about learned helplessness and battered person syndrome. I had it down pat. I knew exactly what went on in a woman's mind when she stayed with an abuser.

But what about her heart? Where is the heart in those textbooks?

Because we don't often enter romantic relationships based on what's going on in our minds. And we don't often stay in them for what we're thinking. We *love*, and because we love, "I would never..." becomes an incredibly inaccurate prediction.

I suspect that Alex is not much different from a lot of women out there, stuck in a relationship with a guy who is really great and would actually be perfect if it weren't for this one horrible thing he does every so often. She loved Cole, and he gave her lots of reasons to love him. She loved their relationship. She loved the good times. She loved the way he made her feel special. And she was willing to forgive him, to make excuses for him, to feel sorry for him, because she loved him so much.

And, also like a lot of women out there, it's this special

ability of Alex's to love that makes it so important that she get out of the relationship before she loses the capacity to feel much at all.

In some ways, I feel like this book, this exploration of the "love" side of abuse, is the completion of a project that I began more than a decade ago in that independent study on domestic violence. And Alex has helped me understand that if you're not actually in the situation, maybe you have no idea what you would do at all.

As always, thank you, reader, for taking this journey with me.

—JB

QUESTIONS ABOUT ABUSE

Q: What are the traits of an abuser?

A: Abusers can be emotionally controlling and manipulative, jealous, cruel, and relentless, without empathy or conscience. An abuser can make you feel insecure, guilty, unworthy, confused, and intimidated and can try to alienate you from your other friends and your family. An abuser can also be physically threatening; boys are more likely to be physically abusive than girls.

Once a person has revealed a violent, mean, or abusive side, he or she is capable of doing it again. The attacking behavior is not caused by you—it happens in spite of who you are, what you mean to the abuser, and what you do. It comes from a problem in the abuser, although he or she may blame the outbursts on you or on external circumstances. If you tolerate, minimize, brush off, or make allowances for the attacks, they will get worse.

An abuser may be mean out of coolness rather than anger (that is, he or she is abusive in an unemotional, mechanical, detached, or indifferent manner). Coolly aggressive abusers can be much more dangerous than emotionally aggressive ones. You should plan to exit the relationship immediately.

Q: I suspect my friend is being abused. What can I do?

A: Tell him or her what you have observed, and ask directly (and privately) if something bad is happening. If your friend's initial response is "nothing" or "I'm okay," ask more specific questions. You can also say "I'm concerned about you" or "You don't seem happy (or relaxed)." If you get no response, but no convincing denial, wait a few days and ask again. Keep asking as long as you keep seeing worrisome behavior.

Q: Some couples just fight a lot, and some people say and do things they don't really mean while they're fighting. How do I know I'm being abused and we're not just having a really nasty fight?
A: Ask yourself these questions:
1. What would you call it if you heard about the same things happening to your best friend?
2. Do you hesitate to tell anyone else what is happening?
3. Do you feel tense or apprehensive when you are about to be with the possibly abusive person?
4. Do you feel guilty when you have been accommodating to the possibly abusive person?
5. Does he or she make you feel worse about yourself?

You can also share with a professional (see "Whom Can I Tell?" on page 364) and get that person's opinion.

Q: But I feel like it's my fault and I'm always the one who starts the fights.
A: Sometimes unhealthy, abusive people—particularly

those who are demanding or controlling—can make you so uncomfortable or fearful that you react by fighting. Your reaction can be a form of protesting, getting distance, or feeling stronger in the face of an abuser's pressure or manipulation. If you have a pattern of starting fights, you may be scared, hurt, frustrated, or threatened, and you need the attention of a helpful person. Happy people do not start fights.

Q: I don't understand how I got into this mess. How do I get out of it?
A: Take steps to get out of it first. You can analyze later, from a distance, how you got into the situation. Here are some suggested steps for exiting an abusive relationship:
1. Write down everything that's happened.
2. Tell an authority figure (for example, a parent, police officer, or principal) what's been happening, and tell that person about your plan to break up with the abuser.
3. Make, and write down, two plans.
   How to break up with the abuser: Try cutting off all contact. If the individual needs a more definitive message, write a letter or an e-mail. Do not signal to the abuser that you are afraid. Let the abuser know you have confided in several other people. Report even the slightest threatening behavior to someone in authority. Do not meet with the abusive person alone under any circumstances or for any reason.
   How to stay safe once you've ended the relationship: You'll

need a contingency plan in case the abuser pursues, confronts, or bothers you after the breakup. Again, seek the help of a person in authority in making this plan.

These questions were answered by Daniel C. Claiborn, PhD, a forensic and police psychologist in private practice in Overland Park, Kansas. He has been a therapist for forty years and has provided consulting and training for the Metropolitan Organization to Counter Sexual Assault (MOCSA) in Kansas City, Missouri, for twenty years. Dr. Claiborn has taught graduate courses in psychotherapy, family therapy, psychological assessment, and hypnosis at Iowa State University and at the University of Missouri-Kansas City and has lectured nationally on psychotherapy, forensic psychology, and the criminal mind.

WHOM CAN I TALK TO?

Nobody deserves to be in an abusive relationship. If you are being abused, it is very important to talk to someone who can help you get out:

- a teacher
- a school counselor
- a police officer, including your school resource officer or campus police
- your doctor
- a minister
- your parents or a trusted friend's parents
- your therapist
- a hotline or helpline representative

National Domestic Violence Hotline:
   1-800-799-SAFE (7233)
   1-800-787-3224 TTY
   www.thehotline.org

National Sexual Violence Resource Center (NSVRC):
   1-877-739-3895
   1-717-909-0715 TTY
   www.nsvrc.org

National Teen Dating Abuse Helpline:
   1-866-331-9474
   1-866-331-8453 TTY
   Live chat at www.loveisrespect.org

Turn the page for a sneak peek
at the next novel by
JENNIFER BROWN.

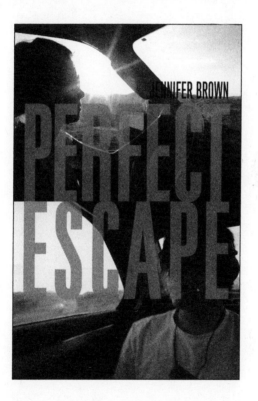

We all knew what Grayson's "difficulties" were.
Grayson's difficulties dominated his life.
And Mom's and Dad's. And mine.
Sometimes it felt like especially mine.
COMING JULY 2012

CHAPTER
ONE

I was six the first time we found Grayson at the quarry. Dad and I had just gotten back from my peewee soccer game, and Mom had met us at the front door, car keys dangling from one hand.

"We won!" I crowed, hopping past her. "And Ashley's mom brought fish crackers!"

But Mom didn't answer. Instead, she muttered something to Dad, whose eyebrows knit together. He turned and peered out the front door into the rapidly approaching night, then stepped outside, cupped his mouth with his hands, and started yelling my brother's name—"Grayson! Graaayson!"—while Mom shrugged into her coat, not even acknowledging that I had gone on to tell her all about the goal I'd scored and the goalie with the freckles who'd gotten a bloody nose when Imogene Sparks accidentally fell on top of her.

Nobody told me what was going on. All I knew was our next-door neighbor Tammy came over and fixed me a cheese sandwich for dinner. We played checkers over and over, and she stroked my braids out with her fingers and didn't make me take a bath so I could go to school with braid-waves the next day.

"Where did Mom and Dad go, anyway?" I asked. "King me."

She shrugged. "To get Grayson. Your move."

"Where is he?" I jumped one of her checkers and picked it up, tucking it into the lap bowl created by my nightgown.

Tammy hesitated the tiniest bit. Her eyes flicked toward the front door, and for a second I thought I might have seen the same worried crease between her eyebrows that I'd seen between Dad's. But she smiled and slid her checker across the board. "They didn't say," she said. "I'm sure they'll be back soon. Your turn."

It wasn't until the next morning when Mom was brushing my hair for school—using the smoothing brush, which destroyed my waves—that I asked again.

"*Ouch.* Mom, where did you guys go last night? *Ow.*"

Unlike Tammy, Mom didn't hesitate one bit—just kept pulling the brush through my hair, all business. "Newman Quarry," she said, as if this were something they did every evening. "The place off the highway, with all the rocks." She pulled particularly hard on a knot at the base of my neck, and I sucked my breath in through my teeth. Staticky strands of my hair were floating outward, following the brush; the whole thing was a fuzz-mess. "I really wish Tammy'd given you a bath last night," she muttered. "You're frizzed."

I frowned. "Why did you go there?" I asked.

She set the brush on the counter, wet her hands in the sink, and smoothed them over my hair, meeting my eyes in the mirror. She sighed, then moved her palms down to my shoulders and patted them lightly. "Your brother is having some difficulties, Kendra. Go get your backpack now. The bus will be coming."

I left the room, my scalp feeling heat-pricked and pulsating, wondering what Mom had meant by "having difficulties" and what that had to do with my parents' going to Newman Quarry the night before in the dark.

But that was eleven years ago. Grayson had been to the quarry hundreds of times since then. Sometimes several times a day, walking three miles down the highway in that precise way of his, muttering under his breath, his fingers hooked like claws while he calculated whatever it was he was calculating.

And we'd all had to go fetch him at one time or another. Stand at the top of the pit and call his name out, knowing he wouldn't answer. Stumble down the rock beds, trying not to lose our footing, trying not to get too many pebbles in our shoes, trying not to get angry. Still calling his name, stupidly. "Grayson! Come on! Mom and Dad are going to be mad if you miss therapy again. Grayson! Graaayson! I know you hear me!"

And we'd all had to try to make him leave the quarry before he was "finished." Which always meant tears for someone. Usually everyone.

I'd been to the bottom of that quarry hundreds of times, starting when I was seven and my parents began sending me over the fence to fetch him, always framing it as "an adventure."

But it didn't feel like an adventure. It felt like a chore. He never wanted to leave. I'd end up doing just about anything to get him out of there. Push him. Pull him. Yell at him. Make promises to him.

I'm not finished, Kendra. I have to count them.

But you have therapy. And there are billions. Come on, just go with me, okay, Gray?

No! I can't! Uh-uh-uh!

Okay, Grayson, okay, okay. Here. I'll help you. I'll count the ones in this pile, okay? Don't cry. We'll count them together....

We all knew what Grayson's "difficulties" were. Grayson's difficulties dominated his life. And Mom's and Dad's.

And mine.

Sometimes, like when Zoe left, it felt like *especially* mine.

CHAPTER TWO

Nobody warned me he'd be coming home today.

I got home from school, dropped my backpack on the floor, and read a text from Shani as I walked into the kitchen.

Then screamed when I bumped face-first into a bony chest. Before my brain could catch up with my reflexes, my phone-wielding hand reached out and punched at the chest with a hollow thump.

"Ouch! Nice to see you, too." My brother, whom I hadn't seen in months, was rubbing the spot where I'd just hit him. He was impossibly skinny, his hair greasy and flopping in his extremely pale face. He always looked like this when he got home from treatment. Probably I should've been used to it, but it's hard to get accustomed to living with someone who looks like an extra in a zombie movie.

"You scared the crap out of me, Grayson. Jeez!"

"I gathered that much when you hit me."

"I'm sorry," I said, pushing past him and heading for the refrigerator, my breath still coming in quick bursts. "Automatic reaction when I think I'm going to be murdered in my kitchen. It is good to see you. I just..." The phone vibrated in my hand, and I glanced at it. Another text from Shani. Major boyfriend issues. "I didn't know you were getting released today. Where's Mom?" I grabbed a slice of cheese out of the refrigerator and unwrapped it, closing the fridge door with my hip, my heartbeat beginning to slow.

"Neither did I. They told me this morning. And the store. She'll be right back."

I tossed the cellophane into the trash, thinking it would have been nice to have gotten some warning, and began folding the cheese slice into little squares, peeling the top square off and shoving it into my mouth. Grayson stood awkwardly in the doorway, staring intently at my hands, his lips moving.

I knew what he was thinking. With Grayson, everything had to be so perfectly lined up. Even if it wasn't his. He was bothered by how I was folding that cheese slice into uneven squares, and I knew by looking at him that he wanted to take a ruler to it before I ate it. I chewed self-consciously, wishing he would stop looking at me like that. Didn't Mom send him to these treatment places to make him stop looking at people like that? "So why the sudden release? Are you better?" I asked, pulling out a chair and sitting. "I mean, is the OCD, you know…?" I trailed off. I didn't know how to finish the question.

I opened Shani's text, pretending that seeing Grayson back in our kitchen was no big deal and that this was a question people asked each other all the time. Pretending he hadn't been in that resident facility Mom had found—the one that was supposed to cure him of his obsessive-compulsive disorder, his depression, the billion anxiety disorders he had, and God knows what else.

Pretending that things hadn't been weird between us ever since his quirks had slowly evolved into full-blown mental illness. Pretending that I could once again overlook his rituals and worries as I had done when we were kids. I wished I could. But the older we got—the worse he got—the harder it was to pretend that he was normal, like the rest of us. People noticed. I noticed. It was impossible not to notice.

How do you not notice someone's mental illness when the whole family constantly revolves around it?

"Yeah, I think so. I guess. Whatever" was his answer. He was probably thinking the same thing I was thinking: *What exactly is better?*

"That's good," I said, and I really meant it, though I wasn't sure if I meant that it was good for him or good for me. Probably a little of both.

There was an awkward silence between us, during which he shifted from foot to foot, mumbling numbers under his breath and knocking the wood frame of the door softly with one knuckle while I stared intently at my phone, as though Shani had written me an engrossing novel.

This was the way it'd been for the past three years.

We couldn't move. We were both trapped by whatever ritual he was struggling with at the moment. Prisoners of the great Obsessive-Compulsive Oppressor.

Who was I kidding? This was the way it'd been for our whole lives.

This is what it's like living with a mentally ill person: everyone afraid to move. Everyone afraid to speak. You don't say certain words like *suicide* or *crazy*, and you do everything in your power to keep the good milliseconds lasting as long as they possibly can. And you don't rush into anything at all, because rushing feels like courting disaster, and you don't even know what that disaster is, because it's never the same disaster twice. A ruined birthday? A scene at a restaurant? Police cars in the driveway in the middle of the night? All of the above?

And you don't ask for attention.

And you get used to it when you don't get any.

And you try really, really hard to forget that not getting attention hurts and that this person—this muttering, shadow-eyed, scabbed patient—was once your hero and best friend in the world. Back when he was just a "weird kid."

And you try to remember that you still love him, even if some days you can't exactly pinpoint why.

After what seemed like forever, he finally moved out of

the doorway, and I could hear his steps, slow and rhythmic, on the floorboards leading to his bedroom. He made it in one try, which meant he must have been feeling better.

Before Mom sent him out to Camp Cure Me, or whatever this one was called, it could sometimes take him two hours to walk from the kitchen to his bedroom, his cries of frustration piercing the hallway. Mom's voice trying to soothe whatever broken part of him told him he couldn't put his foot down until he'd counted every grain in the wood beneath it. Her sobs creeping through the bedroom walls at night. That feeling of fullness behind my eyes all the damn time. And the feeling of resentment that I tried to stuff away because when someone can't even walk through his home normally, resenting him somehow feels mean. Not to mention pointless. Resenting Grayson wasn't going to cure him.

After he was gone, I sat at the table for a few more minutes, taking in deep, even breaths and pressing my forehead into my palms. I could smell the cheese on my fingers, and it made the taste in the back of my throat go sour. I knew I should've been happy that he was back, but all I could think was, *Things have been so calm around here without him.*

I also thought about the night, two months or so before he left, when things had seemed so good. He'd seemed relaxed...or at least relaxed for Grayson. Mom and Dad were really happy, and we'd all spent the evening watching TV together, which hadn't happened in months. We joked with one another. Mom made popcorn. I fell asleep on the couch.

At some point, Grayson had brought in his old alarm clock—the kind that buzzes—set it to go off about thirty seconds later, and propped it right next to my ear. Then sat back and waited for it to go off. When it did, I was so startled and confused, I almost fell off the couch. Grayson laughed until his whole face was red and he was holding his belly and gasping for breath. Mom and Dad, still curled up together on the other couch, were giggling as well.

"Kendra, get up!" he'd said, trying to look serious but gasping too hard to pull it off. "You're late for school!"

I'd punched him in the arm but had laughed, too, because even I had to admit that his prank was a good one. "Paybacks, bro, paybacks," I said sleepily.

The next morning, he'd refused to get out of bed. Said the air was filled with toxins and he couldn't breathe them in or he'd get cancer. And he'd been that way since. I never got the chance to prank him back. He would've been way too anxious to find the humor in it.

Sitting at the kitchen table, I hoped for another evening like the one we'd had before he went away. Only I hoped it would last longer this time.

I sat there until I heard the garage door rumble to life, and then I got up in a hurry, pushing the chair back with my legs, and headed upstairs to my room. I didn't want to deal with Mom right now. She would be in that on-edge place again. No softness. No smile. Forever the woman who had yanked that brush through my hair, saying earnestly, *Your brother's having some difficulties, Kendra*, only not finishing the sentence: *and you've got to make up for them. You've got to be the child with no difficulties at all*.